Bad Dreams

Lucy's Story

Amanda Sheridan

For my own Mum, May Sheridan.
1926 – 2010.
You always loved a good story.

Author's note.

I know that a lot of people considered Lucy Wilson to be their favourite character in *Rapid Eye Movement*. In many ways she was mine because, as Lucy herself said about Jennifer 'she could be a bit up herself.'

If you've read *Rapid Eye Movement* you already know what happened to Lucy in that book, and although I've written two more books about Jennifer and her life—*The Dreaming* and *Dream Catcher*—I never stopped thinking about Lucy.

Now, I've decided it was time we all knew Lucy.

Bad Dreams is her story. In her own words.

This book contains spoilers for the *Rapid Eye Movement* series.

Please note - this book has been written in UK English. As a result, the spelling of certain words differs to that used in the US.

'At the end, we're just a character in someone's memory movie.'

Lucy Wilson

Chapter 1 – Home.

It's weird how my footsteps made no sound as I walked up the stairs. Not even that annoying creaky step, the fifth up from the bottom and ninth down from the top, made a noise. And I knew it wouldn't. But I don't know why I knew that. At least I didn't at first. The realisation came to me slowly and even now I don't completely believe it is possible. I walked up the polished wooden stairs—so familiar, yet so strange now—and I trailed my fingertips lightly along the top of the banister. The stairs had been fitted before we moved in but they had been lovingly sanded, stained and polished by yours truly to give them an aged effect. So had the banisters. It had been painstaking work, my hands ached every day, but it had been a labour of love, and the finished product had been worth all the aches and the hard work.

At the top of the stairs, I turned to the left and walked along the hallway. I couldn't help glancing at the large canvas photo print that hung on the wall. It's my favourite—a close-up of a purple crocus adorned with gentle snowflakes. It was more luck than skill to have found it. The vibrant colour of the flower caught my eye and I captured the fleeting life of the snowflakes, already beginning to melt, as I took the photo of something destined to be beautiful for only a moment before disappearing forever.

Below the canvas sat one of the small tables I'd salvaged from a junkyard. I spent ages refurbishing it until it looked like it had been bought from an expensive furniture store. That had been a learning curve, but I loved discovering all the ins and outs of woodworking. The first few attempts were disasters and ended up as kindling for the fire. I was determined to make a go of it. So, after I'd spent many evenings watching online tutorials—and with just as many practice sessions—I began to get the hang of it. I became hooked, especially knowing I was making stuff for my home. For *our* home, Charlie's and mine, and when the girls came along it became their home too.

~~~

Someone, Charlie most likely, had lit the tealight in the small copper holder that sat on the table. Bless him, he knew I aways loved the smell of sandalwood wafting around the house and I suppose he lit it now to remind him of me.

It was the holder that Claire bought me for Christmas one year. It might have been our first Christmas here, I'm not sure. But I remember squealing like a teenager at a boyband concert when I opened the gift-wrapped package. It was beautiful and it looked so expensive. Claire later told me she'd bought it for a tenner in a charity shop and she felt a bit guilty that she'd spent so little on a present for her bestie.

'That's daft,' I remembered telling her. 'It's beautiful and I absolutely adore it. You always know exactly what to buy me. Not like that lovable big lump over there.' I pointed to Charlie, who was already opening the bottle of Scotch that Gavin had given him. 'Do you know, he spends all of November asking me cryptic questions to try and figure out what to buy me. Then he ends up just asking me.'

I couldn't help smiling as I breathed in the scent. It was good to be home.

~~~

Earlier that day—after a week of wandering around the village, poking my nose in where I shouldn't, and learning all the gossip and goings on that make up the darker underbelly of what, on the surface, looks like a pleasant little village in the Yorkshire countryside—they held my funeral. I turned up for it, of course, it wouldn't be proper not to show up. I was the guest of honour after all.

I stayed for most of the service but I slipped out before it concluded, thankful that nobody would notice me sitting in the back row in the dark old church. It would have been embarrassing to be seen in these tatty jeans and this old sweater—the one that was frayed around the cuffs and had paint splashes on one shoulder. These are my lying-around-the-house clothes. The ones I put on when I can't be arsed doing anything, even though I know I should work on some household project, be it cleaning or laundry, or even cooking. Whenever Charlie saw me stretched out on the sofa in these old togs, he knew it was his turn to make our dinner.

Holding the funeral in a church was a surprise. None of my family are religious, apart from a couple of old aunts on Charlie's mum's side who wouldn't have had a say in the matter anyway. I wondered why Charlie went the full monty—flowers, hymns and a vicar telling them all what a wonderful person the deceased had been, and how I would be even more wonderful now I'm living it up in the afterlife. I listened to his words in disbelief. He never knew me when I was alive and he was hardly likely to get to know me now that I'm a corpse in the coffin on the brass stand in front of him. Plus, he is going to be in for one heck of a shock when he discovers that the afterlife seems to consist of just hanging around watching everyone crying.

But he did say some nice things about me. He probably got them from Charlie or Claire, or some of the people I worked with. It's nice to know they didn't tell him I could be a stubborn bloody cow when I took the notion, or that I liked to drink and occasionally I enjoyed watching a dirty movie. Or maybe they did tell him and he decided it would be prudent to edit those bits out. He finished by saying how sorry he was that I'd died. Not your fault, mate. No need to apologise. Mind you, I'm sorry too.

At that, I slipped out through the double doors before I started bawling my eyes out. I don't think it's proper to cry at your own funeral.

I thought about hanging around for the burial, but that would have been too much. The service was maudlin enough, but the thought of sticking around to watch them lowering my coffin into the cold, wet ground—and everybody standing around weeping and wailing into their paper tissues—would be downright depressing. I've always hated funerals. Most people do. They're awful, lonely heart-breaking moments that acknowledge the end of a life. They're brutal and depressing for everyone involved but, by heck, they're ten times worse to suffer through when they're your own.

Besides, it's raining and I've no blooming coat with

me.

~~~

A bite to eat, with coffee or tea—you could also have booze, if you were prepared to put your hand in your pocket—was provided for everyone at the local pub afterwards. I wasn't hungry, obviously, and I wasn't invited, obviously. I thought that was a bit rude, so I skipped it.

I don't think I could have listened to them for long anyway. Once all the tea and coffee had been drunk, and all the sandwiches and traybakes polished off, some would call it a day, say their goodbyes to Charlie, telling him they were sorry, and they'd slip out quietly to head home—their duty done and their bellies filled. The remainder—those in it for the long haul—would start ordering from the bar, and once the booze started flowing, their tongues would loosen up and they'd start talking about me. They'd say the usual stuff about how sad it was that a woman in her prime could be taken so young. They'd sympathise with the family with the usual sorry-for-your-loss words that mean so little but have to be said because it's the 'done' thing.

They would say things like—what a great mum I was to those poor little girls. There'd be sighs and head shaking and even a tear discretely wiped from the corner of an eye, and they'd say that Charlie and I made such a lovely couple. More sighs, and a few words about how we were the perfect family, living in our lovely home. 'She did so much work on it herself,' they'll say.

'Hidden talents, that lass. Aye, and not too bad looking either.'

10

'Always friendly and up for a chat, and a bloody good teacher. My wee ones loved her to bits.'

'Aye, but then she quit teaching to be a photographer and I think she got a bit up herself, what with all her fancy cameras and her website, and her pictures hanging in all them galleries up in London, and the like.'

See? This is why I don't like funerals. They start off saying the loveliest things about you and then someone says something—nothing very bad—they just point out a wee fault, a wee character flaw. By the time they're on their fourth round of G&T or Pinot Grigio, the floodgates will open and, the next thing you know, they'll be telling everyone that I'm the kind of person who should have been run out of town years ago.

Nah, I can think of a million better things to do on the day of my funeral. Although while I can think of a million, I can only do a much smaller number than that. Five, at best, and wandering around the house on my own is one of them. The solitude is nice. Nobody's looking for me to make them something to eat or help with their homework. I can walk around at my leisure. I can admire my beautiful old farmhouse that Charlie and I bought and had to partially restore.

~~~

I was terrified when we signed on the dotted line because I thought the mortgage would be too much—plus there was so much work that needed to be done to it in order to make it completely habitable. Bloody expensive work, too. Even with Charlie's aunt's money, I still thought it was going to cost us a fortune and I didn't want to spend all of it. Mind you, she left him a lot. I'll not say how much because that's just crass, but it was an eye-watering figure. We did a lot of the work ourselves, in the event, and that cut down on the expenditure so that, on the day we moved in, there was still a fair bit of Auntie Ethel's money in the bank account.

I never told Charlie that I was so frightened. I nodded bravely and smiled when we signed the contract and later that day we celebrated with a bottle of Prosecco, while I kept my fears well and truly hidden. The amount of stuff that needed doing terrified me. I thought it was too much, what with him away at work and me teaching, and I thought it would take months, years even. But we did it. We worked flat-out for the best part of seven months renovating it. We turned it into a modern, comfortable home, but we kept the old-fashioned charm of the original building. And I absolutely loved it.

It was hard work, backbreaking at times, but I loved every moment of it. I loved it with a passion. It was my home. Our home. And when Amy, and then Chloe, came along, it became their home too.

I loved the old exposed stonework, the original beams, the woodstoves we put in the fireplaces and the farmhouse-style stone tiles in the kitchen that extended to most of the ground floor. Perfect for mopping when you have a muddy dog racing inside on a wet day, and splattering the contents of the great outdoors all over the place. I cursed and swore at poor Ross—my border collie—when he dirtied my floors with his wet coat and mucky paws, but I loved him, and I happily got out the mop and pail out to clean up after him.

~~~

My mind flooded with memories as I went upstairs. I opened the door to the girls' room and I was blasted with an explosion of all the moments that were stored away in my mind. Their births. One easy and one agony, but both an experience I would never want to miss out on as I brought them into the world. They are both precious and loved beyond reason.

I remembered their first steps, and their first words. Amy's was 'Da-da' but—and I hate to admit this—Chloe's first words might have been 'for fuck's sake.' I remember both Charlie and myself were horrified when we heard those words coming out of our youngest daughter's angelic mouth. Oh, we laughed about it later and we reckoned she'd picked it up from me. I take swearing to a new level sometimes, but hearing it spill from our baby's lips didn't half make us doubt our parenting skills, and both of us did our very best to curtail what we said in front of them. It wasn't easy.

Chloe came out with that phrase every so often, right up until toddlerhood. Then we sat her down and quietly informed her that those were no-no words and she was never to use them again. Ever.

I don't think I've ever heard Chloe say the word, 'sake' out loud again.

Dammit. It's memories like this that bring a lump to my throat, and I'm pretty sure that's a tear sliding down my cheek. Is this going to happen every time I think about my two darling daughters? My babies. My world. I'll never play with them again. Never take them for walks out on the moors or a trip into town for new clothes. I won't ever do their hair with pretty ribbons and bows and show them how to put on their make-up when they're older. All I'll ever be able to do is watch them.

And it wasn't just the girly stuff. I'd never be able to take them for walks on a frosty day—dressed up in their little welly boots and warm coats. Never take them across the fields to check out the newborn lambs in spring, or pick blackberries in the summer. My girls weren't all about being pretty princesses. They lived in the country and they loved that life, and getting all mucky and wet, just as much as they loved dressing up. But I couldn't do any of those things with them ever again.

Dammit. I'm really crying now. This day is going from bad to worse.

Chapter 2 – Dead.

After I died, I woke up. It was confusing and disorientating at first because I hadn't a bloody clue what was happening. I sat up and discovered I was in a cold, dark place. By cold, I mean icy cold. Like the inside of a fridge. Oh, and I finally discovered that the little light doesn't stay on when the door is closed. Ha, ha.

My head was gripped in the worst headache I'd ever felt—and I've experienced some belters in my day. Usually wine-induced. I thought this was the same. I thought I'd drunk too much and I'd fallen down somewhere, and the coldness was due to me lying unconscious and exposed to the elements because it was wintertime.

But it didn't quite feel like that. I distinctly remember that yesterday was warm and sunny and summer was definitely still around. Besides, I wasn't shivering. I didn't have goosebumps or chattering teeth. No, it went deeper than that—into my bones and my soul. A woolly sweater wasn't going to make a much of a dent in this kind of cold.

It got even colder when I saw myself lying there.

I'm dead, I realised. I've no idea where that notion came from—I could have been asleep or unconscious—and why it came to me so suddenly, but I knew in my heart it was the truth.

All of a sudden, the Grief family showed up, and all five stages of them hit me like a hammer blow. But I can proudly admit that I processed them in less time than it takes to list them. Denial decided there was no point in hanging around, shook his head in disbelief, and flew out the window in a heartbeat. The body lying on the steel table in the morgue was pretty much a smoking gun as far as he was concerned, I thought. I was surprised he even showed up at all. I suppose he has to, in a way. He has to make the deceased—that's me—doubt the whole thing.

Anger frowned and popped his head up, ready to rant and rave about the injustice of it all, and I couldn't help it, I embraced him for a second or before realising there was nobody around to vent my anger on. I told Anger in no uncertain tones to piss off. Which is what you're supposed to do, I guess.

There was no one around for Bargain to haggle with, so he weighed up the pros and cons of it, decided it wasn't worth the hassle and slunk off.

Depression made herself at home in my tear ducts long enough to fill my nose with snot and make me wish I'd brought a tissue. Then Acceptance put her arms around my shoulders and decided to stick around to see what would happen next. I liked Acceptance. She was nice and did her best to keep me from feeling bad or lonely, plus she explained a lot to me about why I was sitting there. Not all of it, but enough to keep me from completely freaking out.

'At the moment, you're nothing more than a figment in someone's dream, or their memory,' she said. 'But at some stage, you'll become an, er—entity—in your own right. That's not so bad now, is it?'

It wasn't great. Being alive and well was better, but it seemed this was my lot now.

Of course, I needed to know more about my situation.

'Will people be able to see me?' I asked.

'No,' she replied.

'Hear me?'

'No.'

'What about other dead people? Are there other ghosts like me I can hang out with?'

'No, sorry. Other deceased persons—we don't like to call them ghosts—have their own stuff to do.'

'Can I eat?'

'No.'

'Have a drink or a smoke?'

'No.'

'Can I have sex?'

'Yuck. No!'

'Can I wash my hair?

'Of course not. You don't need to.'

'Is there anything I can do?'

'Um, not really. You can walk around.'

'Where?'

'Um—mostly around here. For now.'

'That's it? Nothing else?'

'Yes.'

I just sat there. Being dead was so boring. There was literally nothing I could do.

After a while, I noticed that Acceptance kept glancing at her watch.

'Are you in a hurry? Is my session up?' I asked with a raised eyebrow and a note of sarcasm in my voice. Obviously, I hadn't been offered the deluxe 'death-with-benefits' package.

'I'm sorry,' she said. 'I'd really love to stay awhile,

but I do have to be somewhere else. We're er—'

She suddenly became very interested in the pebbles on the ground near her feet.

'You're what?'

'Um—well, we don't really do this sort of thing. Mostly we deal with the living—the ones who have suffered a bereavement. You see, our job is to help them process what they go through. Some deal with it quickly, but for others it can take weeks or months to come to terms with their loss. I've even seen people who never get over the death of someone they were close to, and this means it can be a long-term gig for us. That, plus so many deaths worldwide all the time—continuously, if I'm honest— means we're always busy.'

'I can understand that, but why are you here with me?'

'Staff training,' she mumbled.

'I beg your pardon.'

'We took on a whole new batch of recruits recently and you just happened to be hanging around doing nothing, so I decided you would be an ideal subject for these guys to work on. Hone their skills, you could say.'

'I see.' I wasn't overly pleased that they were using me for training purposes, but I wasn't very mad because it did make sense.

'I hope I haven't upset you, but we have been very short staffed recently.'

'No, I get it. It's okay,'

She smiled with relief, then grinned and gave me a playful punch on the shoulder. She told me she'd come back when she wasn't so busy and we could hang out together. Then off she went.

Staff training? While it sounded a bit far-fetched, I knew that a hell of a lot of people died every day worldwide, so I could accept what she was saying.

~~~

All alone again, I got down off the table and looked around. I was dressed in only a hospital gown, and it was horrible. If only I had something else to wear. I wished I had my jeans and old sweater on—the ones I wore day in, day out when I was at home, mostly at weekends. They were ideal for all the things I did on a Saturday and Sunday. I never could see the need for fancy clothes, especially around the house—unless someone was visiting, of course. But there would be no more old, comfy clothes or even fancy clothes for me ever again, it seemed.

It was a shame really, because I did have some gorgeous outfits in my wardrobe. Dresses and the like that I'd acquired over the years, for nights out and formal events, with all the matching accessories—shoes and bags. I pictured the dresses hanging there that I'd never wear again. Acceptance popped back and gave my hand a reassuring squeeze and, hey presto! I was wearing clothes once more. My jeans and my old, comfy sweater. I even had socks and my hiking boots on my feet. There's no stopping me now, I thought. Acceptance nodded in agreement.

'You can do stuff like this yourself. All you have to do is think about what you're wearing and it'll happen.'

'Really? That is so cool.'

19

'It really is,' she said, and I could see her beginning to fidget.

'Look, I'm so sorry, but I really have to go. Are you sure you'll be okay on your own, lovey?'

'Yeah, I'll be fine. Go. Do your thing.'

I wasn't fine, but there was no point in complaining about it.

'Just so you know, the five stages can be a bit fluid, and we're likely to show up again when you're least expecting it, so you'll find yourself going back and forward. Shout if you need some help. Anytime.' She reached out and pulled me into a tight hug, then patted me on the back and disappeared.

Well, I wasn't going to hang about in this place either. I took one last look at my body lying on the slab—a final farewell glance, you could say—then pushed open the double doors and walked out of the mortuary.

Chapter 3 – Not quite dead and raring to go.

I'm bored. I need something to do. Anything. A hobby of some kind. Trouble is, I can't do anything. I can't touch things or taste anything. I can't speak to anybody. I'd probably frighten them to death if I said hello. Actually, that might be good. I'd have somebody to keep me company. Somebody to chew the fat with.

Afraid of what I might find, I didn't dare go home. The thought of seeing Charlie and the girls without me and missing me would have been too much to bear, so I spent the week until the funeral wandering the earth. It mightn't have been a week. It might have only been a day or two—it was hard to tell how long or how short it had been, as I seemed to have no concept of time and its passage. But it felt like a week had passed. And calling it 'wandering the earth' was stretching it a bit. I didn't wander the earth, or the country or the continent. I just went around the village. As much as I wanted to go farther, something seemed to be holding me here.

It's not a large village. The closest town of a reasonable size is twenty miles away and it's where everyone goes for banking services, non-food shopping such as cars, furniture and, if you're buying or selling a house, or getting a divorce, it has two estate agents and a solicitor's office. That sort of thing. It also has a secondary school, a police station, a doctor's surgery and a dentist. Several restaurants, a cinema and about five pubs. Our village is just that—a village. Not quite quaint, but not a dump either. It has a couple of well-established shops. A butcher's and a baker's—but there's no candlestick maker. He retired years ago because everybody's into wax melts and tealights these days. There's a primary school—the one where I used to teach—and a post office, two good pubs that both serve a decent lunch, and an off-licence. It's been robbed five times in two years. The petrol station beside it was robbed once, and there's a small Tesco Extra just outside the village that has never been robbed.

Statistically, that puts us in the high crime rate. But when I say robbed, I don't mean heavy-set blokes with their faces hidden behind ski-masks and armed with sawn off shotguns, threatening the staff and demanding millions, then speeding off in their getaway car moments before the SWAT teams and the Air Support helicopters arrived to hunt them down. It was more a kid with a knife in his pocket, walking into the off-licence and asking for a bottle of cheap cider, then discovering he didn't have enough money to pay for it. He pulled the knife out while he was checking his pockets for loose change and the guy behind the till panicked. The four other robberies were of a similar vein—kids wanting booze and threatening the staff—and the petrol station robbery wasn't exactly what you'd call breaking news either. It was just an absent-minded old dear who filled up her car and forgot to pay before driving off. She returned the next day, with her purse full of apologies and banknotes.

But people here love to make a big thing out of the high crime statistic because it's a deterrent to the newbies that want to move in. They want out of a high-crime area so the village is spun as an 'out of the frying pan, into the fire' kind of place. By the locals. Not by the estate agents, obviously.

We have a lot of houses in and around the village. The older ones are the traditional Yorkshire stone houses, built using a type of Carboniferous sedimentary rock sandstone known as York stone. I read that somewhere. But quite a few new developments have sprung up, and recently there has been an influx of townies who think it's the bee's knees to live in a semi-rural area, away from the stressful lifestyle of the big cities. Obviously, they don't believe the stories about the above-the-national-average crime rate, but they do however miss their wine bars and coffee shops, and are often heard complaining loudly about the lack of said wine bars and coffee shops. They have to make do with the tea room that adjoins the post office. It's never been robbed because the two old ladies who run it are not the kind of old dears you mess with. I'm serious. They look like kindly old grannies, but try being five pence short when buying stamps and see what happens.

A coffee shop would make a fortune in the first week and I'm genuinely surprised nobody's opened one yet. I'm sure somebody wanted to give it a go and applied for planning permission to either build a coffee shop or re-purpose an older building into one, but those stuffy old farts in Planning, or the Council, or even the Concerned Citizens slash Neighbourhood Watch slash Nosey Old Busybodies would have turned it down and run whoever proposed it out of town before the proposer had finished telling them how good it would be for the village. Or they murdered them and hid the body. Around here, they tend to look on any kind of change as something dark and sinister.

It could have made a mint, though. Get the townies in, serve them their skinny lattes, their macchiatos and their Americanos, or iced lattes and frappés on a hot day. Throw in some muffins and cupcakes, and you'd be rolling in it in no time at all. Mind you, with that amount of money coming in, you'd probably get robbed every Friday. By proper criminals.

And while the newbie coffee addicts were getting their caffeine fix, they could admire my photos for sale displayed on the walls around them. And buy them for their homes. Result!

Well, it would have been a nice little earner—if I'd lived to see the first coffee shop opening.

I bet they'll open one next week, hang a selection of my photos up on the walls—with a hefty price tag—and then milk the soul out of the fact that I'm a dead local artist. They'll tell their customers how tragic it was that the artist's life was cut short in her prime. Such a wonderful talent lost to the world. They'll brag about how I was 'A local woman. Yup, born and bred right here. Aye, she'll be missed.' Then they'll lower their heads in a moment of silence, follow it with a heavy sigh then point at my works on the wall, my masterpieces, and tell the punters they should snap them up before the big galleries get them and the prices skyrocket.

Thankfully there wasn't an arty-farty coffee shop here when I was alive. They'd have buttered me up to get my stuff on the walls in, '*our gallery section, where we love to actively encourage local talent to promote to our discerning clientele.*' Once they had me suckered in, they'd siphon off most of the profits by insisting on a high commission—they always do that. I mean, how expensive is it to rent a wall? Then I'd get all shouty and call them bloodsuckers and rip-off merchants, and they'd call security—or worse yet—the police. Two plods would show up and tell me to settle down, which would be like a red flag to a bull. I'd get worse. I'd shout and swear, and then I'd get thrown out, or arrested for public disorder. Mind you, with my name in the local newspaper and a disorderly conduct charge on my record, my street cred would go up. Crazy, misunderstood artist and all that—the prices would definitely skyrocket.

If a coffee shop ever does open, I hope Charlie isn't daft enough to gift them my photos. He can put them there on loan maybe, but don't give them away Charlie, please. I want you to hold on to them for the girls, to keep or sell as they wish. It mightn't be enough to get them on the property ladder, but it would help with their student loans or they could put it towards their first car. I wish I'd made a will now, but you never think of these things when you're still in your thirties.

It was a good thing I put all the money I earned from the big sales into that savings account in their names. They'll get it when they turn eighteen. They probably won't remember me by then, but it'll be a nice surprise for them.

~~~

I hung around the village for the best part of a week until the funeral and, during that time, I discovered all kinds of things about the occupants. You wouldn't believe who's sleeping with who, and who's on the verge of getting caught. For such an unassuming little village, it's a bloody hotbed of scandal, sexual shenanigans and intrigue. It's more musical beds than musical chairs and, every now and then a bit of a row breaks out, bags are packed—or sometimes belongings are just dumped on the doorstep—and the aggrieved party does a bit of mouthing off in the pub about what his or her ex did. The guilty party will be seen moving in with whoever he or she got caught doing it with, while the aggrieved party moves on to somebody else fairly quickly and everybody else sort of moves up or down the sexual property ladder. It's better than any soap on the telly, but it must play havoc with the electoral register, not to mention who's paying whose electricity and gas bills. I bet the energy companies just address the bills to 'The Current Occupant.'

Apart from the aforesaid robberies, some minor shoplifting and the occasional bout of vandalism, and despite what the locals—and the national statistics—might say, crime isn't too serious here. The robberies themselves were done—as I said before—by the knife-wielding kid with not enough change to buy his scrumpy, or usually just teenagers with scarves around their faces and the attitude that petty cash was theirs for the taking. Apart, that is, from the time a gang from out of the village—allegedly—went on a spree and robbed the petrol station and the off-licence at the same time. That one made the local TV news, but no one was ever caught for it because—as I said—it wasn't an out-of-town gang of hardened criminals. It was an old dear who was a tad forgetful, and a kid with no pocket money. 'Fake news,' as they say. 'Wrong end of the stick,' is more the truth of the matter.

Charlie was always the first to tell me that so and so had left his missus and was now shacked up with such-and-such. He didn't half love a bit of juicy gossip. Sometimes builders are worse than women—the things they talk about.

And hanging onto the coattails of that thought, 'Oh Charlie. I'm so sorry.'

I think I said it aloud, but there was nobody to hear me. Then it hit me again. I'm dead. I'm really, genuinely, absolutely dead.

Depression appeared in front of me.

'No, I'm okay,' I told her before she got upset and started crying. Honestly, I know they're supposed to mirror my emotions, but I'd prefer it if they'd just go away and leave me to come to terms with the whole thing by myself.

'Are you sure?' She asked. 'I have extra tissues if you fancy a good cry.'

'Honestly, I'm fine. It was just a passing moment. Acceptance warned me this might happen, and I accept that. Sorry to bother you.'

'Okay, well, if you're sure—' Depression looked a bit down at my rejection but she squared her shoulders and made the best of it. And took off.

~~~

I wanted to run as far and as fast as I could from Depression and the rest of the Grief gang, as well as from my thoughts. So, like her, I took off. I ran down the road and over the bridge and when I got there something stopped

27

me halfway across. I couldn't put one foot in front of the other in a forward direction. The other side of the bridge beckoned, and about ten or so metres beyond it, I could see the backside of one of the 30mph signs. That was where the village ended on this side. It also led to the road that would take me home. But I couldn't go any further. I was stuck here.

Maybe it was just this side. If I tried the other end of the village it might work.

I didn't hold out much hope, but there was no point in not trying, so I walked along the street towards the invisible boundary at the other end, between the village and the countryside. The only indication that I'd reached the village boundary was the road sign that both welcomed visitors and simultaneously warned them to drive carefully. Charlie had always joked that they should have added 'Or Else' to it, and I remember us spending a long car trip wondering what 'Or Else' would entail.

'Banishment,' Charlie said. 'Or is that too lenient?'

'Well, if they're visitors, it isn't really punishment since they'll be leaving after lunch at the pub anyway.'

'Six months in the slammer then,' Charlie suggested. 'Or execution by firing squad.'

'Nah. That would be if they did it a second time. For a first offence it would be some form of public shaming, probably.'

'Oh, yes please! A day in the stocks where we could throw rotten vegetables at them would be great fun.'

He was joking of course, but there was an amount of glee in his voice that made me think that a couple of hundred years ago this would have been his favourite pastime.

'Definitely. If it was a nice day, we could bring a picnic lunch and sit on the green and watch the show. Maybe bring some past-their-use-by-date eggs and throw them, along with some veggies.'

I remember rubbing my hands gleefully at the thought of it, so it probably would have been my favourite pastime too. 'Village life, eh? It doesn't get this exciting in the big city, what with their fancy magistrates' courts and custodial sentences. They never have any decent public floggings or vegetable throwing these days.'

We carried on with the joke for ages, each suggestion becoming more and more ridiculous. But it was a fun way to pass the time on the journey.

~~~

I hadn't realised it, but I'd walked as far as the village green. This was where Charlie and I would have had our imaginary picnic, without the stocks and the rotten vegetables, of course. There might have been stocks on the green hundreds of years ago, but restraining people in them and throwing old eggs and rotten vegetables at them is frowned on now and the stocks are long gone. Health and Safety probably wouldn't approve either. What if someone got hit in the eye? No, we have to put our eggs and rotten spuds in the recycling bin now, or face a fine from the council.

As I walked along, my musings on mediaeval crime and punishment took me to the other end of the village. I stood a few paces away from the aforesaid 'Welcome' sign.

I decided to skip the mad dash this time and, instead, I took one deliberate step and then another until I was level with the sign. If I leaned forward, I could see the front of it and read it. I could even see faint traces of red paint where someone had spray-painted something on it and not all of the paint had come off, and a dent on the edge where a car had clipped it. One more step would get me out of the village so I lifted my foot and moved forward. Or I tried to.

'Ah, fuck.'

I couldn't move. I was going nowhere.

Am I going to spend the rest of eternity here? In the village where I bought my groceries and dropped the girls off at the primary school? The school where I used to teach? Was I destined to haunt the old post office where I'd stood for ages in a queue to mail the canvas prints of my photographs to buyers all over the world?

The two old dears who ran the post office and adjacent tea room were sisters, both unmarried, and they'd worked there since the days of the horse and cart—they probably remembered the stocks and the village floggings—so it took them a while to understand what international mail meant. At first, they were delighted with the steady custom when I popped in nearly every day to send off a batch of flat parcels. But a Christmas card to the cousins in Australia was one thing, whereas sending parcels that had to be weighed and measured, the price calculated for airmail and international tracking, was another. Then there were customs forms that had to be completed, and of course, I needed receipts. It was hard work and, as the batches of parcels I carried in got bigger, their lips got tighter and the pleasant smiles disappeared, along with the pleasant chit-chat about the weather and the price of milk.

I was so tempted to call in and see them, and surprise them with no parcels. They'd be pleased at that. But my death notice was taped to the front window and they'd probably drop dead from shock if I appeared in front of them. Mind you, I'd have some company. It wouldn't be great company, but I can't be picky nowadays.

Speaking of death notices, they'd kept it plain and simple. Just the date of my death and details of the funeral, including the date. I've no idea what day it is so the funeral could have been held already. Or not.

I'm stuck here anyway so it's not like I could go. But if I've already been buried, I would like to see my final resting place.

So, how do I do that?

I thought about it. Then I tried clicking my heels together like Dorothy did in the old movie. But that didn't work. I tried snapping my fingers. Why I did that, I have no idea. But it didn't work either, so I made a wish—I wish I could go visit my grave. Then another one. I wish I wasn't fucking dead. Neither of them worked.

Then everything went black.

Chapter 4 – Not a real ghost.

When the blackness lifted, I realised what I'd discovered earlier—and it's something awful. I've learned that, other than short distances—around the village mostly—I can't move around of my own free will. Which seriously messed up my plans to see the world and have a stab at deep sea diving. I don't breathe so I wouldn't need all the equipment.

I'm not a ghost. Not in the ordinary sense of the word. At the moment, I seem to be nothing more than a manifestation in people's dreams. That's the sum of my existence.

Right now, I'm in Charlie's dream again, and he's dreaming about my funeral. Again. He seems to be obsessed with it, which is probably to be expected, but it explains how I found myself in the back row of the church, listening to my own funeral service once more.

And let me tell you, that was seriously screwed up, and it's an in-your-face reminder that I'm now properly dead and buried. What a bummer.

Even though he keeps going back to it, Charlie's mind must have prevented him from dreaming too much about the finer details of the funeral—but it gave me a chance to learn a bit more. It allowed him to revisit the nice bits—the words and the hymns and the flowers—but his brain or his psyche decided that reliving the actual burial was too much for him to cope with so soon after my death. That part was tucked away in some dark corner of his big, loveable lump of grey matter until he was in a better mental state to process it. As a result, I was able to slip away before the burial took place but not before I walked up to the front of the church and caught a glimpse of myself lying in the open coffin.

And, of course, my stupid morbid curiosity made me take a quick peek.

'Oh, that is just so freaky.'

But that wasn't enough for me. I had to take a proper look.

'Oh, for fuck's sake.'

I was dressed in that awful dark grey suit I kept for parent/teacher meetings or other people's funerals. I hate that suit and I hate the thought that I'm going to be spending eternity in it, depending on how well they embalmed me. It was cheap so, with a bit of luck, it should decay faster than me. My head was resting on a white pillow—maybe silk, maybe polyester, depends on how much they spent—and I was surrounded by the same white material. My hair didn't look too bad, considering most of it had been shaved. How did I know that? I haven't a clue but I did. I took a closer look and I realised it was a wig. I was wearing make-up and, to be honest, I looked pretty good—if a little pale. What I, or nobody else could see— but I knew it was there—was a long scar on my head that was only partially healed. It was held together with ugly brown stitches and some dried bits of blood stuck to it.

So, it was my head. That was what killed me, I think. But what caused it? A brain aneurysm? Head injury? Was I shot? Who would shoot me anyway? And why? It could have been a car accident, maybe. For some reason that one sounds plausible. I don't know. Perhaps I'll never know. It might be so traumatic that, even dead, I can't cope with the knowledge. That's stupid. Discovering you're dead is worse than discovering how you died. Isn't it?

The wig was of good quality, and it was my natural hair colour but without the red highlights I'd sported for the past few years. Thankfully, it wasn't pink or green and I'm guessing Claire wasn't allowed to choose it. Claire would have gone overboard completely so, thankfully, somebody had managed to put a halt to her inappropriate sense of humour.

My make-up was just right, almost enough to cover my deathly pallor, and I didn't seem to be wearing any jewellery. Good, because I told Charlie years ago that I didn't want a single piece of jewellery buried with me if I died. When I died.

'Why not?' Charlie had asked.

'Duh. Body snatchers.'

'Good point. I'll make a note of it. Any other instructions? Want me to stuff garlic in your mouth and drive a stake through your heart just in case?'

'Only if you see me shopping online for capes, and I have a nasty love bite on my neck.'

'You do have a nasty love bite on your neck.'

'Yeah. You did that on Saturday night. Are you a vampire?'

'Not that I know of.'

'Then you don't have to drive a stake through my heart yet. But I'm famished so could you make me a garlic 'n cheese toastie. Pretty please.'

He'll probably give the girls the less expensive things—the custom earrings and bracelets—when they hit their teens but he'll keep my wedding and engagement rings, and my gold necklace with the matching earrings safely tucked away in a box until they're grown up and sensible enough not to lose them. Or he might sell them on eBay. Nah, I don't think he'd do that. He's far too sentimental.

All the other bits and pieces would go to the charity shops. My cameras and accessories would fetch a good price online and Claire would probably pick through my clothes—we were the same size and exchanged items of clothing all the time—and pack up what she didn't want for the charity shops.

And that would be it. I'd be nothing more than a memory. Decaying flowers on a grave and a framed photo gathering dust on the mantlepiece. I'd be someone it was impossible to talk about without choking up and spilling tears of grief and loss. At least for a while, when the pain of loss was still raw. Gradually though, the emotions would fade and there would be laughter and smiles as stories were told about me. The girls would ask Charlie about me.

'How tall was Mummy?'

'Taller than you, but not as tall as me.'

'Did she fart a lot?'

'Oh, indeed she did. And they were smelly farts. I mean really smelly, stinking farts. Just like yours. She'd let off loud ones, too.'

This answer would always result in eruptions of giggles.

'Was she good at kissing?'

'That's a secret.'

And the worst question of all. 'What did Mummy look like, Daddy? I can't remember her.'

~~~

The church was packed to the gills and I was chuffed to bits to see that so many people turned up to say goodbye to me. I know I wanted to sit at the back but my curiosity got the better of me and that was why I'd made my way up to the front to stand beside my coffin.

As I stood there, admiring my make-up and cursing that horrible trouser suit, I could hear a few nearby sniffles and some polite nose-blowing. I hate to admit it, but my cold, dead heart swelled with pride to know I'd be missed by people outside of family and friends. Neighbours, a few fans and people I didn't even know were there. That was nice.

Claire was in the front row with her head lowered and her face buried in her hands. Gavin had his arm around her. Charlie was—no, I'm sorry love but I can't look at you and the girls right now. That would be too much to bear. Maybe later, pet.

Then a morbid thought crossed my mind. Did they? Had they? I couldn't stop myself and I bent over the coffin and peered in to see if there were any incisions that had been stitched up. Not neat and tidy so they wouldn't leave an ugly scar, but rough and hasty, and done to keep in everything that had been scooped out. Bits of me that they needed to examine and weigh, and take the necessary samples. Then, when they'd finished, they'd gather it all up again and pour my organs and all my innards into a plastic bag—maybe even a 'bag for life' from Asda—and bung it all back into my chest and abdomen cavity. A bit like the bag of giblets you get inside a Christmas turkey. The bag you have to remember to take out before you put the turkey into the oven. I managed to ruin a couple of Christmas dinners by forgetting to remove the bag of giblets, and we ended up eating bangers and mash under the mistletoe.

~~~

I couldn't see anything because they—the people at the funeral parlour—are always careful to cover up those icky bits. But just because I couldn't see any evidence of it, it didn't mean a post mortem wasn't performed on me. An autopsy they call it on American TV shows, but it's always a post mortem—often shortened to PM—in the UK, and on the Beeb, and in coroner's courts. I hope they haven't though, because I hate the thought of lying pale and stiff, and naked, on a mortuary table—like a prop in an episode of *Silent Witness*—with my torso cut open, my face peeled down to my chin and my skull sawn in half. Yuck. And double yuck. The thought of my organs being disconnected from arteries and veins and whatever, and taken out one by one to be plopped onto a set of scale while an attractive pathologist and her tall, and impossibly handsome, male colleague stare at one another meaningfully and nod wisely, was just creepy. And a bit nauseating. On both counts.

There were a lot of nods and meaningful stares on *Silent Witness*. I loved that show, but I did yell at the TV a lot when it was on.

'Hey! A bit more explanation in the dialogue would be a big help. Not all of us have medical degrees, you know.'

It's just occurred to me, I'll never get to watch the next season so I won't know if Nikki and Jack ever get it on, or if they continue to stare meaningfully at one another until one of them gets written out of the show by either dying or going off to a new job.

Is Charlie dreaming about my post mortem or is it just me wondering about it?

I don't know. But either way, it's something I don't want to witness. Not even silently.

Chapter 5 – Death is a theme park.

Everything had gone black again—I really wish I could fix that—and when I opened my eyes, I was strapped into a seat and hurtling through the night sky at high speed. All I could hear was the wind as it whistled in my ears and buffeted my face, and the terrified screams of the people around me.

Ah-ha. Maybe we're getting somewhere. Maybe I died in a plane crash. But no, that doesn't fit. I don't recall making any travel plans recently. So, whose dream am I in? Somebody who survived a plane crash? Or died in one?'

I don't know anyone who fits that description. Charlie and I had a bit of a bumpy landing coming back from a week in Malaga once but, other than that, nothing. I certainly don't remember ever being strapped into a seat and thrown through the air as the plane I was in presumably broke into pieces. Nobody I knew had either.

The closest I'd ever come to this sort of speed was a massive water slide at an aqua park on that same holiday in Malaga. That had been fun, but this was a bit frightening.

Then it dawned on me. I was on a roller coaster at the big theme park we'd all gone to last year.

I looked right and then left, just like the green cross code man—I wonder what happened to him—told us to do at primary school. Both Amy and Chloe were tightly strapped in on either side of me, the delight on their faces contradicting their screams. They loved it and were terrified by it in equal measure as the carriage took us up high at a seemingly impossible angle, stopped still at the top for about five terrifying seconds that seemed like a lifetime and then tipped over to begin its heart-stopping downward journey. My stomach lurched and I gasped aloud. My knuckles were white as I clutched the safety bar in front of me, thankful for the big, solid straps that held me—and my girls—firmly in place. I silently cursed Charlie for chickening out.

Heights didn't bother him at all, but he refused to go on the roller coaster.

'One bolt.' He sucked on his teeth in the way he did when he was talking to a client who was asking the impossible, and he was trying to get out of the job because it was going to be a) too expensive for the person who wanted it done, b) it would leave him out of pocket, and c) a ranch-type floor-to-ceiling stone fireplace might work in a ranch in Texas but it was never going to work in a small, semi-detached bungalow in a village in Yorkshire. Yeah, I knew that sucking-the-teeth thing only too well.

'One loose bolt is all it takes,' he warned us, 'and all this will come crashing down in a tangled heap of metal and mangled, broken bodies. There'll be blood and broken-off arms and legs scattered around everywhere. Eyeballs will pop out and splash into your slushies and there'll be a finger instead of a chocolate flake stuck in your ice cream.'

Both Amy and Chloe were wide-eyed and open-mouthed as Charlie continued. 'The injured and the dying will be howling for help and no one will be able to get near them for all the tangled metal. TV news crews will show up before the ambulances and paramedics get here, and they'll report on the terrible injuries and rising death toll. And it'll be on every news channel all evening and again in the morning. Nope. No way. You couldn't pay me enough to get me to go on one of those death traps.'

The girls were screaming with excited anticipation by this stage. They couldn't wait to see the mangled bodies and get on the telly. I knew right then that they'd be spending years in therapy when they grew up.

'But you'd let your beloved wife and children go on one?' I had my own doubts now but the girls were still screaming, fixing their hair for the TV cameras, and pulling me towards the queue to get on the death trap.

'Why not?' Charlie shrugged. 'If it doesn't collapse, it'll be fun. It probably won't collapse—these things hardly ever happen. Well, you hear about them now and then, but it's once in a blue moon. Hardly worth worrying about. I'll just wait here in case I have to identify your remains.'

Oh, prophetic words, Charlie. Although they didn't need you to do that because I was already in the hospital when I died.

I frowned. Where had that thought come from? And how did I die? I still don't know. I can't remember. I'll have to look into that.

~~~

The roller coaster had been fun. No bolts came loose and killed us, and we enjoyed an exhilarating ride on it. Well, Amy and Chloe enjoyed it, I wasn't so keen. We survived it, got off, and I took each girl by the hand as we walked, a little unsteadily on my part, towards the devoted husband and father who'd left us to risk our lives while he remained on terra firma, tucking into his bag of chips. The girls rushed to him, giggling and shouting that it'd been the

41

'best fun ever' and complaining that 'mummy won't let us go again.'

Okay, I'll admit I enjoyed it a little bit—the adrenaline rush and all, and I was breathless with excitement—but I wasn't going to go through it again. My legs were shaking for ages afterwards and I felt sick. But that could have been the cheeseburger earlier.

It occurred to me then that I was in Amy's dream because she still talked about that day. Her mind took me all though the fairground with her holding my hand, Charlie and Chloe beside us, also holding hands. It was fun. We went on all the rides—some of them twice—though not the roller coaster again. We won lots of prizes and ate so much junk food we all began to feel queasy. It didn't matter that both my daughters were out of their tree on E numbers and sugar and babbling nonsense by the time we got to the car, it was a once-a-year event and we'd all be back to healthy snacks tomorrow.

I couldn't help smiling. At least one of my daughters was having happy dreams in which her mum was still around to take her to the funfair.

Chapter 6 – Out of the dreams and into the rain.

My plan to get out of people's dreams worked like a treat but my timing could have been better.

'This was a really great idea, Lucy. Wasn't it?' I told myself.

It seemed great at the time but now, sitting here on the dry-stone wall as the rain came down in torrents, I was drenched to the skin. It was bucketing down. And even that well-known expression didn't do this rain justice. This was monsoon rain. The kind that backed up drains, left cattle stranded on small hills and had the woman on the TV weather forecast open-mouthed in awe as she described just how much rain was predicted to fall.

My hair was plastered to my scalp and I was soaked right through to my underwear. I was cold, wet and miserable as I sat on the wall, muttering swear words and cursing the weather and my stupid, stupid idea. If it had been sunny and warm, it would have been a belter of an idea. But no, it had to bloody well rain.

The idea—the one that wasn't so great now—was something I'd had been working on. I was tired of winking out of existence every time the person in whose dream I was residing woke up. And to be honest, the whole 'winking out of existence' thing was a bit frightening. It smacked of nothingness. For all eternity. Like the parrot in the old *Monty Python* sketch, I'd shuffled off this mortal coil only to find there was nothing else. That was it. Forever. Unless reincarnation was real and I'd would pop up some day as someone else. Or maybe a tiger. Or a blue parrot.

The idea had been simple in its concept but the actual implementation was bloody tricky. I had to time it to perfection and pinpointing the exact moment someone would wake up was almost impossible. But, with a bit of perseverance—basically, I scrunched my face, closed my eyes and concentrated really hard—and a lot of luck, I managed to not disappear when the dreamer woke up. I turned out to be a fast learner when it came to this death gig, because it took me no time at all to figure out that if I got out of someone's dream, I could leave them to it and go do my own thing. It was limited though, and once my family stopped dreaming, for whatever reason, I blacked-out again. This was another thing I intended to fix at the first opportunity.

Blacked-out made it sound like the curtains had been closed, but it was more than that. I was aware of everything going dark a split second before it happened. Then there was nothing. Just the blackness. And I didn't know how long it had lasted. It could have been five minutes or it could have been five years. There was no way to tell. It was like I blinked completely out of existence.

But while they remained in REM sleep, I could either stay in the dream or take off to explore.

And explore I did.

But, before I went all Captain Kirk—exploring new worlds and discovering new civilisations, or just watching the neighbours shagging and fighting—I spent a while each time in Charlie's dreams. He, or rather his subconscious mind, was reliving his life with me. Is that what people do? I suppose it is. I mean, if we spend our waking hours remembering someone we've lost, it stands to reason that our dreams would follow the same path.

On this occasion, Charlie was dreaming about some of our first dates and, in this particular dream, things were getting hot and heavy in the back of his old van. I remembered it well, and it was mostly pleasurable, if a bit cramped. It was one of many sessions we spent tangled together as our passion for each other grew. God, I sound like a bad romance novelist because, in reality, it was bloody uncomfortable.

Charlie's dream was about the night I nearly wrecked myself when I caught my foot in the seatbelt and went arse over tit into the back seat. Charlie thought I was just in a hurry to get my kit off and start snogging him. I hadn't the heart to tell him I was in agony.

Not only was it the night I pulled a muscle in my thigh, it was also the night we decided it was time to get a place of our own. At least I think it was. I can't quite remember how many times we had sex in the back of the van before deciding to find a place to live.

After the lovemaking, we climbed back into the front seats—rather painfully in my case—and Charlie switched on the engine, turning up the fan to clear the condensation off the windscreen. See, this is a hot romance. I should have written it and published it, and made a few quid off it.

Or maybe not. Apart from the little, nonsensical stories and rhymes, I made up for Amy and Chloe, I'm not much of a writer. Sometimes I struggle to think of something to write on a Christmas or birthday card, and I usually end up just signing it from me, Charlie and the girls. At a push, I'll wish the recipient 'Happy Birthday', or 'Season's Greetings', or something to that effect, but I rarely write anything more elaborate. That is why I never wanted to write a book.

~~~

In this dream of Charlie's, it was wintertime and frosty outside and I wondered if it was condensation or ice on the windscreen. In the dim interior light of his old Ford van, we could see our breath as we engaged in some post-coital conversation before heading home.

Then, out of the blue, Charlie said, 'I love you. I mean, I really love you.'

He turned away from me and stared out of the window, too shy to look at me but he reached for my hand and squeezed it. I suspected he was blushing. I squeezed back and smiled.

'I love you too, Charlie.'

This was the first time either of us had used the L word and it was a big moment for both of us, but I can't remember if that was the night when we made a commitment to each other.

I must ask him. His memory is better than mine sometimes. Oh, wait. I can't ask him. I can't ask him anything again. I can't ask him if he wants a beer, or fancies Indian—I can whip up a mean curry and rice—or a Chinese stir-fry for dinner, or just frozen fish and chips.

I didn't think it was possible, but I started crying again.

Just then Depression's head popped up over the fence and she gave me a forlorn wave.

'You okay, sweetie?' she asked, and her voice was so sad. Almost as sad as me.

Acceptance had been correct when she told me my Grief Stage buddies would appear at random.

'Not really,' I replied.

'Oh, I know how you feel. This is just awful. I don't know what we're going to do. I just want to curl up and cry when I think about it.'

'Whoa, wait a minute. Aren't you supposed to be cheering me up? Not pandering to my misery?'

'Hel-lo. Depression Stage. The clue is in the name, love. It's my calling. I'm here to help you wallow.'

'I don't want to wallow.'

'Eh?' Depression frowned. 'How can you not wallow? This is perfect for wallowing. It'd be a shame to waste such a good wallow. Now I feel even worse.'

She hung her head and tears flowed down her cheeks.

For fuck's sake. I don't wallow. Never did. And now this plonker who thinks she knows how I feel is expecting me to drown in my own misery.

Anger stepped out from behind a tree and tapped me on the shoulder. 'I think you should tell her to piss off.'

'Won't that upset her?'

'Hopefully.' Anger gave me a smile that was also a glare.

'Well, I'm not in the mood to upset anybody, so I want you to piss off.' I glared back. I was angry. Angrier than I ever had been in my life.

Anger's chest puffed up with pride.

'Well, aren't you the bad-tempered cow. Now that

you're in a mood, you should be raging against the injustice of it all. Break stuff and scream and shout. Thump things until your knuckles bleed.'

'Why would I do that? It isn't going to change anything, is it?'

Anger's mouth dropped open. 'Well, of course it isn't. That's not the point.'

'What is the point?'

'You're supposed to be me. I'm Anger. One of the five stages of grief you're supposed to go through.'

'Haven't we done that already?'

Anger stamped his foot and swore loudly. 'What? That five-minute box-ticking session when you became aware you were dead? That was a warm-up, dearie. Now you have to do it properly.'

'No.'

'I beg your pardon?'

'I said no. I'm not going to scream or break anything. I know I'm dead. I don't like it but it's all I have left and there's no point in getting angry about it.'

'You've been talking to that bitch Acceptance again, haven't you?'

'What if I have?'

We stood there, angry glares on both our faces. I was so furious I thought I was going to explode.

Anger laughed, but there was displeasure and bitterness in the sound.

'Then it would seem that my work here is done.'

With that he scowled and disappeared—not quite in a puff of black smoke, but it was close—and he left me ready and willing to kill somebody. But, because he'd gone, the anger went with him and I calmed down.

'Is he gone?' Depression cautiously stood up.

'Yeah. I dunno where to, but he's vanished for now.'

'Thank goodness for that. I get really upset when he's around. All that shouting and swearing, and those angry vibes he gives off, make me so distressed. He blows his top at the slightest thing and I feel like bursting into tears. What do you say we make a deal about not letting our emotions get out of hand?'

Bargain Stage drove up in a flashy sports car, wound down the driver's side window and smiled. 'Did someone mention making a deal? If you're making a deal, I can help. I'm great at haggling. You wouldn't believe how little cash I got the previous owner of this beauty to accept.'

I clenched my fists, then unclenched them as quickly as I could. I didn't want Anger showing up again. These guys were making things worse. All I wanted to do was get on with my life—well, death—but they kept interfering. I wanted to cry, pretend they didn't exist, make them promise to leave me alone and tell them to piss off. All at once.

Instead, I closed my eyes, took a deep breath and counted to ten. When I opened them, I was on my own again and I punched the air in victory. Although it was possible that Acceptance was hovering around somewhere nearby, but that was okay. Acceptance was one of the nicer members of the Grief family.

What if I'm not dead? What if I was in a car accident or a fall and I'm injured and I'm lying in the hospital in a coma, or something? And the funeral and the *Silent Witness* episode—okay scene, I know it wasn't a whole episode—what if all that is Charlie having a nightmare about me dying? He always said he wanted to go first—at the age of ninety-four and shot by a jealous husband. He's a funny guy, my Charlie. Or he was. I expect he's not laughing or cracking bad jokes much these days.

No. I'm fairly certain I'm dead. The funeral was a bit of a clue. But what happens next?

Chapter 7 – Freedom.

I'm not sure how I managed it, or if I even had anything to do with it. I don't care. I wasn't bound by the sleep patterns and the dreams of my family and close friends any more, even when they were awake, and that's all that mattered. This was a big thing for me and it meant I could come and go as I pleased. Not that I didn't like being in their dreams. I did. It was my only interaction with them, and my only way of keeping them close to me. Just the other night, I had a great time in Charlie's dream. He must have been thinking about me when he went to bed. Well, of course he was. Why would he not be thinking about me? But, in this instance, his thoughts must have crept into his subconsciousness when he fell asleep, because there we were, on a beach in Tenerife.

My hair was casually tied up on top of my head. I was skinny and tanned, and I looked a million dollars in my teeny-weeny tiny bikini—black, not yellow. Stretched out on his sun lounger beside me, Charlie looked hotter than hot—fit and tanned—in his denim shorts. He had forsaken the budgie smugglers for a pair of shorts because he couldn't find them when we were packing to go on holiday. The reason he couldn't find them was because I'd binned them. While I was quite happy to stare at my husband's sexy body, I didn't want anybody else looking him up and down. Besides, they were way too small for him.

We'd just been for a swim, I remembered, and we were relaxing in the sun to dry off before going for lunch.

That was a great holiday. It was the first time we'd

been able to splash out because, after scrimping and saving for ages, our finances were a hell of a lot healthier, thanks to two big contracts Charlie had recently finished and the money we'd received from his late aunt. That money was now in our joint savings account, apart from a few grand we'd kept to buy some things we desperately needed and a few luxuries we wanted. This holiday was one of those luxuries.

I rolled over onto my stomach and untied the strap of my bikini top. I would only put it on again when we went for lunch, regardless of which way up I was lying as I wanted my boobs to be as tanned as the rest of me. I nudged Charlie and asked him nicely to rub sunscreen onto my back and shoulders. I closed my eyes as I enjoyed his gentle ministrations, and I felt myself drifting off.

~~~

I was no longer in Charlie's dream, but this time I didn't black out. It was as if some unknown, invisible force that held me inside people's heads had let go of me and I was now free to control my movements. I actually felt lighter but, at the same time, more solid. It's hard to understand, never mind explain. More—unbound—is probably the best way to describe it. And I definitely felt more like me.

~~~

Like all ghosts, I didn't have to walk, run or take the bus. I only had to think about where I wanted to be and I was there immediately. This was so cool and I planned on making the most of my new-found freedom.

What did I do? I went straight back into Charlie's

dream.

Well, why not? He was in Tenerife and the weather was lovely, and that was exactly where I wanted to be.

Of course, I had a moment of panic the second I lay down beside him on the sun-lounger again. What if I got stuck in his dream again? Did going back cancel everything out? I closed my eyes and attempted to jump back out of the dream. Success! It was easy-peasy. I did it a few more times to be sure before I settled down to a spot of sunbathing on the beach with my man beside me. It was heaven.

That holiday in Tenerife had been such a great time. We made the most of the two weeks with lots of swimming, sunbathing and sex. Then sangria, more sex, and sightseeing. All the S's that made the perfect holiday, although we had so much sex, I was sore. I wasn't complaining though, after all, it was another S.

But we did other things, too. We joined a boat tour and went whale watching and we managed to spot one whale—maybe two. It was hard to be sure. We hired jet skis and had a race which I won. We went on an escorted bus tour which included the active volcano of Mount Teide. That was awesome. The whole island was. We had the time of our lives, but the two weeks soon flew by and we left the sun and the sand behind, flying home to rain that quickly turned to sleet. Sleet was another S but not a welcome one. I think my tan faded after a week.

Chapter 8 – Looking back in time.

I had a good life. It was short, but sweet, with only one or two small bumps along the way. And one major one—two, if you count dying. I enjoyed nearly all of it, and it's a shame I only made it to thirty-six. Not quite that even. My birthday is—would have been—next month, I think. I'm not sure what month or year it is, exactly. I had a lot of plans for the next fifty or so years, and that's a real bummer, but there's no point dwelling on it. I'll only get upset or angry and those weirdos will show up again.

Despite being an only child, my upbringing was normal and happy. From what vague memories I have of my early years, my parents doted on me and I can put my hand on my heart—my cold, dead heart as it is now—and say that I wanted for nothing.

Well, I wanted a pony.

This is perhaps my most vivid early memory, and I probably remember it because of the devastating consequences of my desire for a pony.

I was desperate for one. It was all I could think about, and I whined and pleaded constantly with my mum and dad to buy me one. I told them my life would be hell if I didn't get a pony to love and groom and learn to ride. And feed it carrots every day. I was eight, so maybe I stamped my foot and wailed at how cruel they were because they hadn't bought me my pony yet. I even had a name picked out. I was going to call him Bingo—or was it, Jingo? Maybe Joey. Strawberry if it was a girl, unless she was black, and then I'd call her Beauty. Stating the bleeding obvious even at the age of eight, that was me.

After some stern words from my dad for using the word 'hell', he quietly explained that they couldn't possibly buy me a pony because there was nowhere to keep it. I wasn't impressed. I was his only daughter—his only child—so you'd think I'd be more important to him and he'd buy me whatever I wanted. Eight-year-olds can be so self-centred.

'But we have a garden,' I pointed out. 'He could eat all the grass and you wouldn't have to cut it on a hot day. You don't like cutting it, do you? Think of all the hard work you'd save.'

My negotiating skills were legendary, even at that tender age.

'A pony needs more than a small lawn, Lucy. It needs a field and a stable and lots of other things. Our house isn't suitable, darling.'

'Why not?'

My father went on to explain that, although we had a garden, we lived in a town and a pony needed to be in the country.

It was on the tip of my tongue to suggest moving to the country but then I remembered one day in class when the teacher told us all about the countryside. About the owls that lived in the trees and the blind bats that flew around at twilight and ate all the flies. The owls sounded cute but I wasn't so sure about the bats. If they were blind, they might mistake me for a fly and try to eat me.

There were animals like cows and sheep that made strange noises at night and it was always dark because there were no streetlights in the country. I wasn't so keen on this now. Without streetlights, I wouldn't know if the strange noises were coming from a cow or a monster.

I frowned. No, that wouldn't be good at all. I needed to think up some other way of getting a pony. Maybe they'd get streetlights in the country one day soon, my eight-year-old mind reasoned. Then I could move there—to a big house, surrounded by trees and lots of fields where I could have lots of ponies. Maybe even a horse. Maybe it would be an old, stone house that needed work done to make it habitable—I'd learned that word last week when I heard Mum saying it to Dad, and I asked her what it meant. I thought it was about nose-picking, which they kept telling me was a very bad habit. But this word, Mum told me, meant—a place that is suitable to live in. She was quick to answer me, not like the time when I'd asked her what 'wank' meant. On that occasion, Mum got angry, told me it was a very bad word and then asked me where on earth I'd picked up a word like that.

I was so tempted to say I'd picked it up off the floor, but I knew a cheeky remark would only land me in even more trouble and get me sent to my room.

'A boy at school said it,' I replied, 'and everybody laughed.'

'Well, it's a very naughty word and I don't want to ever hear you say it again.' Mum told me with a stern look and a wagged finger. I filed it away with the other naughty words I'd already heard in school.

Despite the weird animals and the even weirder noises I'd learned about, it was probably then that I decided my future house would be in the country and it was my dream for as long as I could remember. I imagined it so many times over the years as I was growing up.

In class, my stories were all about the big house that I pretended I lived in. I imagined it and wrote about it. I told all the stories of the people who lived happily in it. I changed the name of the girl who lived there, but it was really me. I always got an A.

The house I was someday going to live in had a big fireplace where I could hang up my Christmas stocking, and a big hall where there would be enough space for a massive Christmas tree. A real one.

I had it all planned down to the last detail. I was only eight, though so, for the time being, I had to be content to live in our house with my mum and dad. But I still wanted a pony.

~~~

Our home wasn't a council house on an estate, but neither was it a mansion. It was just an ordinary house with three bedrooms and a back garden in a quiet residential cul-de-sac, and only a ten-minute walk to the main road where I got the school bus every morning. It was another ten minutes—in the car—in the other direction to Tesco, where I went shopping with Mum every Saturday morning while Dad had a lie-in.

He was an accountant. I had no idea what that was but it sounded like he counted people's aunts. That didn't make much sense. Who had that many aunts they needed someone to count them?

Mum was a teacher, but not at my school, thankfully.

It would be so embarrassing to have your mum as your teacher. Imagine accidentally calling her Mum instead of Miss. Everyone would laugh at me and I'd never live it down.

Mum taught GCSE maths at the big secondary school, the same one I'd be going to in a few years, and hopefully Mum would be retired by then. She was thirty-two and that was ancient, so she should be close to retirement age by the time I got there.

With both of them working we weren't poor. We weren't rich either, but we were what Dad called 'comfortably well off,' like a sofa, or my old shoes. He said it meant we were able to go to Spain for two weeks every summer, and I could have a cool birthday party every year with all my friends and lots of presents for me, and little thank-you gifts for my friends. There was cake and fizzy drinks and lots of sweets. That was what comfortable meant to me when I was eight.

~~~

It's funny how just thinking about how much I wanted a pony back then brought so many other memories back now. If you'd asked me before I died if I'd ever gone to Spain as a child, I would have said no because I had no recollection of it. Now, it's a bit like a jigsaw puzzle and once I found the pony piece, the other pieces dropped into place and the picture became apparent.

I remember that I never completely stopped asking for a pony, no matter what cool birthday and Christmas presents I received. I always dropped lots of hints in the weeks leading up to my birthday, and I started months before Christmas, promising to be extra good if they'd buy me a pony. I always hid my disappointment as best as I could when the presents with my name on them under the tree on Christmas morning were definitely not pony-shaped.

Then one day—the Saturday after my ninth birthday—Mum said we were all going on a day trip. She wouldn't tell me where we were going—neither of my parents would tell me anything. I dutifully climbed into the car, sat back and gazed out of the window as the world as I knew it sped by.

~~~

Both my parents were killed outright in the accident. A car with R plates on the front and rear windows pulled out of a side road, the driver not bothering to look in both directions because, at eighteen, boys—or the young men they thought they were—knew they were the greatest drivers in the world and invincible. Dad's blue Toyota—the one he lovingly washed and polished every Sunday morning when the weather was dry—ploughed straight into the souped-up black Peugeot that pulled out in front of him.

~~~

As well as my parents, the boy racer was killed. I wasn't hurt, apart from a very minor bruise on my forehead that I didn't even feel.

I'd turned nine years old only three days earlier and I didn't know it but my parents were taking me to a local equestrian centre where they'd paid for riding lessons. It was the closest thing to buying me a pony they could manage. When I learned that fact some years later, I lost all interest in horses.

~~~

With my parents dead, I was placed in temporary foster care until a relative could be found. But neither of my parents had any siblings, nor, it seemed, any aunts or uncles, or cousins. There must have been one aunt or uncle though, because eventually a second cousin on my mother's side was located in Canada—but he had a large family of his own and couldn't afford to take on another child. He politely declined the offer by Social Services to have me shipped like a piece of cargo to Ottawa at the UK taxpayers' expense. I remember imagining myself wrapped up in brown paper with a postage stamp stuck on my forehead and I was glad Cousin Canuck didn't want me.

The year in foster care was okay, nothing special. I was fed and clothed and the couple in whose care I was placed were kind, if not overly affectionate. I was lonely, though. I missed my Mum and Dad terribly. At the same time, I was a bit shell-shocked and withdrawn, simply because I didn't know what was going to happen to me.

Then, less than a year later I was adopted by a lovely couple—Alan and Linda Arnott—and right up until the day I died, I considered them my real mum and dad. They told me early on what had happened to my parents—the ones I knew and loved up until I was nine—and then gradually, in the face of such love from my adoptive parents, my memories of them faded away. I remembered a few bits and pieces. Mum's long, brown hair which she always wore in a ponytail. The two goldfish in the bowl that sat on top of the cabinet in the living room, and the garden where

I played in the sun. It had a big tree and my dad fashioned a swing there for me with two lengths of rope and a square bit of plank for the seat.

~~~

As well as the accident, a lot of memories of my early years with my birth parents began to surface and I felt the tears welling up in my eyes. I quickly wiped them away before Depression showed up with a box of Kleenex and a black cloud trailing along behind her. Why am I remembering so much more now? Before, when I was alive and growing up, the memory of my birth parents had gradually faded away. The sound of their voices. What it felt like to be held by them. The kisses and the cuddles. The games indoors when it rained, or out in the garden when the weather was fine. The last memory to go had been the scent of my mother's perfume—light and floral.

All those early memories had been overwritten by the new ones my adoptive parents made with me. Trips to the beach. As much ice cream as I could eat. Kisses and cuddles for no other reason than they loved me, and sympathy when I fell and skinned my knees. Linda's ample bosom was a comforting pillow where I could lay my head when I was sad, and it was a moment such as this when I first called her Mum. It made her cry, but they were happy tears.

I remember getting a bicycle for Christmas and Alan—now my dad—pretending to hold the saddle to keep me upright. I remember squealing with pride and excitement when I looked back to see him standing on the footpath waving to me, and I realised I'd done it myself, albeit with training wheels still attached. I think he squealed a little bit with pride and excitement that day, too. They loved me so much. I was their pride and joy. It was their love for me that made me mostly forget the two people who brought me into the world but, through no fault of their own, were no longer around to love me.

~~~

As I went from teenager to adult, a confusing memory would occasionally surface. It always came as a bit of a surprise—when I looked up from whatever I was doing at the time—to see my birth mum. She'd be standing in the kitchen or sitting in a chair reading, maybe even outside tending to the garden, and she'd turn around, from the stove, or her book, or she'd glance up from the flowerbeds, and smile at me. But it was a fleeting thing, and the images vanished in the blink of an eye. It bothered me a little and I even thought it was her ghost, although it was most likely a flashback or a repressed memory surfacing, or something like that.

Now here I am, remembering these moments of my life in technicolour detail as if it was yesterday—it's that vivid. All the buried memories of my birth mum and dad who died when I was nine have come back. I can hear their voices, smell Mum's perfume and see Dad's smile. I remember the house and the garden, and my desire for a pony. All of my early life has come back and I'm able to relive those memories again. It's nice, but sad. Very bittersweet.

It occurs to me that they might have been around watching over me all along. Is that what the dead do?

Watch us but don't engage with us? Like we're characters in a play they're watching? Do they? Are they? Were they watching me when I first kissed a boy and let him put his hand inside my knickers? When I got really drunk, threw up in the toilet bowl and slept on the bathroom floor? Oh, I hope not. But, at the same time, were they watching with pride and love in their hearts when I passed all my exams—even though I only managed to scrape through some of them—and went on to university? When Charlie and I got married? When the girls—their grandchildren—were born. Oh, I hope so.

I don't have a religious bone in my body, never have, and nothing I've seen since I died has changed my mind. All I can say is this afterlife—if that's what it is—isn't as good as it's cracked up to be. All the preachers and their fans promise eternal, floaty smiles, sunshine, and lots of harps. But the reality involves a lot of hanging around and, believe me, it's pretty boring. I don't half wish I could appear and tell them so, and maybe yell 'Boo!' at them. But it does make me wonder—since it looks like I'm going to be hanging around for a while—if maybe I could watch over my girls in such a way that they might occasionally look up at me and smile, not quite knowing I was there, but having a feeling that I might be. Charlie, too. I'd love to put my arms around him and rest my head on his shoulder just to let him know that I'm still here and I still love him.

I just have to figure out how.

~~~

I sat on the old stone wall with my elbow on my knee, and my chin resting on my closed fist. I was deep in thought—just like the famous sculpture—and I was trying to figure out how to stay with my family without them screaming in fear and running out of the house every time I appeared. Or Charlie setting off the fire alarms by burning sage and wafting the smoke everywhere to ward off the evil spirit that used to be his wife.

But I couldn't concentrate because one of the large granite stones had a slightly jagged edge and it was digging into my right bum cheek. I shifted slightly but that made it worse and I almost fell off the wall. Just call me the ghost of Humpty Dumpty, for fuck's sake.

Some ghost I am. You'd think I wouldn't be able to feel anything. Actually, I can't. It was more about me knowing the stone was jagged, rather than feeling it. A bit like how I feel about the rain.

Speaking of which, Mother Nature, who seems to be in a bitchy mood today, decided to send me a short, sharp rain shower.

'Are you kidding me?' I shouted as I glared up at the sky.

In no time at all I was soaked to the skin. I sat there, honestly believing I was shivering and could feel my hair plastered to my scalp. I bet I looked a mess. Five minutes later, and typical of our British summer weather, the rain stopped and the sun burst through the clouds. Steam began to rise up off the road surface, and I wrung the water out of my hair as best as I could while I waited for my clothes to dry.

It took less than a minute because I'm a ghost and I don't get wet.

Chapter 9 – Nature v nurture.

Of course, this took me down memory lane again. It was a Saturday and it was a showery summer's afternoon, a bit like the weather today, when my mum and dad—Alan and Linda—called me into the kitchen where they were both sitting at the table. They had their serious faces on. Before I could say anything, they told me they had something they wanted to discuss with me. I was about fifteen then, and the look on their faces was a bit worrying. I wracked my brains to try and figure out what I'd done wrong, and who might have ratted on me about what I'd done. I felt the cold fear settle around me as it dawned on me that maybe they'd got wind of something Claire and I had be up to.

Claire was my best friend ever since primary school and we got up to all kinds of mischief from the very start. Nothing serious, and it was all in good fun, but we often got a good telling off for our behaviour. I was fortunate in that Alan and Linda didn't live too far from where I'd lived with my original parents, so I didn't have to change schools so Claire and I were still best friends.

There were positives and negatives in this scenario, though. Positive, because I didn't have to face a complete upheaval in my life—new parents, new name, new home, new school and new friends. Negative, because I had to face the sympathetic looks and sighs—I was their tragic heroine for a few weeks—and then suffer the cruel gallows humour of the usual Orphan Lucy jokes and comments once the sympathy came to an end. I fought back a few times, which got me in trouble with the teachers a bit, but my classmates soon learned to shut up about me and my dead parents. I was thankful to have Claire by my side, always supporting and defending me.

But, sitting there in front of Mum and Dad, I wondered if this chat—as they called it—was about Claire and me, and a few others that we hung around with, smoking in the shrubbery behind the bus shelter last Friday evening. Someone had ratted on us as two of the gang had already been yelled at by their parents. I figured all the other parents had been informed and now it was my turn to get shouted at and warned about the dangers of smoking.

Or it could be the kiss and cuddle I gave Stuart last weekend. When I let him cop a feel of my boob. Jesus, if it was that, they would murder me.

It was worth dying for, though.

I sat down opposite them, my face the image of wide-eyed innocence and, now when I think back on it, I'm sat on this wall grinning as I imagine my dad switching on a recording device and stating – 'For the purposes of the tape, interview of suspect Lucy Arnott commencing—blah, blah, blah.'

I don't know if equipment such as police interview recording devices existed back then, or if they just wrote it down, but I can easily imagine Dad doing that.

But no, it was nothing to do with me smoking or getting my boobs felt by Stuart. Stuart, by the way, wasn't my boyfriend. He was a mate but I fancied him like crazy and I was working on upgrading him to serious boyfriend status.

No, this must be something much worse because I remember Mum's eyes filling with tears as she pulled a tissue out of her pocket and dabbed her eyes with it.

What the bloody hell was it? It couldn't be the "Sex Talk"—that wouldn't make Mum cry for a start—because they'd sat me down at this very same table when I turned twelve and told me about sex in all its gory details—the ins and outs of it, so to speak—and they'd managed to put me right off it forever. That was probably their intention, and I must say it worked a treat, right up to the moment I snogged Graham Brooks last Christmas. We dated for two weeks, and although we didn't do much in the way of groping or anything like that, we had some great snogging sessions. He wanted to, but I never let it go any further and we broke up in the New Year. He said he had to study because he was getting behind but it was probably because I wouldn't let him into my knickers. I wasn't upset because I'd gone off him anyway and I'd set my eyes, and my heart, on Stuart.

Stuart had gone the farthest so far, the evening he felt my boob. And when I say felt my boob, he didn't just cop a feel. He cupped it in his hand—all 32B of it—and ran his thumb gently over my nipple. Oh, wow. The sensations I felt down *there* from just that one touch. I couldn't believe it, and I sort of got why my mum and dad played it down and said it was bad. If this was bad, I never wanted to be good.

'You know we love you, Lucy,' my dad said.

Unable to speak, I nodded.

'We've loved you since the very moment you came

67

into our lives,' Mum said.

I sensed a "but" coming. But we've stopped loving you. But we know you've let Stuart feel you up and we're disowning you because of it. But we're getting a divorce and neither of us like you enough to want custody of you, so we've decided to give you back to Social Services for a refund. But we're broke and we need one of your kidneys to sell to that nice young man from Black Market Organs Ltd. But. But. But what?

'But we think it's time you knew about your birth parents and who you really are.'

I almost fainted with relief as Mum, still dabbing her eyes with the tissue, got up and opened the kitchen drawer. I watched her as she took out a large file, stuffed almost to bursting, and placed it on the table in front of her.

They must have put the file in the drawer earlier because I knew it hadn't been there before. That drawer was for old batteries, matches, cables, and other odds and ends—stuff you can't bring yourself to throw out in case you might need it one day.

Mum rested her palm on the file and her nails made a clicking noise as she tapped her fingers against it.

'Is that it?' I asked. 'You guys had me really frightened there. I thought you both were dying or something.'

At least it wasn't about the smoking or the snogging, and I was keeping my kidneys.

Their stilted laughter failed to completely dispel the tension that surrounded the three of us as we sat around the kitchen table. I didn't know what to do or what to say to ease it. I lowered my head and stared at the wooden surface of the old farmhouse-style table. It had been scrubbed clean so much over the years that it was almost completely white, apart from the rings made by mugs of coffee, a few pen marks and some food stains that no amount of scrubbing could ever budge. No one minded the marks and stains; they were just part of its story.

So much of our family history could be told around this table. The day I arrived at this house—this home—I'd been encouraged to sit on one of the chairs and was given a glass of milk and a big slice of the most delicious chocolate cake in the world. My mum—Linda as she was then—smiled and said hello, and told me to eat up because there was plenty more where that came from. My hesitation left me and I took a big bite and then another. It really was delicious and I learned later that it was homemade.

The nice lady from Social Services—Jane—was there too, and was smiling as Linda poured her a cup of tea. Alan was hovering in the background when Jane told me that these lovely people wanted to be my new mummy and daddy, but only if I was okay with it and if it was what I wanted.

Other than the chocolate cake, I didn't know what I wanted. I didn't want a pony any more, and the couple I was staying with—my foster parents—were friendly and nice. But a new mum and dad? I didn't know what had happened to my old ones and I still missed them. I missed my own bed in my own house, playing on the swing in the back garden, and going out in the car for an afternoon drive—

The crash. I remembered it.

'Where are my other mummy and daddy?' I asked Jane. 'Why can't I be with them? Why do I need new ones?'

Jane and the lady who gave me the cake and milk exchanged a look. Then Jane took my hand in hers and gave it a gentle squeeze.

'Do you remember being in the car, Lucy?'

I nodded. I eyed the chocolate cake again and the lady pushed the plate closer to me.

'Well, there was an accident and your mummy and daddy were hurt and the doctors couldn't fix them,' Jane said.

'But they'll be coming back for me once they're fixed? Won't they?' I asked between mouthfuls of cake.

'I'm sorry Lucy. That isn't going to happen and that's why we're trying to find you a new mummy and daddy. These lovely people—Linda and Alan—want to be your parents and then you'd be their daughter. But only if you want this as well. It's your decision, sweetheart.'

'I don't know.'

I really didn't. I didn't know these people and I didn't know why they wanted to be my parents. I looked at Jane and my eyes filled with tears.

Linda came over to me and knelt down beside me. She took my small hand in hers and smiled at me. Her smile wasn't just on her lips, it was in her eyes and all over her face. Through my tears, I smiled back at her.

'You don't have to make any decisions just yet, love,' she said. 'You take all the time you need and, if it helps, you can come and visit a few times—maybe stay for tea, or we could go out for ice creams—and that way we can all get to know each other a bit better before we make any big decisions. But, even if you don't want us to be your mum and dad, that's okay too. How does that sound?'

I nodded slowly and her smile got even bigger. Then I don't know why I did it, but I threw my arms around her neck and buried my face against her shoulder. She put her arms around me and hugged me back. I think I knew then that I wanted her to be my new mum.

~~~

That had been a year after my birth parents died. I remembered it like it was yesterday. I spent a year in and out of temporary foster homes—some good, some not so good, but none of them were really bad—until a family member could be found. That didn't materialise, because, although the Canadian cousin didn't want me, he'd be prepared to adopt me if he was given a large sum of money to cover the extra mouth that he and his wife would have to feed, clothe and educate. As a result, Social Services kept me in foster care but placed me on the adoption register where Alan and Linda found me. And wanted me to become their daughter.

The process took around six months, and during that time, I spent afternoons with them under Social Service supervision, with someone always ready to intervene should anything go wrong—like they tried to kill me, or I tried to kill them. I'm sure these things happen now and again. Once they were satisfied there were no issues, I got to spend full days with Alan and Linda. I was getting to know them and they were getting to know me. It didn't take long for me to become happy and comfortable in their company. It was like I'd known them all my life. Once it was finalised and I finally came home with Linda and Alan—now Mum and Dad—for good, I never looked back. They were wonderful. They loved me so much and did everything they could to make me happy. I didn't tell them, but I'd already been won over by the chocolate cake. Mum taught me how to bake one and I make it for my own girls now.

Or at least I did when I was alive.

~~~

It was the day when they told my fifteen-year-old self to sit down because they needed to talk to me that I learned who I really was. I mean, I knew I was adopted and I knew my real name, but other than a few fragmented memories, and a few bits and pieces gleaned from Linda, I had no real recollections of my life before the car accident. I was never curious anyway. These two people sitting opposite me were my parents and I was their daughter. I didn't need anything else.

Mind you, that didn't stop me hoping for some great revelation, and I told them I always thought I was a princess or an heiress, or the forbidden love child of two very important people who had to keep me hidden for my own safety. But, in truth—as I opened the file and read the first page—I was the daughter of Gillian and Harry Blake. A secondary school teacher and an accountant who had both been killed instantly when they were involved in a car crash while taking their only daughter to an equestrian centre on a day trip. I already knew that bit, but it was still a shock to read it again, and I felt the old feelings of guilt bubbling up to the surface once again.

Mum and Dad, as well as the shrink from Social Services, had spoken to me at length about this, and they reiterated time and time again that it wasn't my fault. It was the little git in the Peugeot that killed my parents, but still—

If I hadn't wanted a bloody pony so much, they wouldn't have been on the road that day.

~~~

Mum had pushed the file across the table towards me and smiled at my flippant jokes about being an heiress, but she said nothing, knowing full well that my inappropriate humour was my way of deflecting my fears and concerns. I wondered who I got that from. Gillian or Harry?

Inside the file, I found my birth certificate bearing my original surname of Blake. It was a normal name, nothing special, and l preferred the name I had now—Arnott. I whispered the name Lucy Blake and it didn't resonate in any way. I whispered Lucy Arnott and I knew that was me. This girl known as Lucy Blake was a stranger. In fact, she was more than a stranger—she no longer existed.

My parents' birth certificates, their marriage certificate and their death certificates were there too, along with about twenty photographs in a paper envelope. I lifted the envelope and took out the photos. They were old and faded, and the kind you had to leave into Boots chemists to have them developed. Then call back the following week to get them. I guess my real parents hadn't gone down the digital road back then. I fanned them out on the table in front of me and looked at them. They were all photographs of me—through various stages of my early life, from babyhood to first steps, first day at school, and then a few Christmas and holiday snaps after that. Up until—well, up until it ended. In nearly all of the photos, I was with the two people who had brought me into the world. I stared at the photos of two strangers and a little girl I couldn't remember. I studied each photo for ages, scrutinising their faces, trying to find me in their eyes or the shape of their ears. I kind of recognised me there, but only in a vague sense and I knew nothing about their personalities. I got the feeling from the relaxed body language and their smiles that I was loved and adored. Of course I was loved and adored. I'm that kind of person. Yeah, fifteen-year-old me was a right arrogant little shit. I still am. Or rather I was.

But seriously, no matter how long I stared at the photos, I didn't know these people. They weren't my mum and dad, and they didn't mean anything to me at all.

I gathered them up and put them back in the envelope. I'd seen all I had to see in the photos and, to be honest, I didn't want to look through the rest of the file. What was in there didn't matter to me. I remember that I did read it eventually, but out of curiosity, rather than a desire to find myself.

I remember how tense my parents were when I was looking at the photos, and I remember their sigh of relief when I put them back in the envelope and closed the file.

I glanced at my mum and dad and spread my hands, palms upwards, on the table. Mum clasped my right hand tightly while Dad took my other hand in his and gave it a gentle squeeze.

'You are my parents,' I told them. 'Not these people. I know they were my biological parents. They brought me into the world, but it's you who have brought me up. You taught me to ride a bike, Dad. And when I fell off that bike and skinned my knees and my palms, it was you Mum, you who dabbed TCP or peroxide on my cuts and scrapes, and shushed me when I howled because the TCP or whatever stung more than the cuts hurt at the time. You cleaned me up, stuck a band-aid on the parts that needed one and told me not to pick at the scabs when they formed. And you kissed the pain away, Mum. You. The two people in those old photographs would have done the same but they weren't there. They died and they weren't there to teach me how to ride a bike and kiss me better when I fell off it. You were. You and Dad. You're here. They're not.'

I could see Mum's eyes filling up again, and I hated making her cry but I was on a roll now.

'You tucked me in at night and told me you loved me. You gave me the sex talk and we all got so embarrassed. You scolded me when I did something wrong and you praised me when I did something right. Remember the weird hip-swaying happy dance you did when I got A's in my exams? I honestly thought you were thinking back to your days as a stripper.'

Through her tears, Mum chuckled at the memory and how, ever since that day, it was a standing joke in our house that Mum was an ex-stripper.

'You stood in the rain and the cold at sports day, and

75

cheered me on, and you've made me feel wanted and loved all my life. I've no doubt these people loved me too, but they died. It wasn't their fault they left me, but their deaths brought me to you.'

I smiled at my parents. 'I got lucky twice.'

Mum was furiously dabbing at her eyes now and even Dad was sniffling.

'I mean, it's cool to know where I got my eye and hair colour from and all, but you are the ones who made this bratty teenager sitting in front of you the person she is today. You're the reason I can be cheeky and too sarcastic for my own good sometimes. But you are also the reason I love to read and I'm good at sports and I can bake a mean chocolate cake. If I ever have a daughter, she will be the second-luckiest girl in the whole world because she will have you for her grandparents. I'm the luckiest girl in the world because I have you for parents. And I love you both so very much.'

Neither of my parents could speak by this stage, and I thought they were really going to start bawling their eyes out. I shook my head and smiled at them.

'We could either have a group hug or you could open a bottle of wine. I think I deserve a glass or two after that scare you gave me when you told me to sit down.'

That broke the emotionally-charged atmosphere and the tears in the eyes of both my parents became tears of relieved laughter.

'Not a chance young lady,' my dad said. 'Nice try, though.'

Chapter 10 – The hearts I've broken.

All this reminiscing was nice, but it was also painful and I wondered how my heartbroken parents were coping. At the funeral they didn't look as though they were coping at all. Black circles surrounded my dad's eyes as a testament to a lack of sleep—he probably hadn't slept at all from the moment he was given the news of his only daughter's death. Maybe even before that, when I was in hospital. Was I in hospital? I don't remember, and I don't know why I would think that I was.

I could see that my dad's skin was grey with shock and he seemed to have aged ten years.

Mum hadn't fared any better. Her eyes were red and puffy from all the tears she'd cried. The weight had dropped off her and she was stooped over like an old woman under the heavy burden of her grief.

My heart went out to them and I wished with all my heart that I hadn't died and caused all this heartbreak.

If only I had looked where I was going, I wouldn't have tripped and taken that tumble and hit my head on that rock.

That memory stopped me in my tracks.

I tripped and I died from a fall? How did I manage that? The clumsy cow that I am wasn't looking where I was going, that's how. I tripped and fell down and died. How embarrassing is that? And where did it happen?

I had a suspicion that it happened when I was out for an early morning walk and taking photographs. It was the perfect scenario because I would have been concentrating on the views and possible shots and not looking where I was putting my feet. The sheep and rabbit dung I tracked into the car on the soles of my boots after these hikes bore testament to that, and it did Charlie's head in. He ordered me to keep a plastic carrier bag in the car and put my boots into it after a hike. I did it a couple of times when I remembered, but most of the time I forgot.

So, if I died up there how long was I there before they found me? Was I missing for days and my body became food for the red kites and the kestrels? Was the Air Ambulance called out and did I finally get the ride in a helicopter I always wanted? Didn't Prince William do Air Rescue in a helicopter for a while? Did I miss out on a ride in a helicopter with Prince William, dammit?

I couldn't help thinking about it, not missing out on meeting Prince William—okay, I thought about that, too— but the whole falling down, hitting my head and dying thing. I picked at the memory like a scab because the scenario I was envisaging didn't seem quite correct. The falling down bit seemed genuine, because I do tend to trip a lot, but the notion that I'd died up on the moors didn't ring true because I also had a fleeting memory of sitting out on the patio with Charlie drinking wine while we watched the setting sun. But was that before or after?

And why does the name Jennifer keep popping into my head? Who is she?

Other than a classmate I wasn't particularly friendly with, from way back in secondary school, I don't recall anyone named Jennifer. The Jennifer in school had been a casual acquaintance rather than a friend for no reason other than she was a quiet, studious girl who didn't socialise much. I don't think I ever said more than a dozen words to her in the whole time we'd been at school together. I can barely remember what she looked like.

While I had no idea who this Jennifer could be, it got me thinking about my schooldays and the friends I hung out with during those years. About a dozen of them could be called friends—Sophie, Karen, Mandy, Binita, Meera and Misha—twins who were affectionally nicknamed M&M—Beth, another Karen—known as Karen Two—and of course, Claire. And five boys—Jeff, Billy, Craig, Stuart and Ollie. The guys were strictly off limits as dates because that would have upset the dynamic of our friendship, or gang, or whatever—but Stuart and I got together in our last year, and I did hear some years later that Sophie and Jeff had hooked up and got married. Out of all of them, Claire was my best friend. She was the one who remained my bestie long after school ended and, although I went on to university and Claire moved away for a while, we stayed in touch. Then, when she came back home again, we were as close as we ever were.

We weren't quite the Scooby Gang—either the cartoon characters or the nickname of Buffy's friends. We didn't solve murders by day or hunt vampires by night. If anything, we tended to be the hunted rather than the hunters because, while we weren't exactly juvenile delinquents, we got up to more than our fair share of mischief. Nothing serious, though. Drinking cider and smoking were probably the worst crimes we'd committed. Up until we all decided to go on a minor shoplifting spree one summer. It was a challenge we set and we didn't do it because we needed to hone our skills in preparation for a future life of crime We did it because we were bored. There were no mobile phones in the mid-to-late-nineties—at least not for teenagers in semi-rural Yorkshire. Social media didn't exist so we didn't have Facebook and Instagram to scroll through back then. It was mostly just hanging around talking, smoking and enjoying lager or cider when we could score it. Drugs didn't exist to the extent that they do today and, even if they did, we wouldn't have had a clue how to get them. Boredom was our main thing during the summer hols back then.

I have no idea who came up with it. It wasn't me, officer. Honest. Actually, it might have been me because I was often the instigator but, on this occasion, I can't remember who it was. Somehow, we came up with the idea of this brilliant, and very risky, dare. Brilliant, because it sounded like fun. Risky, because getting caught could land the perpetrator in trouble with the local police as well as the parents.

We weighed up the pros and cons, and decided that the fun far outweighed the risk factor, and we all agreed that each of us would steal something from the corner shop without getting caught. Strict rules were suggested and approved, and points would be awarded for the most daring and successful theft. There wasn't a prize but the winner would be granted the status of a legend, and lesser mortals would bow before his or her skill and magnificence.

One of the rules we set down was that we could only steal one item, and it had to be edible so no evidence would be left—which made sense—and it had to cost less than a pound. We also had to do it in pairs so not only would we would have confirmation that we had carried out the dare, but also our partner in crime would distract the shopkeeper. Our partners were selected by vote and, when my turn came, I was partnered with Karen Two.

Everyone agreed, and we set a time limit of two days for each one to do the dastardly deed. I was crapping myself when my turn came. Karen Two did hers the day before, with me having a rather boring chat with the shopkeeper so he wouldn't see her swiping a bag of crisps, and we were delighted with her selection because we all got a share of the proceeds.

I didn't want to steal crisps or chocolate as I'd been on a health kick that summer because I wanted to lose a couple of pounds, despite my mum telling me it was only puppy fat.

'I'm thirteen, Mum. This is not puppy fat.' I remembered saying.

With healthy eating in mind, an apple was my desired choice but it would be hard to conceal. I plumped for a Mars Bar instead, despite my desire to cut back on tasty goodies. I've done that a lot over the years—an apple or a Mars Bar? Mars Bar or apple? Easy decision. I'd decided that the chocolate was much tastier than the apple and, more importantly, it slipped easily inside my sleeve in a way that a Granny Smith wouldn't. Despite my nerves, I was shaking like a leaf, but I got it, hid it up my sleeve, and it stayed there until I made my getaway.

That had been the extent of my life of crime. And

Mum had been right about the puppy fat.

But this still didn't explain who this Jennifer woman was.

I don't know her but I feel like I do. This is so weird.

Chapter 11 – To do lists can be fun.

I love making lists. To do lists, grocery lists, Christmas card lists, birthday party lists, nice bottles of wine I've drunk lists. Not that I ever bought any of them. I had a habit of losing the scrap of paper I'd written them on, and ended up buying whatever wine was on offer at the local off-licence.

I made a list of things to do on holiday—which we never did as we just took each day as it came with no prior planning. Things to put in the suitcase lists. Places to visit lists—at home and abroad. Cleaning lists—easier and much more fun to do than the actual cleaning. I made all kinds of lists. When we first bought the farmhouse, I made lists of all the things we needed to do to finish it and make it habitable. I had an indoor list and an outdoor list, and they were about three pages each. There was nothing better than putting a line through a job that was finished, and I loved it when there were more lines through the completed work than things written there that we still had to do.

Admittedly, in the first weeks after we signed on the dotted lines to complete the purchase and finally got the house keys, there was more added to my lists each day than we managed to cross off. It was daunting and it worried me. I thought we'd never be finished and, I must admit, it terrified me. Especially when Charlie was miles away on a construction job and had to stay there, sometimes for a week or so. I know he was at the end of a phone if I needed to talk to him, but I still fretted at the enormity of what faced us—or me—when he was away. I didn't complain about it, though. Charlie being away on a big job meant good money was coming in. Money that we needed because we were, or rather I was, spending it like we had a printing press in the back room. Part of that was my fault because, although I loved the house itself with a passion, there were some things I just didn't like, the colour of the tiles in the bathroom for instance, and I insisted on changing them.

I do have a tendency to shout and stamp my foot and insist it's my way or no way when I make up my mind that I want something. Ripping out the perfectly good tiles because I didn't like the colour was one of those things.

Oddly enough, we never made a baby name list for either of the girls before they were born. Probably because we had more or less picked the names and also because we didn't want to tempt fate in any way.

Now that I'm dead, I have plenty of time to make lists for everything. Because being dead is so absolutely boring. I can't eat, sleep, get drunk, drive the car, go swimming, wash my hair, have sex, surf the internet, or do any of the million everyday things people do. So, I pass the time by making lists in my mind. That was the first one—a list of all the things I can't do any more. The list of things I can do is an awful lot shorter. I can't even haunt people, but I did make a list of people I'd love to haunt if I could. It was long, and ranged from famous politicians to just about everyone who'd pissed me off since as far back as I could remember. I spent ages on that one.

But I also made, not so much a list, but a series of mental notes that might help me figure out what happened to me. I was slowly piecing it together in my mind and beginning to understand it. Not everything yet because my memory still had a lot of blanks but, from what I have managed to remember, it wasn't anything spectacular, and it wasn't exactly an exciting revelation.

Basically, I was just unlucky.

From what I remember—and it's still all a bit patchy—I got up early on the Saturday morning, packed a lunch, persuaded Ross to come with me—not that he needed much persuasion—and we drove up in my old Land Rover because I wanted to take a batch of photos for a project I was working on—a few sets of scenic prints that I could sell at the markets and craft fairs in the run up to Christmas. It was summertime—late summer, I think—and the weather was fair, but a little bit chilly. No rain and early morning sunrise meant good sharp images, so it was perfect.

I remember sitting on a big boulder, happily munching my sarnies while Ross raced around chasing whatever his imagination and his nose could conjure up. Then, on the way home I tripped and fell. I must have hurt my ankle because I remember limping back to the Land Rover. And that's all I can remember.

So how did I die?

No matter how hard I thought about it, I couldn't figure it out, and I have a feeling this Jennifer woman is connected, or involved. but I can't get any closer than that.

It wasn't quite giving me a headache, but I was annoyed at myself for not being able to remember, and I wondered if it was part of the brain damage—

Whoa! Is that part of it? Is that why I can't remember? Did my head get banged about so badly that bits of my brain turned to mush, especially the memory bit?

This didn't make for pleasant thinking and I decided to put my lists away for a while and think of something nicer. Besides, I was getting bored with thinking about it and getting nowhere.

Chapter 12 - Pets.

Remember the movie—*The Sixth Sense*? Where the little boy said he could see dead people? Well, most animals can see dead people too. I don't know how or why but they're very good at it.

I first discovered this little-known fact when I was poking around the village one night. Yeah, you've guessed it. I'm a nosey parker. I wander into people's back gardens and peek through their windows. I see all sorts of stuff. And, not surprisingly, most of it consists of the ordinary, mundane things we all get up to in the evenings in the living room. We get comfy on the couch, grab the remote and spend the evening watching television. A cycle of the news first, then maybe a surf through the Sky channels to see if there's a half-decent drama series that's worth either watching live or downloading on catch-up to watch later. Then you have a run through the sports channels and, if nothing there takes your fancy, you go to Netflix or Amazon and select the series you've been watching. Pause it to go into the kitchen and make yourself a brew and then settle down for the rest of the evening with your feet up. Or you could listen to music and read. Catch up on some ironing. Bake a cake or have wild, passionate sex with your significant other. Or all of the above.

I know it sounds boring, but it's life. It's what most of us do after a long day at work. The kids are fed and washed and off to bed. The dinner dishes are in the dishwasher and the dog has been walked and is asleep at your feet. He'll need a few minutes outside later for a pee before bed but he's okay for now. You're tired but it's only a quarter to nine and it's far too early for bed. So, you watch TV, have a bit of a natter, read a few chapters of a book or scroll through Facebook and Instagram on your phone. Evening sorted.

Charlie and I did that most evenings throughout the working week, especially in the winter. And it was nice. Actually, it was more than nice. There was nothing more heart-warming than getting a good fire going in the wood stove, curling up together on the sofa and watching something on the telly. Or Charlie watching something while I read a book on my Kindle, and then maybe sex, if both of us were in the mood. We did it less in the summer, though. Curled up in front of the fire to watch the telly, I mean. The sex was, if anything, more frequent in the summer time.

The way we designed the back patio meant we had some shelter from the breeze that blew down off the hills, and it was south-facing so it caught the sun for most of the day and well into the evening. All it took was a sniff of half-decent weather and we practically moved out there. Lunches, dinners and even breakfasts were all taken out the back when the weather was nice. And we had plenty of barbeques with friends and family—the kids all playing on the lawn in front of us where we could keep an eye on them, and the adults enjoying wine or gin, beer or cider, while Charlie cooked the steaks for our dinner with burgers and sausages for the kids. Salads that had been prepared that morning and kept in the fridge until needed, and plates and cutlery left out with paper napkins and condiments. I was so well-organised I could sit back and enjoy my wine with nothing to disturb me. Claire taught me that. She'd perfected the art of relaxing outdoors in the summer, glass in hand, watching someone else doing the hard work.

I loved those summer evenings with friends over, but I also loved the evenings when it was just Charlie and me. Especially the last one—

The last one? What? What did that mean? Did we have a romantic evening on the patio and I died the next day? Something tells me that was what happened. That, or something similar. I wish I could remember it properly. I remember some of it but it's still full of gaping holes.

I wracked my brain, or at least the parts of it that were still intact, but I couldn't get any more details about my demise. Maybe an image or two, and a thought here and there, but nothing concrete. Nothing by way of an explanation.

~~~

So, back to the good times on the sofa on winter nights. Yeah, we did that like the old married couple we were. Content in the glow of the warm fire and the comfort of familiarity. Those were our weeknights.

Weekends were another thing altogether. We'd organise a babysitter and go out somewhere—usually into town with Claire and Gavin for a meal in a nice restaurant—we had one or two favourites—or an evening in the village pub. Sometimes we went to listen to whatever live music was on. Other times we participated in the twice-a-month a pub quiz. I loved the quizzes because I was good at them. I had a head stuffed to overflowing with trivia and I could pull the answer to the most obscure question out of the 'stupid facts' filing cabinet in my mind. Pub quizzes were fun, and usually organised to raise money for a charity, but you'd be surprised how competitive they sometimes got. Not to the extent of punch-ups, but occasionally things got a bit heated.

Other times we'd pack up the girls, and Ross, and spend the weekend at Claire's. We'd usually alternate—our place one weekend, their place the next.

And speaking of dogs, it's time I got back on-topic again. My attention seems to go everywhere and anywhere all at once these days. My thoughts are all tangled up like socks in a tumble dryer and I haven't a clue how to sort them out.

~~~

Yes, animals can see me. Or at least they can sense me when I'm close to them. It's pretty limited, and mostly they just turn their heads in my direction, but sometimes they flatten their ears and cower down. I hate that, but most of the time they just give me a curious glance, thankfully. I did get a slight wag of a tail once. That made my day.

I discovered that cats are more aware of me than dogs. It happened one evening when I was peeking in through the living room window of a house in what I would describe as a reasonably well-to-do area on the outskirts of the village. Like I said, most people are couch potatoes, content to spend their evenings sitting in front of the TV while sipping from their mug of tea, or their beer, or their glass of wine. But every now and then, oh my—

~~

Although the curtains were pulled across, the occupants of this house hadn't closed them completely and I was able to look through the front window right into the living room. I won't say which house because that would be telling. I know most of the people in the village and the surrounding areas. At least I know their faces, if not all their names, so I don't know who lives here.

I could see that the lights were dimmed and the television was switched off. Music played softly on the stereo—some crooner from the 50's or 60's, I think.

Through the gap in the curtains, I could see a middle-aged man on his hands and knees on the floor. He was naked apart from a ball gag and a studded collar around his neck. I tried to get a look at his face to see who he was—it's a small village and everyone knows everyone, and I'm a nosey cow. So, while I was trying to identify him, a woman, also middle-aged, wearing only a pair of thigh-high boots, a mask, and a strap-on stepped into the—er—cosy living room scene and cracked the whip she was holding. The man whimpered with either terror or excitement. I'd guess terror by the size of the strap-on, but you never know. I whimpered a little myself. Suddenly it dawned on me who they were and it was all I could do to not to burst out laughing.

But, while I'm a little bit kinky, I'm not that kinky. I didn't want to see any more so I stepped back and there was this blood-curdling yowl from a dark corner near the wooden gate that led to the back of the house. I screamed and jumped back. Then there was a hiss and another, sort of angry, but mostly frightened yowl. And I could see two greenish eyes glaring at me from the darkness.

It was a cat.

Now, I love cats. They are the most awesome creatures in the universe, but sometimes the noises they make can turn you into a quivering mass of terrified jelly.

From a relatively safe distance, I calmed down and peered at it. It flattened its ears and peered back at me as it sat there, hunched in the corner on the doorstep. Obviously, it had been chucked outside while Mr and Mrs Kinky Kouple got their jollies on.

'Here, puss,' I said, and made kissy-kissy noises to win it over. Like that would ever work with a cat.

True to form, it growled back at me and backed up even further into the corner.

I knelt down and held out my hand. Some company at last, I thought. I had this vision of me and my black cat familiar have a great old time together.

'Hey, pussy-cat. I'm er—locked out, too. Can't we be friends?'

Growl, meow, hiss. And a paw came up ready to bat or claw at my hand if I came any closer.

He, or she, was as black as a coal cellar at midnight. And he, or she, was terrified of me.

I stood up and took a step back. Darkie, as I've now named him, or her, leapt up onto the wall and disappeared, leaving me lonely and more than a little concerned.

Because it begs the question, am I an evil hell-spawn? An embittered spirit, trapped forever between the worlds, destined to seek out revenge on those who have wronged me? Or was I a lost soul, or even a Chosen One, seeking to right some cosmic wrong before I could find eternal peace?

I hadn't a clue.

But whatever I was now, that cat was terrified of me. And that was depressing.

Ah, shit.

Depression smiled. Believe me, it didn't look good on her at all. She obviously needed the work and was aiming for a more enticing appearance.

'Come here, love.' She held out her hands to me, offering me the comfort of her down-in-the-dumps personality. I was sorely in need of some comfort, so I stepped forward and allowed her to wrap her arms around me as she pulled me into her embrace. I started crying because Depression was here and because the cat didn't like me.

'I love cats,' I managed to say between gasping, heart-broken sobs.

'I know you do.' Depression held me tightly and rubbed my back. 'And they love you. Mostly. You know what cats are like. Feed them on time, or five minutes early, and they adore you. Feed them five minutes late and they're plotting to kill you and dispose of your body. Don't take it personally.'

'Why not?'

'Because, while you're not an evil hell-spawn—there's no such a thing, by the way—you are a lost soul. And, I hate to tell you this, but you are kind of stuck. Here.'

'Why?'

'I have no idea. Call it a mistake. A glitch. Maybe you weren't meant to die but you did, and you're sort of caught halfway in between.'

'In between what?'

'Um—here and there, I suppose. I don't know. It's not like I have a cousin called Explanation that I can just WhatsApp and ask.'

I pulled myself out of her arms.

'So, I'm stuck here—in between here and wherever I'm supposed to be and I can't even have a pet?' I started crying again.

'I know. I know. It's awful. There, there. Have a good cry.'

Depression was at her peak now. I needed to stop her.

'Any animal? Any pet? Not even Ross, my collie?'

She got a bit cagey and couldn't look at me.

'What are you not telling me?'

'Nothing.' She studied the ground at her feet. The grass and the mud from the rain earlier was fascinating.

'Tell me, or I'll get angry.'

Yep. The ground was so very interesting.

'I mean it. I'll get really mad.'

'Okay. Okay.' She held her hands up. 'Don't get angry. You know what will happen when Anger shows up.'

She glanced around, expecting to see him standing behind her. He wasn't, because I wasn't mad. I was sad.

Depression breathed a sigh of relief.

'Talk,' I said.

'Well, I don't know much about it—how it works and all. Some pets and animals will be afraid. But that's rare. You were just unlucky to find a cat that had a nervous disposition. Most pets are only slightly aware of your presence, and a lot of that depends on the time of the year. It's October now, and the veil is thinning—'

'I'm sorry. The what is what?'

'The veil between the worlds grows thin around Halloween and spirits are more—um—visible to those who have the knowledge and the intuition to see them. Animals have it ingrained in their DNA—or their psyche, inner eye, kidneys, or whatever. I don't know how it works, it's not my field of expertise. I only know that it works best when the veil is thin.'

'What about people? Can they see me at this time of the year?'

'Well, some can. It depends.'

'Are you telling me that I could make contact with Charlie at Halloween?'

'Oh, no. No. Definitely not.'

'Why not?'

'Because Charlie would have to be—er—'

She scratched her head and I could tell she hadn't a clue what she was talking about.

'Dead?'

'No—I don't think so.'

'Psychic?'

'Maybe.'

'Drunk?'

'Possibly. You'd be surprised what people see when they've had a few.'

This conversation was going nowhere and I seriously needed Depression to be gone before I got angry with her.

'Okay. I get that it's not your field and I can see you

haven't an answer for what just happened. Darkie, that cat I just met, is highly strung and doesn't like things he or she can't understand. Darkie likes the simple things in life— good quality food, a warm bed, some sort of scratching post, and a litter tray for when it's raining. Having two kinky owners who throw him out while they're getting it on is a bit of a problem for Darkie. But I didn't cause it so he would have screamed and hissed no matter who turned up in the back garden. Am I right?'

Depression blew out a breath and shrugged her shoulders. 'Probably. Yeah.'

'So, this is a rare occurrence and most animals, and maybe the occasional human, would be fine if they saw me? Right?'

'Um—right. I think.'

'That's all I needed to know. And now that I know it, I'm happy again.' I gave her my most cheery smile and she disappeared in the blink of an eye.

I punched the air in victory and set off towards home to see Ross.

Chapter 13 – Dead of the night.

Everybody was asleep, including Ross. He'd forsaken his dog bed and was now stretched out on his back on the sofa. His head was upside down and drooping towards the floor, and one front paw was upright. His tongue was hanging out and he was snoring gently with the occasional soft bark thrown in. I wondered if he was dreaming.

'Ross,' I whispered his name. 'Hey Rossy-Wossy. How's my big, beautiful boy?'

He gave a few short woofs in response to whatever he was dreaming about—maybe me—and stretched his legs a bit, but he didn't open his eyes, so I left him to his slumber and took a walk around the house.

Calling him by one of his many nicknames—some good, some bad—reminded me of the little rhyme I made up as a bedtime story for the girls. It was titled *Rossy-Wossy, you're so bossy.* and it went like this—

'Rossy-Wossy, you're so bossy.
You bark all day and you bark all night.
You bark behind me and give me a fright.
You bark at trees and you bark at cars.
You bark at people and even the stars.
You beg for a treat, and sit there so sweet.
And then you lie down, asleep at my feet.
Rossy-Wossy, we love you.
Even when you roll in poo!'

The girls would chant the last line and there'd be a fit of giggles and I would have to read another, more sedate one, to get them off to sleep.

Although it didn't have the desired effect of lulling them off to sleep, Charlie thought my *Rossy-Wossy* poem was good and he said I should make up some more and write them down.

'Oh, I couldn't,' I told him. 'I wouldn't know what to write.'

'Something that will have them nodding off in seconds,' he replied.

'Like maybe—a song? Or a lullaby?'

I thought about it for a moment.

'Okay, what about this one?' I grinned and began to sing softly.

'Go to sleep little babies, else the monsters will get you.

Close your eyes. If you don't, they will steal you away.

To a land full of monsters who will chase you all day.'

'Perfect,' Charlie laughed. 'But, unless you want them hiding in the wardrobe for the remainder of their childhood, I'd stick with more traditional lullabies and save the horror-movie theme songs for when they are asleep. That one is more Stephen King than Brahams Lullaby.'

I never did sing that one to them, but I did make up lots of silly little songs and rhymes about so many things that they loved. Later, when they were too old for rhymes and songs, I made up stories about dogs and cats, the pheasants that came into the garden, and the birds at the feeder. I gave names and histories to some of the sheep in the fields around us and the foxes as they played with their cubs. All good, healthy stories that wouldn't traumatise them.

Charlie reckoned I should put them all together and think about publishing them.

'Obviously not the horror stories. You don't want to get sued by the parents of some kid who thinks *The Littlest Vampire* or *Werewolf Puppies Who Eat Naughty Children* might be real.'

'Amy thinks they're real,' I said with a straight, innocent face.

Charlie stared at me until I burst out laughing.

~~~

I loved being here in the dead of night. I could roam to my heart's content. I could make sure the girls were tucked in and fast asleep, and give them a ghostly goodnight kiss, then I'd go and check on Charlie. He's been drinking a bit more recently, and more often. Not to the point where I'm worried about him, but his alcohol intake has definitely increased. Until now, he'd always been a beer or cider bloke and really only took spirits on special occasions—Christmas, birthdays, that sort of thing—and he didn't like wine.

But he'd taken to drinking a glass or two of whiskey at night, just before bed. I expect it helps him sleep. Dulls the pain of loneliness. Don't get me wrong, it isn't an issue—he's not drinking more than two small glasses, and he isn't a neglectful father or anything like that, but I hate to see him sitting there, staring into the fire or at the TV screen, drowning his sorrows. I don't blame him. I'd be doing the same thing if he was dead and I was sitting there all alone. I'd probably be much worse. Yeah, I'd definitely be much worse.

I stayed with him until he finished his drink and, although tempted to remain until he went to bed, I slipped quietly out of the room. I did stay one night, I even stretched out on the bed alongside him and watched him go to sleep. It wasn't a happy moment for me.

~~~

On the surface, Charlie is okay. His days are the same as they've always been but without me to share them with him now. He gets up, lets Ross out to do his business, gets the girls up and ready for school, feeds them and has a bite himself. He's is a picky eater now and he has lost weight, but I suppose that's normal under the circumstances. Then they're all off out the door to school and to work, and I'm alone in the house. The way it was when I was alive, except I had more to do then—housework, laundry, paperwork, and of course, my photography business. Now, the laundry is piling up because he can only do it at the weekends, regardless of the weather, and he has to tumble dry everything if it's raining. I hated the tumble dryer, preferring to line-dry my clothes, and I only used it if I had no other choice, although the UK weather made sure I used it often enough. I can see that the kitchen needs a good tidying up and everything needs to be dusted. He'll get around to it in time. He knows he has to.

~~~

He herds them out the door and into the car. He'll be taking them to school, giving each of them a kiss and a hug, and a warning to behave themselves, as he drops them off at the gate. Then he'll go to work. I've watched him there, too. He acts as he always has—hard-working, fastidious, and he even indulges in the usual workplace banter. Typical builders and their jokes about everything. Some of them can be quite rude.

So says me, the prude.

OMG. LOL. Who's kidding who? That would be the barrage of text messages that'd be sent back and forth if anybody heard me saying that, because everyone who knew me knew that I frequently came up with dirtier jokes than any brickie ever could.

Charlie is slowly getting to grips with doing nearly everything on his own now—especially where the girls are concerned. Claire will collect them from school, take them to her house where she'll make a light snack for them, and then Charlie picks them up as soon as he finishes work. He parks them at the table and tells them he'll send them to the workhouse if they don't do their homework while he takes Ross out for a walk. Not so far now—even I can see signs of Ross slowing down as the years begin to take their toll on him. Amy and Chloe don't know exactly what the workhouse is, other than it's not good, but they know they need to do their homework if they don't want to find out.

Then everyone has dinner, including Ross—his own dinner and whatever scraps he can beg from the table—and the three of them settle down until bedtime. This is the part where Charlie is more like his normal self. He engages with the girls. He'll ask them about their day. He'll laugh at something Amy tells him, and he'll answer all of Chloe's 'Why does?' and 'Why is?' questions as best as he can.

Once the girls are bathed and off to bed, Charlie is on

his own. This is the worst time for him as he has no distractions and too much time to think. This is when I see what my death has done to him. He's not quite broken, but he is seriously battered—I can see it on his face and in his eyes. He misses me and he wants me back. He wants to close his eyes and when he opens them again, I'll be standing in front of him and he'll be happy once more.

Oh, Charlie. I wish I could be with you. I wish I could hold you again, laugh and joke with you, work out the monthly bills with you. Curl up in front of the telly with you. Make love to you. Do all the normal things we did together as a couple and as a family with two young children. I want all of that back as much as you do. But we can't. I'm gone and there's nothing that can change that. I'm so sorry.

It was moments like this that kept me from lingering too long in this house I called home. I loved the place with a passion, and I felt I was still tied to it because no matter how much I promised myself I wouldn't go back—seeing Charlie and my lovely daughters without me was almost too much to bear—I was still drawn to this place. It made sense on some level because it had been my home. Charlie and I had worked hard to make it the way we wanted it and, in my eyes, it was perfect.

But most of the time I went there at night when they were fast asleep, or during the day when they were at school and at work. I needed to be there on my own. That way I could pretend I was still alive and they'd gone off to school and work. Or they'd be home any minute now, looking for their dinner and telling me all about their day as

I dished out their food. I even imagined what I was making for them—something nice, that they'd enjoy and praise me over how tasty it was.

To be honest, I was never that good a housewife when I was alive. There were dozens of times when I got caught up in a work project, maybe looking for the perfect photo to put on a canvas, and time got away from me. I'd look up in surprise when I heard the door opening, and there'd be a moment of panic before I dug some oven chips and frozen battered fish out of the freezer to feed my family.

~~~

In the wee small hours, I loved walking through the house, listening to it creak and groan as though—now that its occupants were safely tucked in and fast asleep—it too could settle down for the night. A gust of wind whistled and made the leaves of the nearby trees rustle, and I could hear an owl hooting in the distance as I glided down the stairs—the way any self-respecting ghost in a scary movie would. Except I didn't actually glide. I wasn't that sort of ghost. I walked down them the same way I always did, being careful not to trip and fall because I did that once. I was fortunate in that I was almost at the bottom when my foot slid off the step. Down I went, banging my knee and wrenching my shoulder in the process. I was okay after a couple of days, limping around and not using my left arm too much. Do ghosts trip and fall over like regular folk? If they were clumsy in real life, would they be the same when they're dead? Or should that be undead?

That thought made me stop halfway down the stairs, and almost caused me to fall down them. What exactly is undead anyway? I'd watched enough horrors movies and read enough horror books over the years to know what the word meant in a fictional context, but what if it was real?

I turned and ran back up the stairs and into the bathroom, closed the door without making any noise and switched on the small strip light over the mirror above the wash-hand basin. There I was, staring back at myself.

I peered at myself, considering my features, and turning my head this way and that to see if there was anything different about me. I scrunched my face to the left and the right, opened my eyes wide and leaned forward to get a closer look. There was nothing out of the ordinary that I could see. My eyes were a little bloodshot and tired-looking but I had downed a bottle and a half of wine the night before when Charlie and I were sitting out on the patio after dinner—so maybe my slight hangover appearance had carried over into death, and bleary-eyed me was to be expected. I just hope wasn't permanent.

Charlie and I were sitting out on the patio? When?

I concentrated on trying to remember. I had a sore ankle and a bump on my head. What had I done to cause that? I'm not sure. It might have been a fall. I don't know. I remembered us laughing and joking over dinner, and I remember sitting with a bag of frozen peas on my ankle. He'd grilled the steaks on the barbeque, and we ate them outside while he drank beer and I got stuck into the wine. The girls were nowhere to be seen. Then it came back to me. Charlie had packed them off to Claire's for a sleepover. It was the weekend and he'd planned a romantic Saturday evening for just the two of us.

And romantic it had been, despite my ankle which didn't hurt so much thanks to the bag of petit pois that were no longer on tomorrow night's dinner menu, and a few large glasses of my favourite chardonnay. I had totally forgotten about the bump on my head, but I remembered now that I'd been out all that day taking photographs. I'd tripped and fallen, twisting my ankle and hitting my head on a rock on my way back down to the carpark. That was me to a T, never looking where I was going.

But we watched the sun setting and sat out long after darkness had fallen. We shared a wonderful evening together, the two of us.

The rest of the night had been just as good. Charlie took me in his arms and made beautiful love to me, and I fell asleep basking in the glow of our love-making and wishing every night could be as perfect as this one.

~~~

I could see my eyes filling with tears as I looked at my reflection in the mirror, and something told me that had been our last night together, but I still couldn't figure out how I died. That didn't matter because, right now, I needed to figure out this undead thing. And whether or not I was one of them.

I checked my appearance, my teeth in particular, and I wasn't a vampire because I didn't have fangs—although I did look a bit pale, but that could be my ghostly face and the poor lighting probably didn't help. I'd told Charlie lots of times that we needed a stronger light above the mirror. He'd replied that my wrinkles would be more obvious in better light. I was well-behaved and didn't thump him.

My flesh wasn't hanging off me, so I could rule out being a zombie. I hadn't turned hairy, apart from one or two annoying ones on my chin that I am not going to talk about. Nor was I baying at the moon or lifting my leg to pee, so I hadn't been turned into a werewolf.

Ghost it is, then.

I reached up to switch off the light and just for a second, as I was pulling the cord, I saw someone else in the mirror. A woman with spiky, short blonde hair and piercing blue eyes. I jumped back as the light went off. I ran out of the bathroom and down the stairs as quickly as I could.

Chapter 14 – Scaredy-cat.

Imagine a ghost being afraid of a reflection in a mirror. How pathetic is that?

I turned and ran down the stairs, along the hall and into the snug, almost slamming the door behind me. It was a good thing I didn't because I might have wakened the whole household, and then there'd be screams and a big fuss. It would all result in Googling to find a reputable local exorcist. Then the press would get wind of it and it would make the nationals. Next thing you know, Ghost Finders or whatever they're called, would be knocking on the door and wanting to set up camera equipment and all sorts of paraphernalia, if not to capture the alleged ghost, at least to snap a grainy image of it—I mean me.

Imagine the headline – 'Ghost of Dead Photographer Photographed.' Yuck.

I didn't slam the door, thankfully, but that's how terrified I felt. Okay, my heart wasn't pounding and I wasn't gasping for breath, obviously, but it did scare the hell out of me. Who or what was that? Did I really see it, or was it a trick of the light? I didn't think so. I definitely caught a glimpse of someone other than me in the mirror, and she was vaguely familiar. I knew her from somewhere but I couldn't place her, no matter how hard I tried.

It was frustrating, but I couldn't conjure up a name to match the face. I couldn't even remember the face properly now. It had been just a fleeting glance to begin with and it was already fading from my mind. No amount of concentration I could muster up would bring it back.

Apart from the fright, and the knowledge that I knew her from somewhere, I was more interested in my reaction to the shock than what caused it in the first place. While I felt scared, it was more a mental fear than a physical thing, and this was something I'd known but hadn't really thought much about until now. I didn't feel anything. I couldn't touch or taste, but I could see and hear. I wasn't hungry, yet I sometimes craved food—but it was more the thought of the taste of my favourite foods, rather than a need for them. Especially tea and coffee. I could murder a mug of tea right now. Or better yet, a big glass of ice-cold wine. But that's all it was. A thought. Or maybe more a memory of what I wanted.

~~~

I sat down on the old leather sofa—Ross had moved to the armchair while I was upstairs—and I pretended that the fire burning was brightly in the woodstove. The curtains were closed, keeping the night out and, in my imagination, I could tell that it was warm and cosy. The lamp in the corner—made from an antique brass fire extinguisher of all things—was switched on but dimmed down low, and it cast a warm and gentle glow around the room. The lamp was one I'd bought at a craft fair, and the instant I spotted it, I knew I had to have it. I didn't even haggle with the seller, I just whipped out the correct amount of cash. Luckily, I had a couple of hundred quid in my bag, and I pointed to the lamp and told to him, 'I'll take it.' He looked a bit taken aback when I didn't even ask him about the price, but I could tell he was delighted to have made a sale. As he wrapped it up, he told me that he'd found it at a salvage yard and polished it up, then reconfigured it into a lamp.

It was only later when I remembered him talking about salvage yards that something clicked in my mind, and I thought it might be something I could try. A couple of weeks later I did a bit of research, found a few that weren't too far away and off I went. Charlie was aghast at the thought of me bringing home a boot load of old junk that he would end up having to dispose of, but I found some really great stuff. I knew I could make something out of what really did look like a pile of junk rather than buy things at fairs, and I was pleased with what I'd gathered on my salvage yard foraging day out.

It was mostly old furniture that I'd bought and restored, but I also made a small lamp out of an old brass blow torch that I bought for a fiver. It really looked the part, with a candle-shaped bulb attached that looked as though a flame was coming out of it. My own creation was a firm favourite, but I still loved this old lamp.

As I sat there, I looked around the room. I took in all the familiar sights, and I felt right at home again. I could almost see the glass of white wine on a coaster on the coffee table with the condensation already running down the edge, as the cold in the glass met the warm air. I even licked my lips.

But, in reality, there was no glass of wine. The fire was cold and dark, it wasn't even set, and the curtains were open because the lights weren't on. It was just my imagination.

But it used to be like that. This was my room. My snug. This was where, a couple of evenings a week, especially in the wintertime, I would light the fire, get comfy under a throw, sip my wine or drink my tea, and binge-watch something on either Amazon, Netflix or Sky. Charlie would be glued to a football match in the other room and, at half-time, he would pop his head around the door and join me for a few minutes. I'd hit the pause button on the remote when he asked me if I needed a refill—tea or wine—and he'd throw some more wood on the fire for me. Then he'd disappear to watch the second half and I'd go back to the thriller I was watching.

Other times I'd put on some music, turn it down low, open my Kindle and just spend the evening reading.

I could do neither tonight, but it was good to be here with my memories. I closed my eyes and laid my head against the back of the sofa, remembering all the good times in my life.

Chapter 15 – Driving ambition.

'Stop yelling at me, Dad,' I yelled.

'Then do what I told you to do. Or we're going to hit that wall. And I'm not yelling,' he yelled.

'You're not showing me properly. I have no idea what to do next.'

'Brake!'

'What?'

'The middle pedal. Hit the middle pedal. Now!'

I slammed my foot down hard on the brake and the car stopped dead, throwing us forward in our seats. The front bumper was only a foot from the wall. I burst into tears.

'Jesus Christ, Lucy. That was fucking close.'

~~~

As I watched the unknown man counting out a wad of banknotes and placing them in Charlie's hand, I felt sad because I was watching him sell my old Land Rover. I had that old girl for many years and I'd clocked up many thousands of miles in her, and in all those years, over all those miles, she'd never let me down once.

I was never much of a car fanatic until I got the Land Rover. It was fifteen years old and had seventy-five thousand miles on the clock yet the engine ran as sweetly as one ten years it's junior. There was a whiff of wet dog in the interior that no amount of cleaning would ever remove because Ross always came with me. We clocked up many more miles—Ross, the Landi and me—as it took me all over the place on my travels around the countryside, my camera at the ready on the passenger seat beside me.

Oh, she had plenty of dents and scrapes, but that was the beauty of an old vehicle—one more dent didn't matter.

Now she was off to a new home and I hoped she'd be happy and be loved as much as she had been with me.

Watching her new owner drive off reminded me of that day when my dad gave me my first driving lesson. He'd taken me, one Sunday morning, to a large shopping-centre carpark on the outskirts of town, stuck my 'L' plates on the front and back windscreens and told me to get into the driver's seat.

That first time was a complete disaster because I almost hit a wall in the empty car park. I got out of the car and refused to try again. Dad was so angry at me and he yelled a fair bit. I yelled back and then he drove us back home in an angry silence that lasted for the rest of the day.

You could cut the atmosphere with a knife, and Mum wisely picked up her book and got out of our way. I think she decided it was best not to interfere and just let us work it out ourselves.

We did, but it took a few days, one shopping trip and a promise that he wouldn't yell at me ever again. That was never going to happen.

He'd been angry with me many times over the years, usually when I got into a bit of bother at school—getting caught smoking, bunking off from classes, the usual stuff— and I remember one hum-dinger of a row when I got a disastrous exam result. It wasn't the result so much, but more the fact that I hadn't bothered studying for it and he knew I hadn't.

He was blowing this out of all proportion and it wasn't like him at all, because my dad was a kind man, full of love, and normally of a happy-go-lucky disposition. But when he got really angry—which was rare—he got shouty and loud.

By the next morning, he still wasn't speaking to me. I got Mum alone and asked her what I'd done wrong because he was being very unreasonable and I wondered if there was more to it.

'I think you frightened him, love,' she said.

'Frightened him? How? It was his fault I nearly crashed because he didn't tell me what to do.'

'I don't mean that, Lucy. Your dad teaching you to drive is just another milestone in our lives. He sees that you're growing up—you'll be eighteen soon—and you're becoming a young woman—an adult in your own right— and you'll no longer be his little girl. You'll go out into the world and make your own path, and I think he believes that you'll leave us behind.'

'He's nuts if he thinks that.'

Mum smiled. 'I know that and he probably does too, but his heart is ruling his head in this instance.'

I knew I had to fix it with my dad so as soon as Sunday morning came around again, I stood in front of him, dangling the car keys in my hand and a big grin on my face.

'If you want me to be the first female Formula One World Champion, you need to take me out to the car park and teach me to drive.'

~~~

My second attempt was just as disastrous as the first. As was my third and fourth. But then, one morning something clicked in my brain and I suddenly got what Dad had been trying to explain about the clutch biting point— that moment when you slowly raise the clutch pedal, press on the accelerator at the same time and you know the car is about to move. You don't just know it, you feel it, and you understand it. No more lurching forward in bumps, only to stall and have to begin all over again.

I got it. I could drive.

Dad wasn't as pleased as I thought he'd be.

'Now you need to learn how to steer it and find your way up and down the gears,' he said with what looked like an evil grin.

It only took a few attempts before I got the hang of it and it only took me a couple more lessons in the car park before he suggested we take a drive up the road. Time to reset my fear meter.

Surprisingly, I did okay. I mean I was no Jensen Button, but I was able to drive with confidence and I remembered everything he—Dad, not Jensen Button—told me as we stuck to the quieter back roads. I looked in my mirrors. I paid attention to what was going on around me— the side roads, other vehicles, cyclists, and anything else that could cause an issue. Dad called it an 'issue' but what he meant was a massive pile-up with bodies strewn everywhere and the sounds of many emergency services sirens in the distance.

I did crunch the gears a few times and I'm fairly sure Dad felt physical pain every time. It was his car after all, and he was probably wondering how much a new clutch and gearbox were going to cost him.

As I pulled into the carpark of a small café, I was proud of myself and I could tell Dad was too. He even bought me lunch and, a week later, he booked a couple of lessons with a driving instructor.

A month later I passed my test on the first attempt. Dad was as pleased as punch and, while he was in such a celebratory mood, I suggested he should buy me a car. He burst out laughing as though it was the funniest joke he'd ever heard.

~~~

Prior to buying the Land Rover, my one and only car had been a little Toyota and, while I was fond of it, I never thought much of it other than it was mine and it was a necessary tool to get me to where I needed, or wanted, to be. But watching the Landi—my Landi—drive off was a sad sight. It was another thing in my life that was gone. Another thing my family had no need of now that I was no longer with them. Another nail in my coffin, you could say.

Chapter 16 – The big, bad world.

University was the coolest place in the world in my opinion and I couldn't wait to get there and begin to enjoy myself. Of course, as Mum warned me, I would have to buckle down and study hard for my degree if I wanted to become a teacher.

Dad butted in, in agreement with Mum, and reminded me that they hadn't scrimped and saved all these years for me to go nuts with the parties and the booze and piss it all up against a wall.

'No, Dad. I won't do that,' I told him. 'I'm a girl and we girls sit down to piss. Don't we, Mum?'

He was trying to keep a straight face but I could see a grin threatening to appear at the corners of his mouth. Mum was trying to hold it together too, and some of the tension that had been building—as the minutes ticked by to signify the moment when I would be leaving home—eased considerably.

The car was stuffed with my belongings—everything I would be needing in my new digs. When I say new, I don't mean that, not even sightly. It was a grotty room in a grotty house, in a grotty street half a mile from the university. I'd have my own bedroom but I'd be sharing a bathroom, a kitchen and a living room with three other girls. It would be my home for the next couple of years and, despite my sadness at leaving home for the first time, I was looking forward to it and I couldn't wait to begin this new chapter in my life.

But I had to give my mum and dad their moment. A

proper goodbye in our house, before they drove me to my new place and said a second goodbye.

Dad must have read my mind because he took both my hands in his and smiled at me. This was his serious-talk face.

'Three things I want you to promise me you won't do. One, don't do drugs. Two, don't get pregnant. Three, don't binge-drink. That's all I ask, love.'

I could feel tears welling up and I smiled a watery smile back at him. Mum was blowing her nose by this stage.

'One and two are not going to be a problem, but could we maybe negotiate the third one?'

Dad took a deep breath. 'Okay, if you must binge-drink, always fall asleep in the recovery position. Nothing kills you quicker than choking on your own vomit.'

'Alan—' Mum warned.

'She'll be fine, Linda. Our girl can hold her liquor. I taught her well.'

He was kidding. The reprimands I'd had over the years when I was caught drinking underage told a different story. But my dad was wise and he knew I'd already had my fair share of booze with my mates. He also knew what students did during their evenings, whether in the local pub where "student's rates" was applied to the booze, or at parties. He'd been a student himself, they both had, in the not-so-distant past, so they knew what I had in front of me.

'Also,' he sniffled. 'Don't walk the streets on your own, night or day. Study hard and do the work, it'll be worth it in the end. Oh, and don't be dating any serial killers.' He took a deep breath. 'You've plenty of common sense, girl, and I know you'll be okay. You will.'

He nodded a few times, more to convince himself than me and then he pulled me into his embrace, hugged me tightly and refused to let me go. My face was buried in the fabric of his sweater and, if he didn't let me go, I was going to suffocate before any serial killer ever got a chance to ask me out. I could hear Mum blowing her nose again.

'Dad? Let go. I can't breathe.' My voice was muffled but he heard me and loosened his grip.

He stepped back and looked at his watch.

'Yes. Sorry. Anyway, it's time we were off, I suppose.'

~~~

A couple of hours later, with a quick stop along the way for a coffee, a sandwich and a trip to the toilets, they dropped me off at the place I would call home for the next three years. Just looking at it made me want to tell Dad to turn the car around and take me home. I didn't need a degree. I could get a job in Asda.

But I gritted my teeth, got out of the car and went in.

It looked better inside. It was a bit like the Tardis—bigger on the inside—and it was clean and didn't smell of anything dead or decaying. It was definitely better on the inside that it looked from the street. Two of the people I'd be sharing this house with were already in the living room when I walked in followed by Mum while Dad began to carry my belongings in from the car. Both of my new housemates looked me up and down and smiled, sort of.

They looked okay-ish. Jesus, I missed Claire. Why couldn't we have gone to university together?

Mum was giving the place a once-over with her eyes, and she kept her face expressionless so I couldn't tell what she was thinking. She checked out the kitchen, running her finger along the worktop, checking for dust and dirt. She didn't find any and nodded in approval.

I remember how they lingered as long as they could after they'd helped me unpack. But eventually Dad stood up and told my mum it was time to go.

She didn't look too pleased at the prospect, but she grabbed her handbag and got to her feet. I gritted my teeth and took a deep breath. This was the moment, and I hated the thought of it. I was leaving home. I had left home. Mind you, they were still here and the car was outside. I could pack up my stuff in ten minutes and be in the car and heading home with them in fifteen. A job on the check-out in Asda, or even stacking shelves, was looking more and more appealing by the second.

Suddenly we all developed stiff upper lips. There were lots of nods and clearing of throats as we said our gruff goodbyes. I stood on the doorstep and waved as my parents got into the car, spent maybe too long doing up their seatbelts and getting comfortable for the journey. Mum looked back and waved as Dad started up the engine, put it in gear and drove off. My eye filled with tears and I whimpered like a puppy that had been abandoned at the side of the road. I wanted to run after them, promising that I wouldn't chew the furniture or pee on the carpet ever again.

~~~

119

Speaking of abandoned puppies, the first weekend I was home, laundry in tow, I walked through the front door and was greeted with a barking, snarling, tiny, brown and white creature hell bent on defending its home from this intruder who'd just walked in. Mum and Dad had replaced me with a three-year-old Jack Russell terrier named Cracker they'd adopted from the local RSPCA. They'd even made up a bed for the adorable little monster in my room and he wasn't too pleased when he had to share it with me, at least not until I'd won his affection by bribing him with treats.

~~~

I didn't run after Mum and Dad as they sped off, obviously in a hurry to go and get their new dog to replace the daughter they'd dropped off at the roadside. I turned back and went inside, and closed the door behind me.

I had planned on going to my room and crying myself to sleep, but two out of three of my new housemates had other plans. One of them took three cans of lager out of the fridge, handed one to me and one to the other girl who'd joined us in the kitchen.

She pulled the ring on her can and took a long swig.

'I'm Laura,' she said in, what I think, was a London accent as we all raised our cans in a toast and I wondered if they would laugh at my strong Yorkshire brogue. 'This here is Sunita. Onia is still sleeping off her hangover so you'll meet her tomorrow. Probably. Maybe. Getting the parents to piss off is the hardest part, isn't it? But don't worry, it's all great from here on in.'

And it was.

Chapter 17 - Yuletide tears.

Despite Charlie's best efforts to give them as normal a Christmas as possible—a bit difficult, considering it was their first without me—both Amy and Chloe were down in the dumps and stared at him as he struggled to get the enormous tree in through the front door. It was wrapped in fine netting so it didn't catch on the doorframe but, it was so large and heavy, it was really a two-person job to lift it and haul it into the house. Charlie and I always manoeuvred it out of the car and indoors together, with the girls holding the doors for us and shouting instructions along the way. Most of those instructions would be them telling us to hurry up so they could get it decorated.

Until now, I hadn't been aware that the holiday period was on us and I stood in the hallway, itching to help Charlie lift the big tree into the holder. This was going to be tricky and I was worried he would ask Amy to help him lock it in place while he held the tree upright. The ratchet on the holder tended to snap shut and it would be easy to lose a finger in the mechanism. I cringed at the thought of it and I could almost hear Amy howling in agony as the cold metal wire cut through her finger.

As always, Charlie knew what he was doing and managed to get the tree upright and the bottom of the trunk into the holder. He motioned both girls to come and hold it upright and keep it steady, then he got down and locked it in place. I silently applauded both him and the girls as the three of them stood watching to see of it was too big and too heavy for the holder and would keel right over. That did happen one year and guess who was underneath it? Yeah, me. I was trying to plug the lights into the wall socket when over it went and I was stuck with only my arse visible. Charlie was laughing so hard he wasn't able to help me out.

Once it was obvious this tree wasn't going to fall, he sent Amy to get the scissors out of the kitchen drawer, then he carefully cut away the netting. The girls watched and smiled as, clear of its constraints, it slowly began to unfold into its natural shape.

'Can we decorate it now, Daddy?' Amy asked.

'Let's leave it a while, pet. It needs to open out properly. We'll go and have lunch, and it'll be ready by the time we're finished.'

Normally the girls would argue back that they wanted to do it now, and they'd begin to take tinsel and ornaments out of the nearby boxes in which we stored the decorations, but they didn't. Instead, they quietly followed Charlie into the kitchen. It was as if the fight had gone out of them and they didn't care if the tree was decorated or not. The spirit of Christmas was missing this year, along with their mum. My heart broke once again as I watched them walk away, and I remembered the fun we always had decorating it together.

~~~

Our big thing—once we had finished decorating the tree on the eve of the Solstice—was to place cushions on the floor in front of the tree and we'd all sit down together after we finished our dinner. We'd have a nice family-only evening, away from the usual distractions such as games and phones and the TV.

We turned off the lights and lit some scented candles. We weren't religious so, in order to balance what the girls picked up in school and from some of their peers, I'd tell them about the Winter Solstice and how it celebrated the birth of the Sun, so that from now on the days would get a little bit longer and the nights a little bit shorter. I'd explain that we bring trees and holly and mistletoe indoors to make us think of new growth and life. These were also thought to ward off evil spirits but I didn't mention that—no point in having them think we had evil spirits in the house. I told them we had a feast because, in the old days, people celebrated still being alive at the halfway point of the winter, and that spring would bring food and better days.

It was a magical time, I told them. My two little girls lapped it up, and I hope I managed to instil in them some beautiful Pagan beliefs and celebrations, which they'd hold onto as they grew to adulthood, and they would celebrate the Yule traditions in a similar fashion with their own children one day.

Charlie and I started it for the two of us on our first Christmas in the house before Claire and Gavin joined us the following day, staying for a couple of days before going home to their own festivities that, like ours, mostly involved food and drink and relaxing.

When the girls were born and old enough to participate, they joined Charlie and I sitting on the floor in front of the tree. They loved it.

We still did the Christmas part of the holidays, with a big dinner and lots of presents from Santa, but I always loved our quiet Solstice celebration the most.

~~~

After they'd eaten their lunch, they began to decorate the tree. I watched them for a short while. It was sweet but oh so painful, and I disappeared up the stairs to the bedroom at the far end of the house where I couldn't hear them. Not that there was much to hear. Normally, there'd be jokes and laughter, and the occasional argument over where to put a certain bauble or a little decorative bird, but this year it was like they were on automatic pilot, completing a task they had to do rather than taking part in a much-loved family tradition. It was a subdued affair, and I suspect it was uppermost in their minds that this was their first Christmas without me.

I couldn't stay in the house so I slipped out—unnoticed, obviously—and went for a walk with my memories for company.

Chapter 18 – Finding Charlie.

Charlie was a semi-regular at the pub where I worked and he'd in come every Saturday evening, and one or two nights through the week. I'd started working there to earn a bit extra, but mostly to keep me from the temptation of partying every weekend when I wasn't home. I pulled pints three evenings a week, sometimes four, from six o'clock until last orders were called. It was an okay job and the wages were reasonable. Not that I needed too much as Mum and Dad had been putting money into a savings account for me for years. It meant my student loans weren't exorbitant and I could spend some of the money I earned from the pub on myself.

It was a typical pub-type pub, traditionally dark and smelling of beer and many years of tobacco smoke. Most of the patrons were men—calling in for a pint or two after work before they headed home to more beer in front of the television. They didn't serve food, other than bags of crisps. Nothing too fancy either. Mostly cheese and onion, smoky bacon, and salt and vinegar with packets of dry roasted peanuts for a bit of variation. The beer was surprisingly good for such a dingy-looking establishment. The landlord kept it clean and tidy, and there were hardly any fights—one or two on a Saturday night, maybe—but they were never serious and the police had only been called once in the time I worked there.

I'd only been there for a week when I noticed him coming in. I took one look at him and almost melted. He was that gorgeous. He wore his hair tied back in a ponytail, and his blue eyes were filled with humour. I gave him the once over and noticed he had a fit body to complete the package. Yummy. Of course, he could be a proper dickhead, or the charming, but crazed, killer that my dad kept warning me about, so I decided to play it cool for a while to see how things developed. I must admit though, I fancied him like crazy.

He must have had the same reservations about me, because for the first few weeks all I got out of him was a quick smile and a brief nod as he sat there sipping his pint.

One day he looked up from his pint, smiled and said, 'Weather's a bit shite, innit?'

'Aye,' I replied. 'Forecast for the whole week's pretty shite, too.'

He smiled again, nodded, and went back to sipping his beer.

I was busy with two other customers for the next five minutes and when I glanced towards the end of the bar, he was gone.

Over the next couple of weeks on the few nights he came in, the conversation didn't quite expand beyond the weather and I decided he just wasn't interested. A shame really, because I fancied him a lot. I still said hello and gave him a cheery smile every evening but other than the weather and occasionally the football, he didn't talk about anything else.

Now and then he would tell me I was looking nice, or he liked the way I had my hair up. Then one evening he took a big slug of his beer, smiled at me and asked me if I'd like to go out with him sometime. And he told me his name was Charlie.

It was all I could do not to grab him, haul him over the bar and snog the living daylights out of him on the floor, despite the spilled beer on the tiles. Oh, the fantasies I've had about doing just that. But I behaved myself, although I did pretend to hesitate before I demurely told him that yes, I'd love to go out with him.

We went to see a movie that first date. I don't remember much about the film, other than it had far too many car chases for my liking. I was just happy to be out on a date with Charlie. The next night he asked me out again, and this time he took me for a meal and a few drinks. Mostly we chatted—we were still getting to know one another—but I definitely felt attracted to him and, from the looks he was giving me, I suspected felt the same. Still, we both behaved ourselves and he gave me a chaste kiss on the cheek when he took me back to my flat. He couldn't have come in anyway as the gang was in residence. I could hear the music and the sounds of everyone talking through the half-open window.

Of course, the moment I closed the front door and walked into the living room I was subjected to the third degree. Laura's interrogation skills were subtle and worthy of every TV cop who got the baddie to 'fess up so, in a sense, she was Good Cop. Onia was definitely Bad Cop, because she tried every trick in the book—and some that weren't—to con me into telling them all the biz about my new boyfriend. New boyfriend? I liked the sound of that. Sunita was the silent observer. She wasn't making notes but I wouldn't be surprised if she was recording the whole interview.

'It was just a meal,' I told them. 'I had chicken in garlic sauce and Charlie had a sirloin. That's it. And yes, we had dessert afterwards. I suppose you want to know what.'

'Dessert, you say.' Detective Inspector Laura nodded wisely. 'We all know what *dessert* means. Nudge, nudge, wink, wink. Isn't that right, DS Onia?'

Detective Sergeant Onia also nodded wisely.

'It means bugger all. I had crème brulé and Charlie had—er—an Arctic roll.'

My reply was met with hoots of laughter and I gave up, went to the kitchen and got a bottle of plonk from the fridge. I poured a glass, and by the time I came back, the conversation had moved on.

~~~

A week or so later Charlie and I were at it like rabbits in the back of his old van. By heck it was great, but it was so bloody uncomfortable. Though it wasn't quite as bad as doing it in his old car, it was still not the best place for us. There was a lot of twisting and turning and getting cramp, although we always got there in the end. This went on for a couple of months, and by now we were seriously in love. It was more than a teen romance, or even lust, because when we weren't at it like bunnies, we talked and laughed and snuggled up together and, when I wasn't with him, I felt as if a part of me was missing.

We were young—I was nineteen and he was twenty-three—and I'm sure everybody would tell us we were far too young to be serious about each other. But I knew I was in love with him and I always would be. Despite our youth, both of us had previous relationships with other people. Although, for me, a few dates here and there, and the occasional weekend away at a festival or something, hardly counted as actual relationships. One or two came close, but they didn't last. Charlie, on the other hand, had almost gotten engaged when he was twenty-one but, instead of buying her a ring, he ended the relationship. When I asked him why, he told me it just didn't feel right.

'I looked at her and tried to imagine spending the next fifty-odd years with her. I couldn't even imagine spending the next five months with her,' he said. 'Don't get me wrong, she was a lovely lass and we had great times together but, for me, there was something missing. Some spark I needed to convince me that I loved her. It just wasn't there. It had been her idea to get engaged and she was a bit upset when I told her I didn't want to go out with her again.'

'I can imagine,' I replied.

'Aye, we had a flaming row and she accused me of leading her on—making promises to get her into bed. Blah, blah, blah. Then she stormed off, out of my life.'

'She didn't go psycho on you, then?'

'Nope. I never heard a peep out of her. Then I met her by chance about six months later, maybe a little more than that, and she was fine. She told me she realised I wasn't the one for her either and she was glad I broke up with her. We ended up good friends until she got a job down in London and moved down there. I haven't seen or heard from her since.'

Other than that, he'd only ever had casual dates. I was the same. My longest relationship had lasted two months, and it was hot and heavy for a while but then it just naturally fizzled out. No one got hurt and we just moved on with our lives.

But this was different and we both knew it. Charlie told me he felt the same, and I knew we were young— probably too young in everybody's eyes—but we knew how we felt. He was the one person I could imagine spending the next fifty-plus years of my life with. When I said this to him, he took my hand in his and replied that he felt the same.

Making love in the back of his old van might have been romantic, but it wasn't ideal. It was all we had at that point in time, but it wasn't long before we both wanted something more comfortable. I wanted to wake up in his arms on a Sunday morning. Or have him waken me with a brew, then have him climb into bed beside me—carefully so as not to spill his own tea—and we'd switch the telly on and watch the early news. Or we'd get back under the covers and make love again.

It wasn't all about finding a comfy place to make love, though. We both wanted to spend all of our time together—or at least as much time as we possibly could. We wanted evenings together as well as mornings. I wanted to cook his dinner for him—just as soon as I learned to cook properly. I could manage a few simple recipes but I wanted to learn more, so we could save money by cooking fresh, healthy food rather than relying on ready meals and takeaways.

The thought of the two of us setting up home together was something I was thinking about quite a lot, but it was Charlie who first suggested we take our relationship a step further by pooling our finances, finding somewhere to live and moving in together. He said we should do it before he wrecked his back completely. That's my Charlie. All hearts and flowers, and romantic proposals. Not likely!

I'm actually laughing as I remember it.

Telling Mum and Dad about my—our—plans one evening after dinner wasn't a laughing matter, though. They hit the roof. They said I was throwing my life away. They asked me if I was pregnant. They ranted and raved about my education and asked me if I was chucking the towel in, and told me I would never get a decent job if I didn't finish my degree. Supermarket check-out till it is, then.

Then they stopped and stared at me as it occurred to them that they hadn't even known I was seeing someone, let alone in a relationship that couldn't possibly be serious at my age. It was a serious relationship—to me and Charlie—and I told them so.

Then explaining that he was some bloke I met in the pub made things worse.

Dad went ballistic. Mum started crying. And me, well I knew I'd screwed up by not introducing them to Charlie before telling them that we'd already planned a life together. Naturally I started back-tracking. I told them I was joking and that the look on their faces was priceless. I told them I had met someone, that he was really nice, and I would love them to meet him, and—I lied at this bit—we had no plans to live together. Yet.

They weren't even slightly mollified and I had visions of them throwing me out and telling me to 'Never darken their door again.'

Fine, I'll just go ahead and move in with Charlie then.

But they didn't throw me out. Mum put the kettle on, and Dad made me sit down at the kitchen table. We were going to have a nice chat over a cup of tea, because tea resolved everything in Mum's opinion.

It mostly did. But only because I put my sensible head on—yes, I do actually have one—and I told them that I had no intention of quitting uni. I was looking forward to becoming a teacher, and I told them that Charlie had a good job as a builder and, although he wasn't making much money yet, he had a lot saved and he planned to start his own business very soon. It would be small at first, I explained. He was intending to take on mainly minor building work like fixing other people's DIY fuck-ups— you'd be surprised at how lucrative that was—but he planned to expand into housing contracts in time, and he hoped to take on staff such as plasterers, roofers, plumbers and joiners. I told them he had a five-year goal to get his business up and running and with me working as a teacher and contributing my income, we could probably reduce that to two, maybe three, years.

Although Charlie did have a business plan of sorts, it was nowhere near as elaborate and likely to succeed as I'd painted it and I was lying through my teeth when I told my parents all this. But I'd done it so well that it even sounded plausible to me, and I was going to run it past Charlie as soon as I got a chance. They weren't completely convinced, but I could tell I'd planted a seed in their minds. I decided to quit while I was ahead and let them work it through in their minds.

'Are you sure you're not pregnant?' Dad asked.

'Of course not,' I told him. 'You know I don't like kids.'

'Yet you want to be a primary school teacher?' He frowned.

'I don't like the thought of having my own kids, I mean.'

'Ever?' Mum asked in a sort of panicky voice, and I could see her lip trembling at the thought of never having grandchildren that she could bounce on her knees and make them giggle with her funny faces and coochy-coos.

'Oh no. I definitely want to have children someday. Just not yet.'

Her lip stopped trembling. I was getting there but it was like playing tennis, having to jump back and forth between them as I backtracked my way into total confusion. I was beginning to think I'd already given birth to three of Mum's much longed-for grandchildren and they were all brickies by the time they were five.

Thankfully Dad—who always liked to make the best of a situation no matter how bad it seemed—suddenly switched to my team. He got up and went to the larder, took out a bottle of Scotch, set it on the table and then got three glasses from the cupboard. Not the good glasses, though. He kept those for big celebrations. My news obviously wasn't a big enough celebration.

Mum and I watched him open the bottle and pour the whiskey into the glasses. Was he celebrating me having an actual boyfriend instead of a series of dates that usually ended in a hangover, or was he just so traumatised by what I'd told him that he needed a stiff one?

I was traumatised too, so I lifted my glass and gulped down nearly half of it.

'When do we meet this Charlie, then?' Dad asked.

'Er—Friday evening. No. I'm working on Friday. How about Saturday evening?'

And that was it. Mum insisted I bring him round for dinner—she made lasagne with a side salad and garlic bread. Charlie arrived at seven-thirty on the dot—I'd warned him to be on time. He brought flowers for Mum and a bottle of whiskey for Dad—I'd told him which brand to get. They questioned him over dinner—okay, they interrogated him over dinner. The poor lad could hardly manage to swallow a single mouthful of lasagne in between answering rapid-fire questions about his parents, his childhood, his police record—he didn't have one—and his future. I thought they were going to bring in a set of jumper cables and a car battery to encourage him to give more detailed answers, and a polygraph machine to check he was telling the truth. He was. At least he was telling the truth they wanted to hear because I'd spent a couple of hours with him earlier, helping him rehearse his story.

And by heck, it worked. They took to him like ducks to water. He was the son they never had. By the time Mum brought out the dessert—her famous, at least in our house, homemade Bailey's and chocolate cheesecake—they loved him to bits. He liked football and rugby league, and when Dad discovered that fact, I think *he* wanted to marry Charlie.

~~~

It wasn't too long before we found a place with rent that we could just about afford. It was a tiny two-bedroom cottage with a bathroom that was smaller than some cupboards I've seen, and an open-plan kitchen and living room that worked better than I thought it would. It was clean and freshly painted. There was no damp and it was well-insulated so the central heating didn't cost us too much. We moved in together as soon as we had everything signed and sealed. His Mum and Dad paid the deposit, while my Mum and Dad treated us to some nice furniture— a sofa and two armchairs, a small table and chairs for our kitchen-slash-dining-room-slash-living-room, and a television. The cottage was already curtained and carpeted, and the white goods came with it, so we didn't have to fork out on those items. We bought the bedroom furniture ourselves and moved in as soon as we could.

Six months after that we got married. It was just a small wedding, with close friends and family, followed by a slap-up meal that didn't cost the earth as we refused to let either set of parents spend any more money on us. We were determined to prove that we could do it all ourselves—and we didn't splash out on a honeymoon. It was the happiest day of my life.

Not long afterwards, I graduated and I became a qualified teacher, but I couldn't get a job anywhere so I did some home tutoring and did a few shifts in Tesco to tide me over until I could find something, which I did eventually, but more about that later.

Between us, we earned enough to stay afloat and Charlie got his business up and running properly about a year later. Life was more or less going the way we wanted it to go.

Chapter 19 – Puppy love.

I stretched out on the sofa and closed my eyes as I allowed myself to imagine I was really there, in my home, and relaxing in my favourite room. In my mind, the girls would be asleep upstairs and Charlie would be watching a football match on the big television in the front room. If the match went to extra time, I'd have to get up and let Ross out for his nightly pee and I'd call for Berfa—named by Chloe, who couldn't pronounce 'Bertha' properly. She would either be out hunting or sitting on a nearby windowsill, patiently waiting to be let in. If the weather was bad, she'd race in, worried that I might change my mind and leave her out there. Like I'd do that. She'd go straight to the cupboard where I kept the cat food and she'd miaow at me, her front paws impatiently kneading the floor as she waited for me to dish out her food. Then she'd settle down somewhere warm and cosy for the night. If the weather was to her liking, she'd most likely remain outside so I'd leave the bowl of cat food on the back doorstep for her as soon as Ross came back inside.

She was a big cat—half calico and half tortoiseshell in colour, half Manx in breed. Manx cats don't have tails but Berfa being a mixed breed had a small tail—about an inch and a half long. The vet told us that this particular mixed breed was known as a Stumpy. Charlie and I joked that her mother was motorcycle racing fan and had spent a fun-filled week at the TT races, lying in the arms of her Manx cat lover and watching the bikes whizz by. As it so often happens with holiday flings, she'd returned home pregnant and alone—because once she showed him the results of the pregnancy test, her Manx lover didn't want to know and our Berfa was the result of that crazy, high-octane-fuelled week on the Isle of Man.

She didn't let her dubious parentage hold her back. Berfa was her own person—cat, I mean. Independent and a keen hunter, she frequently and proudly, it seemed, left the remains of her victims on the back patio door step. Sometimes, she'd leave a leg or what looked like a tiny set of lungs, or maybe kidneys—I'm no expert on rodent or avian internal organs, so I could never be sure. Then maybe a wing or a tail the next day, and often she'd leave nothing more than a sinister bloodstain. Her offerings were always mangled enough to be tricky to identify, like a jigsaw puzzle for serial killers where the murderer was leaving only one piece at a time on my doorstep. I wasn't squeamish but I had no intention of ever trying to complete that jigsaw puzzle.

I disposed of the pieces quickly before Ross got a chance to snarf them down. He had a bit of a sensitive tummy and if he ate anything he shouldn't, it usually came out the other end very quickly.

Although she was a friendly cat, used to being lifted and cuddled and, of course, well fed, Berfa decided where she wanted to be—outdoors if it was a mild night or asleep in front of the fire or snuggled in our bed if it was colder.

While it wasn't bitterly cold tonight, it was a bit chilly and I was surprised she wasn't inside. I was disappointed because, if she had been in the house, she might have seen me. Maybe she would have hopped up onto the sofa and curled up beside me, purring contentedly, pleased to have me home again.

But I was getting used to being on my own and, since it was something that I was never going to be able to change, there was no point in moaning about it. Instead, I looked at it in a positive light because, with two young girls, a husband and a rather boisterous dog in the house, I rarely got time to chill on my own. Even when I was sitting down with a glass of wine or a good book to read, my thoughts were always on what needed doing. Laundry, if the weather was fine and ironing, which I hated with a vengeance. Once I quit teaching to take up my photography hobby as a business, the ironing board was confined to a rarely-opened cupboard in the utility room. Cleaning the house—this was something I actually enjoyed. Grocery lists—mental ones that always needed to be written down because, the moment I stepped into Tesco, my mind went blank and I couldn't think what I needed for dinner that evening, never mind the rest of the week. Charlie's accounts. My accounts. Photos to be printed out or put onto canvas. Locations to be sussed out and photos to be taken before I even thought about what to do with them. Advertising—mostly on social media. Website updates. Sales that had to be mailed. Bathing the dog. Baking. Homework. After-school activities. New clothes and shoes for both Amy and Chloe. Bathing the dog again when he rolled in fox poo or something dead. Fox crap was like cologne to Ross. He loved it and thought he smelled like a handsome millionaire hunk and a millionaire. He hated getting bathed but he never made the connection between rolling in dead, smelly things to the indignity of getting plunged into a tub of warm suds.

Even my so-called quiet time was filled with thinking about all this and a zillion other little things that made up our daily lives.

So, it was actually nice to be able to sit in the dark and, apart from the wind in the trees and the sound of rain hitting the back window, the only thing I could hear inside was the noises an old house makes as it settles down for the night. Although it had been extensively modernised, the walls and foundations, floors and ceilings were still those of an old farmhouse and, like every old farmhouse, it creaked and groaned as if the ghosts of all its previous occupants still walked the floors. Ghosts even I couldn't see.

~~~

I thought about Charlie again, and all the good times we had together over the years. While most of it was good and we were so happy together, it wasn't all plain sailing. It took Mum and Dad a while to get over the shock of my marriage to Charlie. They were okay with me dating him, and even living with him but getting married and settling down at our age was a step too far and, for a while after the wedding, they were cool and distant with him. But it wasn't long before they began to thaw, although Mum occasionally still repeated the old adage—marry in haste, repent at leisure.

Also, money was tight for the first few years. There were some weeks, months even when we had barely enough to buy food and I remember many evenings when we feasted on beans and toast, or shared a portion of fish and chips between us. Alternating Sunday dinner at Mum and Dad's one week and with Charlie's parents, Kate and Johnny, the following Sunday kept us from starving.

Both sets of parents vied with each other in the amounts they were prepared to offer to help us out financially, and while they were good offers, we were stubborn and determined to prove to them, and us, that we could manage. We turned down their offers and saved every penny we could. We both quit smoking and only had a bottle of cheap wine and a couple of beers on a Saturday night—at home. We kept the heating off unless it got very cold—we were young and passionately in love, so we didn't need the heating on much, if you get my drift. We were careful to switch off lights and not leave appliances on stand-by to keep the leccy meter from ticking over too fast. We did all this and slowly we began to get our heads above water. The rent was the most expensive outlay and, as long as we kept in front of that, we managed.

Then Charlie got his first big contract. It was a new development and there'd be enough work to keep him going for over six months. Trouble was, it was miles away, and I hated the thought of being apart from him and only seeing him at weekends. But it made sense for him to stay there and not travel back and forth every day.

What did help dispel my loneliness was Claire—my best friend from primary and secondary school—moving back to the area. She had quit university after six months and since then she'd been travelling around Europe and Asia, working in bars and restaurants along the way. She even took a job as a tour guide for a while. In her eyes, she received all the education she needed by seeing the world, experiencing many different cultures and learning how to fend for herself. She learned to cook, had a smattering of several different languages—enough to get by in some of them—several boyfriends, and she still managed to earn enough money not only to get by, but to bring a healthy savings pot back with her. Eventually she'd grown travel weary and knew it was time to come home and settle down, but she was at a loss to know what to do. Find a job? Go back to uni? She just didn't know and, as a result, she hung out with me a lot.

I hated that Charlie was away so much, and I would have gone nuts if it wasn't for Claire—she practically moved in and, best of all, she always brought wine and snacks. So, with her help, I stuck it out.

About four months later, things began to look up when Charlie got several more contracts, one after the other, and had to take on staff. Suddenly, we were in business and, while we weren't exactly rolling in it, we didn't have to worry so much about putting food on the table or paying the bills.

We weren't rich but we were no longer struggling and things were definitely on the up for us.

~~~

Six months went by, give or take, and one morning we got a letter in the post that we were afraid to open. I remember us sitting at the table, our hands cupped around our mugs of tea, the plate of toast and marmalade forgotten, as we stared at the white envelope lying on the table in front of us. A well-known local solicitor's name and address was embossed on the top left-hand corner. We had no idea what could be in it and we were afraid to find out. Charlie was especially worried as it was addressed to him and might be from a client unsatisfied with a job he'd done, but he couldn't think of anyone who would be disgruntled. He was well-thought of and always in demand because his work was excellent and always a hundred per cent professional.

'What's it about?' I asked.

'I haven't a clue,' Charlie said.

'I mean, who's it from?'

'Some solicitor, by the looks of it.' He just looked at me and my heart started thumping. Was he in some sort of trouble? Was he being sued?

Neither of us could muster up the courage to open it and we sat there holding onto our mugs of tea for dear life. Claire sauntered in, hair in disarray and wearing her dressing gown over her pyjamas—she'd stayed over as we'd had a few drinks last night. She switched on the kettle and turned to look at us while we stared at the letter.

'What's this then?' she asked as she snatched the letter up and noticed the solicitor's name on the envelope. 'Are you two getting a divorce?'

Neither of us spoke.

'If you are, can I have Charlie?' She grinned and stuck her tongue out at me, then winked at Charlie.

We still couldn't speak.

'Oh, for fuck's sake.' She ripped open the envelope and read the letter inside.

'What is it?' I asked.

But Claire was speechless herself now. She stood there with her mouth open in shock.

'What is it?' I asked again.

'Who's Ethel Mason?'

Charlie and I looked at each other and shrugged. We had no idea.

'Lemme see it,' Charlie said, as he held out his hand. He took the letter and read it twice before putting it down and looking at me.

'Well?'

'It's about Auntie Ethel. I didn't know her surname,' he said. 'She's died and she's left a will. Apparently, I'm mentioned in it.'

'Who's Auntie Ethel? I didn't think you had any aunts. I certainly don't remember ever meeting her.'

'I've two but she's me great-aunt. One of me mum's aunties, I think. I've a vague memory of when I was a nipper, of Dad and me going to her house to cut the grass and fix up her fence and stuff. I think I remember her giving me sweeties but, other than that, I can't really remember much about her.'

'Well, she obviously remembered you,' I said. 'How much do you think she's left you?'

I was already spending it. A heated swimming pool. Luxury holidays. A sports car. Two, maybe. Caviar for breakfast. Champagne for lunch. Diamonds, designer clothes and a five-star restaurant for dinner. Trips to Paris and Milan in the new jet to buy said designer clothes.

'Probably not much. No one in our family was ever

rich.' Charlie sent my impending luxury lifestyle crashing down with his words.

I drained the pool and cancelled my travel insurance. I handed the car keys back and sacked the jet pilot after I'd returned the clothes to the designer capitals of the world. It'd be fish fingers instead of caviar and tea instead of champagne tonight.

'Enough to pay next month's gas bill, then?'

'Maybe. Probably not.'

Oh, well. It was good while it lasted.

'Well?' Claire was standing there, arms folded, watching the two of us. I looked at her and shrugged.

'Aren't you going to phone them and make an appointment? Maybe see what's what?'

'Uh, yeah. I suppose that would be a good idea.'

'I'd say it's a bloody terrific idea,' Claire replied.

~~~

We were gobsmacked when the solicitor read out the will. I remember us sitting there like two statues, not able to blink, and not knowing what to say. And not being capable of saying anything even if we knew what we wanted to say, because Charlie's great-aunt had left him a considerable amount of money. To us it felt like a mind-blowing, lottery-winning amount. Not a double rollover jackpot or anything like that, and we couldn't say that we were millionaires. More like half-millionaires, which was close enough in my book. Anything more would be too frightening to contemplate.

The solicitor babbled a bit about what Ethel had written. It turned out that, from when she was a child, she'd thought the world of 'her wee Charles,' and even though she hadn't laid eyes on him since he was a wee lad, she thought he was worthy of inheriting her money. His parents got her house and he got the cash.

We didn't ask how Auntie Ethel got all this money. For all we knew she could have been a drug lord—or should that be drug lady? Maybe she laundered money for them. Or she bet on the horses, or kidnapped people and sold their organs on the black market. With just a quick glance at one another, we both came to the same conclusion—that it was best not to ask in case we jinxed it. While it would be nice to see the police solve a big case that had tormented them for years, it would be a shame if all that money ended up in evidence bags in the local nick instead of in our bank account.

We left the solicitor's office still in shock. I wasn't even sure either of us were in a fit state to drive home so I suggested we grab a coffee somewhere. Charlie nodded in agreement and we held each other's hands in mutual support as we walked to the nearest café, where we ordered two coffees and two slices of apple tart.

With cream, because we were rich now.

~~~

While I was lying there reminiscing about what Auntie Ethel's last will and testament meant to us, the door creaked and began to open. At first, I thought it was a real ghost—not that I'm not a real ghost—coming to either haunt me or tell me that he, or she, had been haunting this house since it had been a working farmhouse, and to get the hell out of his, or her, home.

I sat bolt upright on the sofa, wondering what was about to appear, when I saw a wet nose push open the door a bit more and in walked Ross.

I gasped with relief and swore under my breath. I felt a bit stupid because I should have known he'd appear at some stage during the night. This was what Ross always did. He'd follow Charlie and me upstairs when we went to bed, walk down the hall and look into Amy and Chloe's bedroom, and give his tail a satisfied wag when he saw that his charges were safe and sound. Then he'd come back into our room where he'd settle down on the floor at the foot of the bed, curl up, and go to sleep.

Or so we thought.

I discovered Ross's nocturnal habits when I couldn't sleep one night. I'd been working in the garden all day and my muscles were stiff and sore. I couldn't get comfortable. I tossed and turned for ages, but I just couldn't get over. Not wanting to disturb Charlie—who had an early start in the morning—I decided to make myself a cup of tea and maybe read for half an hour, in the hope that it would relax me enough to get me off to sleep.

I put on my dressing gown, then crept downstairs into the kitchen. While I was waiting for the kettle to boil, I went into the back room to retrieve my kindle which I'd left there earlier. I switched on the light and there he was, stretched out almost the full length of the sofa. His head was resting on one cushion and he'd pushed the other onto the floor—he was always nudging cushions off the sofa and carrying them around, only to leave them lying on the floor. We reckoned it was a *feng shui* thing he had going.

He was dead to the world but opened one eye when I turned the light on. He wagged his tail, happy to see me, but it was obvious he had no intention of getting up. He wasn't doing any harm so I smiled, grabbed my e-reader and left him to his comfy sofa.

Ross did this almost every night, especially in the winter. In summer, when we had a rare heatwave, he mostly slept by the back door, the tiled floor giving him some welcome relief from the heat.

~~~

Tonight, it was obvious he was sticking to his usual routine and I wondered if he would react to my presence. Or even notice I was there.

In the darkness—darkness that my eyes had become accustomed to—I could see him stop as though something wasn't quite right. He sniffed the air and looked around the room. My heart leapt with joy when his eyes softened into a relaxed, all-is-right-with-the-world gaze, and his tail wagged slowly. I swear he looked at me when he did that. I was tempted to call to him but I was afraid of frightening him off. It was better to just have his silent company, without the slurpy kisses and the excited barks, than risk him kicking off on one of his barking sprees and disturbing Charlie and the girls.

He must have known I was there though, because he ignored his usual spot on the sofa where he could stretch out and snore his head off. Instead, he hopped up onto the armchair beside the fireplace, did his usual two or three turns—as if he was channelling his ancestors, the wolves in the wild as they made their bed in the snow—then settled

148

down with a loud, contented groan. Our eyes met briefly, and it seemed he was happy to have me back with him. Then he closed his eyes and went to sleep.

I did the same, settling down on the sofa and closing my eyes. I didn't fall asleep, though. It was more a drowsy sense of calm and peace that washed over me. I was in my home with my dog nearby and my husband and daughters were asleep upstairs. I imagined the dying fire still glowing as it gave off the last of its heat, keeping back the chill of winter that threatened to creep unbidden into my favourite room. I was in my world, where I wanted to be.

I ignored the fact that I was dead.

Chapter 20 – Do ghosts sleep?

When I opened my eyes, it was daylight, and it did feel as though I'd been asleep. Maybe not normal sleep, but it was definitely sleep of some kind because I was aware that time had passed and I was also aware that I'd been dreaming.

Ross was gone from his chair by the fire and the day outside looked cold and damp and miserable. 'Driech,' was the word Gavin, Claire's Scottish husband, would use. It was the perfect word to describe the bleak, dreary world outside the window. Winter didn't seem to be going away any time soon, by the look of it.

If I'd been alive, I would have woken up cold and shivering, and cursing myself for falling asleep on the sofa and not in my nice, comfortable bed with my husband beside me to keep me warm. Right now, though, it felt great to have experienced a semblance of sleeping and waking. And dreaming. I'm fairly certain I had a dream during the night, although I hadn't the foggiest notion of what it was about because dreams so often disappear from memory as soon as we open our eyes. I hated when that happened. I'd wake up with the sensation of having a really good dream and I'd be buggered if I could remember even a tiny part of it.

That's what I was experiencing right now. The dream was somewhere in the back of my head, almost on the tip of my tongue. It felt as though it was lurking behind some early-morning mist and I could remember it, if I just concentrated hard enough. But the mist refused to budge and the dream was gone, seemingly never to return.

But hey, at least I *had* a dream.

~~~

The family was up and about. I could hear them going about their morning routine. The scraping of chairs on the floor. The clatter of spoons against cereal bowls, and the arguments over using too much milk. All this could easily grow into a full-blown row until Charlie stepped in and nipped it in the bud with a stern warning. I could hear Ross yapping for his own breakfast and the radio blaring out the news while the usual mini-drama played out like it did each morning in our kitchen.

I would have been there in the thick of it—getting the lunches ready while I tried to grab a slice of toast for myself and cursing under my breath because it had gone cold. I'd make sure they had their schoolbags and their PE kits and whatever else it was my responsibility to make sure they had for school. Charlie would roll his eyes at me as he told them to hurry up. I'd ask him if he wanted more toast and I'd roll my eyes back at him when he said he'd get a breakfast bap or a fry-up at a café later. I'd kiss them all goodbye and they'd be off. I'd turn off the radio, gather up the plates and bowls and mugs to stack them in the dishwasher and breathe a sigh of relief as calm descended and the house would be mine for a few hours. I loved them dearly but, by heck, they could be a noisy bunch first thing in the morning.

I watched from the window as the van drove along our bumpy lane to the main road—calling it a main road was a stretch because it was barely wider than the lane and it had just as many potholes. Charlie turned right towards the village, where he would drop the girls off at school then carry on to his own work. They disappeared out of sight after a few yards as the road went downhill past a line of trees.

Out of sight, but not out of mind. Oh, no. Never that.

~~~

I turned away from the window and glanced around what had once been my home. The kitchen looked as though a bomb had gone off and the windows were too grimy for my liking. The laundry was piled up in the utility room and the fire needed to be cleaned out and set. The log basket was empty, and the whole place could do with a good going over with a vacuum cleaner and a duster. I'd no doubt that the bedrooms, the playroom and the bathroom could do with a bit of a tidy up and a good cleaning as well.

Not my problem any more, I thought with a shrug. Then I mentally slapped my wrist and felt a bit guilty for relishing the fact that I couldn't do the housework. I would love to do it, but I couldn't. There was no point in thinking otherwise and I hoped Charlie would get something sorted soon. He was normally so neat and tidy himself so this was a bit out of character for him.

'He's depressed,' Depression said, and I whirled around in fright at the voice.

'Don't sneak up on me like that. You almost gave me a heart attack.' I glared at her.

'Sorry. I thought you'd heard me come in.'

'Okay, you're here now. What do you want? And what makes you think Charlie is depressed?'

'I don't want anything in particular. Mind you, I wouldn't turn down a brew.'

'I can't make tea and you know that.'

'I probably shouldn't be telling you this, but actually you can, although it takes an awful lot of practice, and I wouldn't recommend it in case any of the family see you. It's not so much that they see a kettle boiling when it shouldn't be boiling, but you can't appear to them, and them seeing mugs and milk cartons and teabags appearing to float around the kitchen would probably concern them.'

'Concern them? That's a bit of an understatement. It would scare the living daylights out of them.'

'Which is why I'm recommending you don't try it.'

'I won't. So why do you say Charlie's depressed? He looks okay to me. A bit quiet maybe.'

'He hides it well in front of your daughters but I'm sure you already know—what with all the time you spend wandering around the house, especially at night—he only shows his true feelings when he's alone with his glass of whiskey before bed.'

I couldn't argue with that because I'd seen it with my own eyes and it broke my heart.

'So, what do I do about it?'

'There's nothing you can do, love. Charlie will just have to come to terms with your death in his own time. He will be okay, but he just needs time to get over you and I don't mean that harshly. It's just the natural progression of things—someone dies, their loved ones grieve and then they come to terms with it. They'll always miss you—always be sad that you're gone—but they'll get over it.'

'I know. And, in truth, I hope he does. I hope he finds someone who makes him happy again.'

'Oh, that is so sad.' Depression pulled a paper tissue out of her pocket, blew her nose and wiped her tear-filled eyes. It was obvious she was planning a good old-fashioned cryfest for the two of us and that was the last thing on earth I wanted right now.

'I appreciate all you've said, but I have to go,' I told her, hoping she wouldn't offer to come with me. How would I get out of that? 'I need to go for a walk, or something, and clear my head.'

'Sure. No problem. We can do that.'

She bloody did want to come with me. I could tell by the way she perked up and almost smiled. I needed to nip this in the bud before we ended up joined at the hip. I couldn't think of anything worse than having Depression following me around like the proverbial black cloud she was. I figured diplomacy was my best option. Well, that and lying through my teeth.

'Oh, that is so kind of you,' I said with a big smile and as much saccharin as I could muster. 'It'll cheer me up no end.'

The frown of confusion came first and I had to bite my tongue to keep from whooping in delight, but it was the horrified expression that slid across her face at the thought of cheering somebody up that caused me to snort with laughter.

'Um—I don't think I can. I—erm—I have to be somewhere.' She pulled her sleeve up and pretended to look at her watch. 'Goodness. Is that the time? I'm late. I'm going to be so late. This is terrible.'

She could have been the white rabbit to my Alice.

'That's a shame. But just go. Don't worry about me,' I told her, and off she went—head down in despair, wiping her eyes with her sleeve. I guess she'd used up all her paper tissues.

~~~

I needed to get out of the house, but when I looked out the window, the visibility wasn't great—that was the understatement of the year, it was almost non-existent—but it didn't matter all that much to me. It was one of those colourless winter days where the grey clouds were so low you could reach out and touch them. Early morning mist was one thing—for a start, it looked pretty, the way it hung just above ground level and you could still see trees and buildings over it as it crept around them—but low rainclouds were another. They made you want to shout at them to just get on with it but, no, they refused to budge— always threatening rain, but only ever producing a miserable, cold mizzle.

Mizzle is a great word. It's a combination of mist and drizzle that was not quite rain but plenty wet enough to dampen your clothes and make your hair go frizzy.

I could have done with a more suitable attire than what I was wearing. The old sweater and jeans didn't look right as I set off on my early morning walk.

Hey presto! I was wearing my waxed jacket, my waterproof trousers—expensive, yes, but God, I loved them—and my good hiking boots. I even had my blue beanie on my head. I was all kitted out for a good hike.

The only things missing was my backpack containing my camera and accessories, my flask of coffee and some sarnies, and faithful Ross by my side.

~~~

Despite the lack of visibility, I knew where I was as I steadily walked along the narrow pathways and tracks, my route taking me higher up the hills. I could hear the gentle sounds of a small stream as it journeyed in the opposite direction. It trickled over rocks, twisting and turning, as it made its way down the tree-covered hill towards the river it would eventually join. It was a stream that I had photographed on many occasions—in the summer with the sunlight glinting off the water. In the autumn, with leaves of red and brown floating along on its path. In winter, surrounded by snow, almost completely frozen and reduced to steady drips as it fought to survive to reach the river below. I think I even had a recording of the running water on my phone. It was one of several nature sounds that I'd recorded there—running water, birds, a rainstorm, even the sound of the wind. I'd also recorded the fire crackling as it burned in the hearth, and the sounds of the windchimes Charlie had bought me. They hung on a tree in the back garden and, on a summer's evening, I loved to sit outside and listen to them tinkle in the gentle breeze. I had planned on compiling an hour-long CD of all the different recordings and maybe selling copies at craft fairs, along with my photographs, calendars, cards and notebooks.

~~~

Going to craft fairs was something I'd been planning for some time, since the idea came into my head when I watched a TV show on arts and crafts as a small business. It was on one of those lifestyle channels that you only ever see when you stop scrolling because your thumb is starting to cramp. I almost went past it but I stopped to pick up my glass of wine. Thirty minutes and two glasses of wine later, I thought this might be something I could try for the upcoming Christmas markets.

Sales through my photography website gave me a good income, but I loved the idea of getting out and about, setting up my table, and meeting the public. I realised I would need some new and innovative ideas to attract customers—something fresh and different, but still within my remit as a landscape photographer. And something not too expensive to make, that I could sell for a reasonable price yet still turn a bit of a profit.

The more I thought about it, the more I liked the idea. Public liability insurance wasn't as expensive as I'd thought it might be, so I took out a one-year policy. I already had the table and it wouldn't take me long to design a pop-up banner to advertise myself and my wares—even this was a decent price. I planned on selling at the local markets and craft fairs, beginning with prints in various sizes, plus postcards, Christmas cards and greeting cards for any occasion. I also wanted to try some photos on slates, and coasters—for Christmas again—plus general images, and I even considered coffee mugs, although I read on various crafters' forums that they didn't sell very well, so I scrapped that idea pretty quickly.

I remember mentioning it to Charlie in bed one evening while the idea was still in the 'thinking about it stage.'

He looked at me as though I had a screw loose.

'Why? You're making plenty through the website. You don't need to spend your Saturdays freezing to death in the winter at a market stall.'

'I know I don't,' I replied. 'But it's something I want to do as a hobby. I've heard it's interesting—there's always a good selection of different crafts and the people are lovely.'

'What if you don't sell anything?'

'Well, I won't know how well or how badly I'll do until I try it. I want to give it a go, and if it doesn't work, I can quit. No harm, no foul.'

Charlie knew me well enough to know that once I'd gotten an idea in my head it would be nearly impossible to talk me out of it. I could see his mind ticking over.

'You'll need a table.'

'Got one.'

'And one of those pop-up banners with your photo and some of your stuff on it.'

'Working on it.'

'And don't forget public liability insurance.'

'Sorted. It was cheaper than you think.'

'A card reader for people who don't like to carry cash.'

'Already have one.'

Charlie folded his arms across his chest and looked at me with a grin.

'You've it all planned out, haven't you?'

'Mostly in my head so far, but I can be up and ready

for the first craft fair two weeks from now. I've already applied and been accepted.'

'Of course you have,' he grinned. 'I'm guessing you have a babysitter all lined up, too.'

'Well—I know a bloke—'

He put his arm around me and pulled me close to him, then kissed my neck.

'Go for it, babe,' he whispered in my ear.

Naturally, the kissing and the whispering and his hand on my leg led to other more important things, and my future career as a crafter was forgotten about for the rest of the night.

~~~

I was a nervous wreck the night before the first fair. I tossed and turned in bed, and I think I got about five minutes sleep the whole night as I kept jerking awake out of a stress-related dream in which it rained or snowed, or there was a howling gale and no one turned up and everything got blown away.

But this was just a dream, wasn't it? And where did I hear that before?

I put my dream out of my mind. It was going to be calm and sunny today, I told myself over and over as I crawled out of bed at five-thirty, on a cold, dark morning and staggered into the shower, bleary-eyed and exhausted.

What happened in my dream can happen in real life, especially with our weather. I discovered this at the end of November on only my third excursion into the world of craft fairs. It was freezing, wet and windy. The gazebos almost blew away and the public stayed at home where they were warm and cosy, and could buy what they wanted online with just a click or two. I sold nothing. I wasn't disheartened, though because no one else sold anything. The woman beside me shrugged her shoulders and muttered something about the 'bloody rubbish British weather and the even more rubbish weather man.' She'd listened to the weather while eating breakfast that morning and the forecast said it was going to be cold, though dry.

~~~

Why was I so stressed about it? I don't know. I think I wanted to do well and I was worried that I wouldn't because, although I had Charlie's full support, I knew he was a bit dubious about the whole thing. I wanted to show him that I could make a go of selling smaller, cheaper products that were still good quality, as well as my high-end photos.

I set off earlier than I needed to, found a nearby parking place and got everything set up on my allocated spot. I secured my banner against the gentle breeze, and laid my wares out on the table—I rearranged them three times before I was satisfied. I had my flask of coffee tucked tidily under the table and enough sandwiches to see me through until packing up time at four o'clock, and I was bloody freezing because it was the first week of November.

Before I left, Charlie had said he might pop down later with the girls to see how I was getting on so I sent him a text telling him to bring my woolly gloves, my fur-lined boots and my parka. And a flask of hot whiskey, and a hot water bottle. I was only joking about the last two items. Well, mostly joking.

By the time they arrived, I was numb with the cold but a very happy bunny. I sold most of the Christmas cards and three sets of coasters as well as nine calendars. Just as I spotted him walking towards my stall, a woman who'd been looking through my selection of small mounted prints, selected a dozen and set them in front of me while she dug her credit card out of her purse.

'All of them?' I tried, and failed, not to squeak with a mixture of surprise and delight.

'Yes, please,' she replied. 'I have friends and family all over the world—America, Canada, Australia, even Egypt. I also have a cousin living in Peru of all places and before you ask, she isn't in prison for drug running. She's an English language teacher, but everyone just assumes she's doing time there.'

It was information I didn't really need so I just smiled politely as I carefully put the prints into a bag.

'Everyone will adore some pictures of home and these are stunning. They'll make ideal Christmas gifts to send to them. Flat and easy to post, too.'

I beamed with pride when she paid in full and gathered up her purchases. I thought she was done and about to walk away when she stopped and had a look at the slate coasters again.

'I'll take these as well. For my sister.'

Cool, I thought as I enveloped them in bubble wrap and popped them into her bag. I could see Charlie watching me with a smile on his face and my parka draped over his arm.

Once the woman with the jailbird-slash-English-language-teacher cousin in Peru had left, Charlie nipped behind my table, stole my seat and took Chloe on his knee. Amy was more interested in my table that sitting on her dad's knee and I had to warn her not to touch anything. Charlie handed me the coat and boots, and I couldn't get them on quickly enough.

'You're doing all right by the look of it,' he said.

'I am, Charlie. I'm delighted.' Despite the cold, I had a grin on my face and a gleam in my eye that would have melted snow. I wiped a smear of chocolate off Chloe's face and watched Amy as she checked out the nearby tables. She was as good as gold and didn't touch anything, which wasn't like her, the little monster that she is. I kept a close eye on her and called her back to my table when she began to stray too far from my line of sight. Both girls were bundled up against the cold and looked comfy and warm, while I shivered.

'I knew you would, sweetheart. You're a star. But then, I know that.' Charlie smiled and kissed me on the cheek.

'It's been great, Charlie. Some of the other traders even bought things from me. They're a lovely bunch. Always happy to keep an eye on your stall when you need to nip to the loo, or go for a look around. But I have a confession to make.' I pulled the bags out from below my table. 'I—um—bought a few things.'

'I don't doubt it for a second.'

'All sensible purchases, though.' I pulled some of my haul out of the bag to show him. 'A matching woolly hat and scarf for me because I'll need them here to keep me warm. The same for you, but not such a girly colour. Unless you want a girly colour. I can get them exchanged.'

'Nah.' Charlie took off his beanie, put the woolly hat on his head and wrapped the scarf around his neck. He grinned at me. 'I mean pink would have been awesome. It brings out the colour in my eyes, but navy blue is good.'

'Yeah, I thought you'd prefer that one. Look at what else I got.' I held the bag open. 'Some handmade soaps because they're lovely, and who doesn't need soap? And these delicious scented candles. And I have some homemade sweet chilli sausage rolls, and I also got white chocolate and raspberry scones. They're your favourite, aren't they?'

'No, they're your favourite. I like cherry scones.'

'I'll get those next time, I promise.'

~~~

He hung around for about an hour before boredom caught up with all three of them and he took his leave, promising to have a hot dinner and a hot drink ready for me when I came home. He was true to his word. Dinner was on the table along with a mug of steaming hot tea. I was delighted with how well my first day at a craft fair had turned out, but I was starving and cold, and very glad to be home.

~~~

I did really well at the craft fairs. Too well sometimes, as I almost sold out completely on a couple of occasions, especially in the run-up to Christmas. The card reader was perfect because the money went straight into my business account and I didn't have to worry about it. I kept a record of any cash sales in a little notebook and, at the end of the month, I emailed the totals to my accountant to keep my finances in order.

~~~

The hardest part was keeping up with my stock. I was working flat-out during the week to make sure I had enough prints and coasters and cards in my boxes for the weekends. I'd only planned on attending a couple of fairs each month but there were so many in November and December, plus I was suddenly getting so popular that I was being invited to different fairs throughout the region, and I hated saying no.

I knew it would die down once the Christmas panic was over so I took it in my stride, neglected my family and the housework, and spent my weekends standing in the cold and the wind and the rain—and I loved it.

Charlie took it all in good humour. He enjoyed joining me for an hour or two, often bringing the girls with him, at other times leaving them with Claire or his parents and mine too, if they were available. My mum and dad showed up a few times and Mum even bought some Christmas cards.

Although I usually took sandwiches with me, I got into the habit of buying hot food from several of the vendors—foodies, as they're known. It was impossible to resist the temptation of all the delicious smells that surrounded me and the hot food was great on a cold day.

Claire got in on the act a couple of times. She'd bring her own chair and a book to read and she'd join me for the day. She didn't have any artistic talents—in her own words, she said she 'couldn't draw the curtains' and 'couldn't write a shopping list.' She was a fantastic cook though, and also enjoyed baking, but it was behind my stall that we discovered Claire's previously unknown talent—in retail. She was the best bloody salesperson I've ever known and she could charm money out of anybody. She had the 'market stall' banter down to perfection—Del Boy Trotter would be in awe of her—and I found myself sitting back, open-mouthed as she persuaded people to hand over their money in exchange for my wares.

We joked that I could stay at home making the calendars and mounting the prints, while she went out and sold them.

Every now and then there'd be a slight lull, and we'd take the time to sit back, pour ourselves a brew and enjoy a bite to eat. This was when we engaged in our favourite method of passing the time—people watching.

We'd cast our critical eyes over the public as they passed by, with those that ignored our stall coming in for the worst criticism.

'She won't buy a thing because she spent all her money on gin and horse-racing bets, and now she hasn't two pennies to rub together.'

'See the way he takes sneaky photos of all the stuff on the stalls? He's planning to copy everything and sell it online.'

'Would you look at her, all dressed up like it's Ladies Day at Ascot. She's already murdered two husbands and is planning on offing the third very soon. That's why she's buying all those herbs and spices.' Claire nodded wisely as though she'd murdered two husbands and knew what was what.

'How can you murder someone with coriander?' I'd ask.

'It disguises the taste of the arsenic in his dinner. You watch all those crime shows. Haven't you learned anything from them?'

We tried not to laugh but it was hard to keep the giggles at bay sometimes, and now and then we'd be eating our lunch and choking with laughter. As Claire was such a great salesperson I always paid for our food. It was my way of thanking her, but she said she didn't need to be thanked—she enjoyed being there with me as it gave her a well-earned break from Gavin and her three very boisterous children. Claire and Gavin have a girl and two boys. They're lovely kids but they have far too much energy.

'I love them to bits. But sometimes they're just too outdoorsy for me. I like to lie about the house on a Saturday, or do something like this which is mostly sitting around and not expending any energy. All they want to do is play football or climb trees, or some such nonsense. Even Lily. She's as bad as the boys. It's great to get a day here for a break.'

~~~

I smiled as I remembered all the good times we had at the markets and craft fairs. They were crazy busy in the run up to Christmas and even during the first two weeks in January there could be a surprisingly high footfall. But after that, they died a death and most crafters took a well-earned break through February and March before they started again—usually around Easter, when they'd continue all through the summer and up to Christmas again.

One of the nicest things about the craft fairs was the people I got to know. They were genuine people, hardworking, honest and lovely, and always eager to help a newbie like me. I made some wonderful friends among the regulars—Carolyn, Jackie, Judith, Deborah, Suzanne and Keith, and Richard and Nat with their Viking-inspired wood craft. There was the bloke who made lovely live-edge wood tables, and lamps out of old fire extinguishers—I got mine from him—and tealight holders out of old car and motorcycle pistons. I remember Graham with his quirky signs, the lady who sold homemade dog treats—Ross loved them—as well as Sharon, who organised everything. I've mentioned only a few, but there were many more. The banter was hilarious and we had many, many laughs.

Sadly, Carolyn passed away not long after my second Christmas being a part of the craft fair community. She was missed terribly.

~~~

It was when I was out on one of my walks through a nearby forest that I hit on the idea of recording various sounds of nature onto a CD. I'd found a little stream and spent about an hour photographing both the stream and the nearby woods. When I took a break, I sat down on an old fallen tree, closed my eyes and just listened to the sounds all around me—the water as it meandered over and around the small rocks, the leaves on the trees, rustling in the breeze, and the birds. There were so many different bird sounds and I could only identify a few of them—a chiffchaff and a wood pigeon were the easiest, and the rapid thumping of a woodpecker some distance away. I couldn't be sure of the others—maybe a blackbird or a thrush. I didn't know and it didn't matter, they were beautiful and so relaxing to listen to, as all the sounds were.

If only I could bottle this up, I thought.

Well, of course I could bottle it up. Not in an actual bottle, but in a high-tech, twenty-first century way.

I whipped out my phone, opened the voice recorder app, and sat there very quietly while I captured the beautiful—and peaceful—sounds of nature. I even considered that for the title of my CD, even though I wasn't planning on mass-producing them.

~~~

It was only a trial run so I let the recorder run for just a few minutes. When I got home, I played it back and it sounded pretty good, if I ignored the sound of myself breathing. It never occurred to me that the voice recorder would pick that up, too. I wasn't concerned because it was an issue that I could easily rectify the next time I tried it.

~~~

I got to thinking about different sounds that would make a relaxing CD that people would love, and I decided on three or four. A gentle stream, bird song—because everybody loves the sounds of birds—and the sound of the wind. These would give a nice autumn feeling. A crackling fire would stir up images of either a fire burning outside on a summer's evening or a hearth in the depths of winter, warming and comforting those gathered around it. A thunderstorm would be great, too.

I was on a roll, and thinking ahead of myself. I even had the CD cover designed in my imagination. More than one in fact, because by now I was now planning a couple of one-hour discs. I reckoned I could sell them for a fiver each, or maybe six quid each and ten pounds if they bought two. Oh yes, I could hear the constant 'cha-ching' of the cash register as people jumped queues and punched others out of the way to get one of my '*Gentle Sounds of Nature*' CD's. I even considered how many bouncers I'd need to hire.

I didn't half love aiming high.

I deleted my first attempt and went back the next morning to the same place. This time I held my phone at arm's length and breathed as quietly as I could while I recorded twenty minutes of birds singing only for me—and my buyers—as the little stream accompanied them.

I came home and played it back. It sounded great.

~~~

It dawned on me now that I'd made a few more recordings over the next couple of weeks, before real life— otherwise known as the school holidays—got in the way. I reluctantly set my little project aside and then—well, that death thing came along and really buggered up every single one of my plans for the next fifty or so years, never mind my successful and highly-sought-after nature CD's. I knew that I'd already transferred most of them to my laptop—as they were taking up too much space on my phone and it made me wonder what happened to my laptop and phone. The laptop is probably still on my desk and who knows where the phone could be. I expect Charlie has it, and he'll have to transfer all my photos and recordings and everything on it to the lappy to save them—just another one of the many tasks I've left him to deal with.

These were all jobs I normally did without a second thought but Charlie wasn't as tech-savvy as me. He wouldn't have a clue how to move everything on my phone to my laptop and would probably get Amy to do it for him. She was a whizz with that sort of stuff and she's even pulled me out of a bind a couple of times when I downloaded images from my camera and couldn't find them afterwards. Two clicks and a smirk from Amy, and there they were.

Kids these days. Bloody know-it-alls.

Chapter 21 – Family fun.

Other than the sounds of the little stream, it was deathly quiet up here this morning. There was no wind. Not even a gentle breeze to chase away the fog and bring out the sun, and I couldn't hear a single bird, or the raspy sore-throat sounds of sheep bleating. It was eerie, but I found it peaceful and comforting.

I walked on, thinking about my life with each step.

~~~

I did fewer markets and fairs in the summer—usually only once a month—than I did in winter. What I sold was more for the gift shoppers, and my sales dropped off enough in the summertime to make it not worth my while attending them every week. I was happy enough about that. It gave me more time to spend out and about, taking photos and planning themes for my website as well as building up stock for my calendars and cards. When I wasn't out working—as I called it—I spent all of my time with Charlie and the girls—out in the garden when the weather was fine, but struggling to keep them from getting bored indoors when it rained.

While my girls weren't exactly feral, they did love the outdoors. They spent their days outside from morning until evening, when the weather was suitable. Both of them had learned to swim, and one day Charlie came home with a swimming pool. I don't mean an inflatable paddling pool, this one had a steel frame that had to be erected first, then the liner attached before it could be filled. Which took ages.

'It'll be autumn by the time we can use it.'

Charlie shrugged. 'I can't make the water come out of the hose any faster.'

Claire and Gavin brought their brood over to try out our new water feature—as she called it—and all five youngsters stood there watching the water not rising. After a while they got bored and ran off to play.

By dinner time it was nearly full and, after dinner, we all went out to try it. It was bloody freezing. I climbed out as quickly as I'd climbed in.

'I'll be the lifeguard.' I told them. Claire dipped one toe in, shook her head, and joined me on the patio.

Being children, they didn't let the cold water deter them, and they splashed and played for ages—their dads keeping an eye on them. It was unanimous—our swimming pool was the coolest thing in the whole world.

Charlie did persuade me to get in a couple of times, in the evening when the sun had warmed the water a bit and it was more comfortable. I enjoyed it. I closed my eyes and pretended it was a real pool—Olympic-sized—and I even pretended there was a wine waiter nearby who'd appear with a fresh glass when I clicked my fingers. There was. His name was Charlie.

Of course, the hot weather didn't last for more than a few days and it wasn't long before we drained the pool and put it in the shed, where it stayed until the next hot spell, a week or two later.

At other times, the girls just spent their days running about and playing. And exploring. They loved to explore. They were happy to spend their days looking for newts, tadpoles—though they were only found in the springtime—

and small fish in the nearby streams and ponds. Under our supervision, of course. They watched the animals—the sheep and the cows—in the nearby fields and they had named them all. We made up many stories about them.

At holiday times, they played with Claire and Gavin's kids. They chased each other, had water fights in the summer, or spent the day splashing in the pool. In the winter, they had snowball fights.

My girls were either rosy-cheeked or tanned, and they slept well every night from all that fresh air and exercise.

During one particularly hot summer spell, when it was so hot in bed that none of us could get a decent night's sleep, I dug out the two tents we'd bought and we set up a little campsite at the bottom of the garden. The girls had one tent, Charlie and I had the other. We added a firepit and built a campfire, and we placed several LED camping lights around us so that later on it wouldn't be completely dark beyond the reach of the firelight. Charlie had found a large tree trunk on a property he was renovating and brought it home, thinking it would be ideal firewood for the stoves but he decided to cut a section along the length of it to make it seat-shaped and it was already in place where we set up our camp. With a blanket added for comfort, it made a great natural seating area in front of the open fire, where we toasted marshmallows and ate snacks from the cool box.

~~~

We had some lovely summer evenings spent at 'Camp Wilson' when the days were hot, the nights were pleasantly comfortable and the lawn was freshly mown. It was a good thing none of us had allergies because there wasn't anything we loved more than being outdoors during the long summer evenings, either camping or just sitting around. We had the scent of newly mown grass and the woodsmoke from the fire all around us—the smoke helped to keep the midges at bay. Yeah okay, we got the occasional whiff of slurry that had been sprayed on the nearby fields, but that was okay—it was all part and parcel of living in the country.

It didn't get dark until after eleven o'clock and, as night approached, I'd tell the girls stories. They'd scream at the scary ones and giggle at the funny ones, then they'd begin to yawn and rub their sleepy eyes. I'd pack them off to their tent and into their sleeping bags and, once they were settled and off to sleep, Charlie would pour a beer, switch on the camping lights and select some quiet, easy-listening music on his phone while I opened a bottle of wine. We sat there forever it seemed, stargazing and chatting as the fire crackled and burned, and gave off warmth to stave off the coolness of the evening. We'd sit there until there were only embers left, before finishing our drinks and settling down in our own tent. Ross slept outside the girls' tent like the faithful guard dog he was.

~~~

One January, we had a bad snowstorm. About five inches of snow had accumulated overnight and some more fell the next morning. The high winds had caused it to drift and the roads were blocked. The girls were ecstatic at the thought of no school for a few days and Charlie had to cancel his work plans. As a result, he was as happy as the girls. We had plenty of supplies in the house, as I always kept the freezer and the larder well-stocked in the winter for exactly this reason, so I was happy too.

~~~

By late afternoon the snow clouds rolled away, leaving the darkening sky clear and the temperatures plummeting. Naturally, the girls thought it would be great fun to camp outside overnight. I said no and of course there were scowls and cries of 'Why not, Mummy?' emphasised by the stamping of feet.

I was adamant. I had no intention of risking an arrest for child cruelty or 'causing unnecessary suffering' or whatever charge they would get me on if I took my daughters camping in January with snow on the ground and temperatures of -6C. Believe it or not, I had more sense than that.

Chloe argued that, if we used the four-person tent so we could all snuggle together and if we got the warm sleeping bags down from the attic, put on our warmest pyjamas and if I made flasks of hot chocolate and if Daddy lit a really big fire, we would all be nice and warm.

Chloe said all this in once sentence and without pausing to draw a breath. I took a deep breath in lieu of hers, counted to ten and told her no. Cue more scowls and stamping of feet.

I glanced at Charlie and I could tell he wasn't on my side. He shrugged his shoulders in a 'why not?' gesture and I mouthed the word 'no' back at him. I couldn't believe he actually wanted to do this.

'I don't mean we spend the whole night in a tent. I'm not that daft. But I could light the firepit and we could huddle around it for a while. Then we go back indoors when they get cold and bored. If we don't let them stay out for a while, they'll complain until March about us being mean parents. This'll shut them up. Besides, it's not like it snows every day, so it's an experience for them. Something different and maybe even fun.'

I mulled it over. It was seven o'clock at night, in the middle of January. It had snowed for most of the day and there was about five inches on the ground, but it was a lovely evening—clear and frosty. There was probably a law against taking young children outside at night in this kind of weather, but the roads were closed so Social Services weren't going to be swooping in to arrest us and take my daughters off to a place of safety any time soon. Charlie's idea actually did sound like fun, provided we limited it to an hour or so.

I told him to go and light the fire, told the girls to bundle up and remember to put their gloves and beanies on, then set about making flasks of hot chocolate.

One flask contained only hot chocolate, but the other one was laced with rum—the trick was to not get the flasks mixed up. I didn't want to add permitting underaged drinking to the list of crimes Social Services were going to hit me with.

As soon as we were all dressed in our warmest clothes and Charlie had the fire burning brightly, I gathered everything up, including some extra blankets, and off we went to the very bottom corner of the garden. The part that was sheltered by large fir trees.

We'd invited Ross to join us but he gave me a 'Fuck,

no.' look and snuggled even deeper into his warm bed by the radiator in the kitchen. I could see his point.

It was lovely while the fire was blazing. We were warm enough, and we could see a vast swathe of the Milky Way. I pointed out the different constellations to the girls as we drank our hot chocolate—the added rum made an excellent drink for Charlie and myself, and the girls didn't know what they were missing—and I taught them the names of the constellations. The ones I could remember, at least.

'C'mere Amy. Sit close to me and lean your head on my arm, then look at where my finger is pointing.' She climbed onto my knee. I put one arm around her and pointed up to the sky with the other as her head rested against me. 'Now see those stars—that one up there is the Big Dipper. It's also known as The Plough or the Great Bear, but its proper name is Ursa Major.'

'I don't see a bear, Mummy.'

'What do you see then?'

'It looks like a big saucepan.'

I snorted with laughter because she was so correct. It had always looked like a saucepan to me.

'Don't tell anyone but all I can see is a saucepan. But if you look at the star just at the edge of the saucepan, then look upwards until you see a bright-ish star on its own. That's the North Star and it never moves in the sky. It's always right there, and all the other stars, as well as us, revolve around it. No matter where you are, if you're here or at school, or at Auntie Claire's, that star will always be in the same position and it always points to the north.'

'Unless you're in Australia. I wish I was in Australia,' Charlie muttered. Chloe was nestled in his arms, listening intently but not saying anything. That was my Chloe. She but listened to everything. Listened and learned.

Charlie kept his arm around Chloe as he sipped his rum-infused mug of hot chocolate and fantasised about a warm Australian winter.

'This was your idea so don't moan and complain about it,' I told him.

~~~

Despite the cold, it was a beautiful evening, and I taught Amy and Chloe the names of some of the other constellations, explaining in primary school terms how they moved around the sky at different times of the year. Then we saw a shooting star, and there were lots of oohs and aahs as it flared across the night sky. I told them to close their eyes and make a wish on it.

'I wish I was warm,' Charlie said under his breath.

'Me, too,' I mouthed back to him.

Both my girls soon began to rub their tired eyes and yawn for some much-needed sleep, or it could have been hypothermia setting in—I was shivering too by this stage—so we decided it was time to gather everything up and get back indoors where we could warm up properly.

Ross lifted his head when he saw us coming in—stamping our feet and complaining about the cold—and I swear he gave me a 'told you so' look.

I got the girls bathed and into their pyjama's, then tucked them into their beds under their warm duvets. I made sure they were warm and cosy and I quickly made up a story about the biggest snowman in the world, promising them that we'd build the biggest snowman in the world after breakfast tomorrow. They drifted off to sleep on that promise and I went back downstairs. Charlie was making hot toddies. He pulled me close to him and put his arms around me.

'Don't go booking any Antarctic expeditions, please.'

'Not a chance,' I said. 'It's the Bahamas or nothing for me.'

Chapter 22 -Time flies like an arrow. Fruit flies like a banana.

They say dogs live in the present—in the here and now—although they can remember the past. Otherwise, we couldn't train them, or an abused dog wouldn't cower in fear when approached by someone he thought was going to hit him again—but they can't really visualise the future.

Dogs, from what I've observed, have a sense of time passing—a feeling, rather than a concept—even though they know, almost to the minute, when it's time for their dinner or to go out for a walk. In reality, it's because they are so exceptionally good at picking up on behavioural cues—even those we're not aware we are giving. It could be a slight movement like taking off your glasses, or glancing up at the clock on the mantlepiece—a cue that you are about to take them out for their evening walk.

Regardless of what it is, if you make a habit of it, a dog sees it and understands what it means.

But mostly, a dog lives in the now—and when you leave them you are gone for good. If you nip to the village shop for twenty minutes to get milk and eggs, or you spend half a day in town, shopping and meeting a friend for lunch and a good old catch-up natter, it's all the same to them because, as far as your dog is concerned, you are gone. End of story.

That could be why, on your return, they greet you like you've been on a six-month cruise around the world. They go absolutely nuts.

'Oh my God! You're back! You've been gone so

long. I've missed you sooo much. There was a postman outside and a white van, and a leaf blew past the window and I had to bark and defend the house all on my own! Where've you been?'

This is what they say in Dog language as they bark loudly while they sniff your jeans and give you a reproachful glare. 'You smell of dog. You've been with another dog. You are actually seeing another dog. How could you?'

Then you mollify them, tell them you've missed them too and next thing you know, they've got their noses in your grocery bag and it's all, 'Oh, what did you get me? Anything nice?'

~~~

I don't know if it's true that dogs only live in the present as I'm no dog psychologist, but I'm definitely living in the present these days. While I can see time passing—in the difference between day and night, or the change in the weather and the landscape as the seasons move from one to the other—I'm not really aware of it. I'm firmly in the here and now, but time is moving around me at its usual pace and I see it mostly in my family. I see how their emotions change, and while their grief hasn't gone away, it has settled on them like a comfortable coat. Sometimes they're normal—they laugh and joke and do the usual things that make up a family dynamic—until something reminds them that a vital part of their family is missing and will never come back.

Then they're suddenly—and without warning—pulled into the here and now. Their concept of me never coming back stops them in their tracks and their grief is once again fresh and raw, and as painful as the wound they suffered on the day they said goodbye to me.

I hate it when that happens but, thankfully, those moments occur a little less often as the time passes.

~~~

My time is different from theirs now. It stretches and shrinks, and I have no control over it. Tomorrow could be several weeks away, or it could happen in five minutes. It's no longer linear. I can look back and remember, even though some of my memories are missing—especially the most recent ones—and I put that down to the trauma I suffered before I died, but I can't see anything if I look forward. It's probably because there is no forward for me. I can think about it, but only in terms of my family's future. I can't see my future because there isn't one to see.

Which is a really depressing thought and I'd better think of something more pleasant before my old buddy Depression shows up with a bumper-sized box of Kleenex. It was time—ha, ha—to put my musings aside for now and think back on the good moments in my life.

Chapter 23 – Teacher's pet.

So, there I was, a fully-fledged primary school teacher, all ready to go out into the big, bad world and impart knowledge to young, impressionable minds for them to soak up like a sponge. What I taught them would one day make them better people who would go forward and make the world a better place. Or so I was told at my graduation ceremony. Other students, and even teachers, said it was more a case of handing out paper and crayons, washing hands and wiping away tears, while dreaming of the long holidays we get every year.

In reality, it was somewhere in between.

Charlie reckoned the movie '*Bad Teacher*' was based on me. Charlie got a hard but playful punch to his arm for his witty quip.

Seriously though, it was all very well thinking I was about to make the world a better place by teaching four and five-year-olds their ABC's and 123's, but the reality of actually doing so was somewhat different.

For a start, finding somewhere that had an abundance of kids willing and eager to learn all I could teach them, along with a vacancy for a teacher, was proving nigh on impossible. There was only one primary school in our neck of the woods—or moors, I suppose—and it had a thirty-mile catchment area. That still only amounted to around thirty to forty children between four and eleven.

Occasionally the number was higher but, more often than not, it dropped to below thirty. People with young families and a dream of living in the countryside would move in and the numbers went up. When they found they couldn't cope with the ruggedness, the poor roads, the harsh winters and the crappy WiFi, they stopped and had a think about it. A major concern was that their kids might be missing out on a more expansive pool of friends and acquaintances, and the opportunities that went along with it. This led them to decide rural life wasn't for them, so they sold up and moved to a larger town, and the numbers went down again.

Additionally, jobs—or the lack thereof—meant a lot of young local families had no choice but to move away, to towns and cities, near and far, because their need for a decent income just wasn't available here.

There were three teachers in the local primary school, two of them having been there so long that they'd taken root. Mrs. Lyttle, the longest-serving, showed no sign of ever retiring and I suspected she would die in her classroom with a piece of chalk in her hand. She was a lovely old dear who put me in mind of *'Miss Jean Brodie'* but with a Yorkshire accent and obviously not from the 1930's—the time in which both the book and the movie were set. She was a bloody good teacher and the wee ones loved her. Although she was the oldest and had been there the longest—technically, she was the headmistress—she didn't like to play the boss and treated her two younger colleagues as equals and good friends. They were Miss Kerr, who was only a few years younger than Mrs Lyttle, and the youthful, by about fifteen years, Mr Tate, or Modern as he was nicknamed—Tate Modern—get it? They all lived locally and we'd often see them in the pub on quiz night, joining in and winning enough times to show they were intelligent enough to be called teachers, but not enough to make us hate them when they pocketed the prize money.

As nice as they were, I really needed one of them to die as soon as possible so I could get a job at the school and not be forced to travel farther afield to seek employment.

About three months after I'd graduated, Charlie and I were debating whether or not I should apply for some primary schools in various towns in the region and how far I should spread my net. We really needed the money—Charlie's business was still only in its infancy and the income from the jobs he did take on was barely enough to keep us afloat. We were weighing up the cost of fuel and the long commute, and trying to decide what I should do, when, as luck would have it, Miss Kerr fell and broke her hip.

Lucky for me that is, not so lucky for her.

I immediately applied for the post of stand-in teacher while she was off on sick leave and I got it. Not so much on my qualifications—though they were good—but more on the fact that I was the only show in town and they needed someone, anyone, to fill the spot left by Miss Kerr.

I sent her a 'get well soon' card, and I sort of meant every word I wrote.

A few weeks later, I got word that my position was to be made permanent. Miss Kerr's physiotherapist had introduced her to his widowed father. The two had hit it off and she'd decided to take her retirement as soon as her period of sick leave ran out and sail off into the sunset with her new beau. They really did sail off. A whirlwind courtship, then a wedding followed by a Caribbean-cruise honeymoon, and her job was mine.

~~~

Being a teacher was okay. I didn't love it but I didn't hate it either. It was easy work teaching five and six-year-olds to remember their letters and their numbers then put them together to form words and sums.

Most of the kids caught on pretty quickly—one or two excelled and were reading and writing well above their age—and the class was well-balanced in terms of ability. I could do this with my eyes shut and one hand tied behind my back. The holidays were great and the pay was okay. It was a welcome addition to our finances as this was back when Charlie didn't even remember having an old aunt, never mind her dying and leaving him a small fortune.

Between what Charlie was earning and my salary, we were able to keep the bills paid and food on the table, with just enough left over at the end of the month for a treat or two—usually a trip to the cinema or a nice meal somewhere. Occasionally both.

The only aspect of being a teacher that I hated were the monthly parent/teacher evenings and I hated them with a vengeance. When one was coming up, I'd try to think of an illness that would get me out of going, but not confine me to bed for a couple of weeks. A cold or flu, or a sprained ankle, wouldn't cut it and I'd already used the migraine excuse twice. I had no choice but to grit my teeth, slap some make-up and a fake smile on my face and show up.

One thing I did enjoy was that they laid on a half-decent spread of tea and coffee with the usual nibbles – tiny sandwiches with a variety of fillings—cucumber, egg and cress, salmon—as well as bowls filled with cheese and onion crisps. And tray bakes—delicious fifteens and caramel shortbread squares. I always managed to discretely scoff a good portion of all three, especially the crisps. I could never walk past a bag or a bowl of cheese and onion crisps without grabbing some before I braced myself to smile as I went to meet and greet the parents of the little shits—darlings, I mean darlings—I was tasked with educating.

My big problem back then was that—and this was a real big problem for a teacher—I didn't like children all that much. I didn't *dislike* them, but I really couldn't get all gooey-eyed over them and I often had to refrain from rolling my eyes when someone talked about the miracle of birth. Every bloody species on the planet gives birth and has done so since we first crawled out of the oceans onto dry land. It's hardly a bloody miracle if you ask me. I remember once saying this to Mum—I think it was when I announced I was getting married to Charlie—after both she and Dad made it clear that they thought I was up the duff.

Mum was shocked when I also said that there was no way I'd ever be daft enough to have a kid. She adored them—babies, toddlers, teenagers—she went gooey-eyed over them all, and she couldn't imagine someone not feeling the same way. I remember her looking at me as though I was another species from another planet—one that grew their offspring on tall stalks in a field, or something. Of course, Mum couldn't have children and maybe that's why she loved every baby within a two-metre range.

My attitude did change after I gave birth to Amy, and later Chloe. I adored them. I wanted to spend the rest of my life kissing and hugging them, making funny noises to them, sniffing their hair—oh, that adorable baby smell—and watching them smile and burp and poop. I loved everything about them.

But they were mine, so I was allowed to adore and cherish them. I didn't have to like other people's kids, so I didn't.

The trouble was, other people's kids liked me. I was a magnet to them and I was their favourite teacher. How weird is that? Of course, every chance she got, Mum said that I'd make a great mother because I was so good with children—I used to babysit the neighbours' kids and they squealed with delight when I arrived. The two of them would latch onto my legs, asking to be hugged and begging me to read to them. I was in it for the money, they were in it for love.

I told Mum to be patient, but that didn't stop her always dropping hints about what a wonderful grandmother she'd make and how I should be getting on with it before it was too late.

'Before all your eggs shrivel up and die. Those lovely baby-making eggs. What a waste,' she said, putting me right off scrambled eggs for ages.

'Or it could be a problem with Charlie. I mean, he wears those tight jeans and I've read somewhere that this causes—'

'I'm on the pill, Mum.'

'Oh. Oh, I see.' Her face fell in disappointment.

A few years later, when I found out I was pregnant with Amy and I told her the good news, her reply was, 'It's about bloody time.'

~~~

I could tolerate the children in my classes—I even liked one or two of them—but the parents were another matter. They were hard work for all kinds of reasons. Some because they were simply obnoxious, but I knew a few of them were really struggling as parents and in life in general. One young lass, the mother of twin boys, had lost her husband and her job within the space of two months. Imagine being a widow at twenty-four with twin five-year olds and no prospects. Yet the boys were always in school on time and wearing clean, though shabby clothes. They were good-mannered, attentive and eager to learn. They had a ham sandwich and an apple in their lunch boxes and their faces were always washed and their hair combed.

Their mum was a shy girl—too young to be called a woman—and always respectful and interested in her boys' well-being. I'd spoken to her many times and she broke my heart when she admitted that she was struggling to make ends meet—but her boys came first and she'd starve before she allowed them to go without. I didn't doubt her. I could see how thin and tired she was and it was obvious she was sacrificing her health and well-being to give her children as much as she could. She was on benefits but they were meagre, so she was looking for work, but she needed something she could work in around school times. I suggested that perhaps she could find something she could do at home—maybe online—and she said she was going to check it out at the Jobcentre that week.

On top of all that, she was still grieving for her man and my heart went out to her.

~~~

Most of the parents were nice, a few were overbearing, but there was one—there's always one—that we always tried to hide from. She was the ultimate pain in the arse. Snooty and obnoxious, and so full of herself.

I hadn't noticed her this evening, so maybe she wasn't here. I breathed a sigh of relief and popped half a cucumber sandwich into my mouth. I almost choked on it when someone tapped me on the shoulder and screeched, 'Hello,' in my ear.

I turned around.

Oh, shite. It was her.

I dry-swallowed my sarnie and smiled. It hurt. It wasn't only the smile that hurt. The sandwich was stuck and I had to keep swallowing to try and get it down. It was bloody painful. I reached for my coffee and took a mouthful. It helped, but I was fairly certain I'd ruptured my oesophagus. I drank some more coffee and finally the sandwich slid on down and the pain began to go away.

She was still there with that tight-lipped 'I am so much better than you,' smile on her face. It was like she was impatiently waiting for me to stop choking to death so she could talk to me about her precious little darling.

'You're Lucy Wilson, right?' she said with a simpering giggle that I know she thought was cute. It wasn't, but it didn't half impress me. I could laugh, snort and choke all at once but to be able to giggle and simper at the same time took multi-tasking to a whole new level. I wanted to kill her, but she was a parent and I was a teacher so they wouldn't let me.

She was tall, with long blonde hair that had been straightened and styled to perfection. Her skin was flawless and she wore only a hint of make-up. She was slim and dressed in a tweed designer jacket over a dark blue V-neck jumper, with jeans that I swear were tattooed on.

I could, and sometimes did, dress like that. Not in designer clothes, obviously, but I could spray on a pair of jeans like the best of them and I had a nice jacket or two in my wardrobe. If I could be bothered to use my straighteners more often, my hair would be just as sleek.

It was the boots that made me hate her. They were tan leather that came up to just under her knees. Cowboy boots, but with flatter heels and I knew they had cost her a couple of hundred quid because I'd googled them. I craved those boots so badly I wanted to lure her out behind the toilet block, kill her and steal the boots off her still-warm corpse.

I'm fairly certain they were my size.

'Yes. I'm Lucy Wilson. You're Jason's mum, aren't you?'

'I am indeed. I was hoping to catch a word with you. I think it's high time the school introduced languages such as Latin and maybe French or Spanish. Jason will be expected to have some basic knowledge of them when he goes to grammar school and I hate that he could be struggling.'

She said that all in one breath.

Jason was five. He was reading above the class age,

though still getting to grips with his maths—some kids were better at one than the other—but he was doing great. He was a lovely little boy—intuitive, well-spoken, eager to learn and always polite—and I couldn't think of any struggles he'd be facing, other than possibly a dead mother with nice socks but no boots on her feet.

'Yes, of course. That's what I'm here for.'

'Great. I really wanted to speak to Mrs Lyttle but she's always so busy. The poor woman can't even fit me in for an appointment. I decided the next—erm—best thing would be to speak to you and maybe you can have a word or two with her for me.'

I refused to let the brief pause between the words 'next' and 'best' get to me, but it was close. She couldn't speak to Mrs Lyttle because Mrs Lyttle avoided her like the plague, and it was poor me that had to face her. I needed to keep my job so I smiled and told her to carry on.

'Well, Geoffrey and I discussed this and, while we appreciate that the school curriculum is already in place, it's hardly written in stone. We think that there should be more to it than basic reading and writing. Certainly, languages should be included, and maybe some introduction to the classics—Shakespeare, Keats, maybe Chaucer and such. I've made some notes and I would appreciate your email address so you can go over them at your leisure then get back to me. ASAP.'

Yeah, right, I thought. The kid is five, for crying out loud. He's more interested in cuddly toys and little red car stories than bloody Keats or Chaucer. I kept my smile firmly in place on my face but I really wanted to tell her to piss off. Then I could turn around, head for the door and make for the nearest pub. The coffee and cucumber sandwiches needed a glass of red to go with them as soon as possible, but I kept reminding myself that I needed this job and I had to be nice to her. Nice, but firm.

'I'm afraid I couldn't do that, Cynthia. It's against school policy to give out our email details, and besides—'

'Just call me Cyn,' she cut in and I almost snarled at her. 'It would only take you an hour or so this evening and you can email me back with your thoughts first thing in the morning.'

Fuck no. I get paid little enough as it is. My time is my time and if she thinks I'm going to spend it reading her email and then reply to her, in my *own* time, she has another think coming. I clamped my mouth tightly shut as I almost said that out loud.

'Just email it to the school. You should have it on your copy of Jason's registration papers, or any of the school literature. It's even on your invitation for tonight.'

'But I never get a reply when I do that,' she told me with a pout.

'Oh, dear. Maybe you're typing it incorrectly.' She never gets a reply because we've marked her emails as spam, that's why. We get enough of them that they are spam.

Just then, Abby—our teaching assistant—tapped me on the shoulder and told me I was needed elsewhere. Abby was actually the school secretary but, since our budget didn't stretch to any more employees, she doubled up as a TA and this was part of her job on these evenings. It was her job to watch for over-enthusiastic parents and give us no more than five minutes with them before calling us away out of their clutches. I muttered an appreciative 'thank you' to Abby once we were far enough from Cynthia that she couldn't hear us, and promised to buy her a drink at our next pub quiz. Abby was worth her weight in gold.

The rest of the evening passed off without a hitch and, as soon as I got the chance, I was out of there and on my way home to Charlie. No doubt Just Call Me Cyn would be going home in a mood to her 'Did I Mention We Were Almost on *Grand Designs*?' luxury home—far enough out of the village to give them the privacy they desired, but close enough to be able to nip in for some basic groceries when they ran out of their truffles and champagne. Her husband, Geoffrey, was a banker—no, seriously he was, I'm not using rhyming slang—and he was a nice enough bloke. I couldn't help feel some sympathy for him and Jason having 'Just Call Me Cyn' in their lives on a daily basis.

I still wanted her cowboy boots, though.

~~~

A couple of years later, class numbers increased dramatically with all the new developments in the area, and the influx of new families—thankfully, there were only one or two Cynthia types. As a result, more staff were recruited and I was moved into the class for the ten-year olds. I loved it. It meant I had a little bit more pay in my pocket each month, and Charlie and I were now earning enough to stay ahead of the bills and even begin to put money in a savings account. More importantly, it was interesting work—more of a challenge—and I found real pleasure in teaching for the first time.

One of my favourite things—and it's strange, because creative writing was never my thing—was that I loved setting my ten-year olds something to write. I didn't set them anything too elaborate, just the usual *'What I Did During My Summer Holiday's'* essay—we've all had to do them at school when we were that age—and I gave them two afternoons in class to write them. Of course, I got the usual groans and screwed up faces but, once they got stuck in, their creative juices began to flow and they came up with some great stories. A few were most likely fictional—I mean, what ten-year old goes into space or shoots a grizzly bear—with a grain of truth added here and there, but most were genuine accounts of what they did before their holiday ended and they started back to school in September.

I always found that they were still in holiday mode for the first week or so, and this was a tried and trusted way to settle them down and transition them from the freedom they'd enjoyed to the routine of being back in the classroom.

It did have an unfortunate—and unintended—inherent social class bias, in that the more well-to-do kids wrote about their holidays abroad, while the kids who lived on farms told the story of the work they had to do each day—work that left little room for play—and holidays just weren't on their radar.

I loved the farm kids. Although not well off in the

financial sense, they were richer in their attitudes—keen to learn and more inclined to adapt to changes in their lives. Most of them could drive a tractor by the age of ten. This might cause the heads of the jobsworths at Health and Safety to explode but, in reality, it was all a necessary part and parcel of growing up on a farm, along with feeding chickens and birthing calves. I couldn't imagine a townie ten-year-old on a tractor towing a trailer from one field to another or helping to pull a calf out of its mother's back end. I couldn't imagine their parents doing it either. Cynthia would just die if her boots got dirty, and a fair few other of the parents would, too.

~~~

All in all, it was fun, and I found my class enjoyed it more than I'd expected. I repeated the exercise a few times over the school year with my highly popular '*Letter to Santa*' and '*What I Want To Be When I Grow Up.*' The kids loved it and I discovered that both their reading and their writing skills improved considerably because of it.

And Charlie has the cheek to call me '*Bad Teacher.*' I think not, sunshine.

A month after that parent/teacher evening I found Cynthia's boots in a charity shop—she'd probably decided they were now too old for her to be seen in and had donated them. They had a price tag of twenty pounds and were a perfect fit. I slapped the money down on the counter and made off with them before I could talk myself out of it.

I loved them, and I wore them as much as I could.

Chapter 24 – A day in their lives.

Although I wasn't aware of the time passing, it occurred to me that I'd been dead for just over two years. I also realised that I hadn't been spending as much time at home as I used to.

I wanted to see my family again. I wanted to spend some time with them and catch up on how they were managing without me. Were they over me? Did they still talk about me over the dinner table, in between healthy forkfuls of roast beef and green vegetables? Or were their nutritional needs going to pot as they snacked on frozen pizza that hadn't been heated properly? Did they get upset, or was I merely another topic of conversation? It was time to find out.

I went from the bench seat on the village green to my living room in the space of a heartbeat. Since I'd discovered how, I loved being able to do it. I could have walked, but that would have taken real time and I was in a hurry to go home.

~~~

It was a Saturday morning and they were up and about. A stack of plates, mugs and cereal bowls—with accompanying cutlery—was soaking in the kitchen sink and I gathered they'd just finished breakfast. Charlie was rifling through the morning post and the girls were fussing over our cat, Berfa. It transpired that she'd been missing for over two weeks, and just when they'd given up on ever seeing her again, she'd walked in through the open window, miaowing for food. Charlie checked her over and, although she was thinner than she had been, and there were a few burrs stuck to her coat, she was none the worse for a moggy who's been away from home for so long.

~~~

Although she'd been spayed just after we got her as a kitten, she had always been inclined to stray and we reckoned she had a man-cat friend somewhere that she went to visit every now and then.

'When his missus is off on a business trip,' Charlie theorised.

'So, she goes to work and he lies around the house all day, then?'

Charlie nodded.

'Bloody Toms. They're as bad as men,' I replied.

'I wonder if our puss came home early because his wife cut her trip short and caught them in the act.'

'Oh no,' I gasped in mock horror. 'That would be a catastrophe.'

'Yeah. I bet there was a lot of caterwauling when the wife, Catherine—Cat for short—came back and found them high on his stash of catnip and playing hide-the-toy-mouse together.'

We were grinning like two Cheshire cats by this stage.

'Do you think she deliberately came back early to catch them in the act?' Charlie asked. 'Hey, that's an anagram of cat.'

'A three-letter anagram. Wow. Good one, Charlie. Yeah, I think she did. Which was a really catty thing to do. And our poor puss had to consider her vacation over and hightail it home on a Ducati.'

'Oh, that's catchy,' Charlie grinned.

I giggled, but we ran out of steam as we couldn't be bothered to think of any more words with 'cat' in them to keep the funny going.

~~~

It seemed Berfa was still slipping off to see her man-cat friend even now. Good on ya, Berfa!

~~~

I watched the girls fussing over her as she ate her food, then Charlie told them to leave her in peace for a while, and she settled down on the sofa for a good sleep. Ross came over and sniffed her for a moment then, apparently satisfied she was the correct cat, he ambled off to leave her alone. I noticed how stiff he was getting as he walked, and his muzzle was almost totally white now. Although his tail still wagged, his eyes had lost a lot of their shine, and something told me that my poor old boy's time would soon be up.

Charlie, Amy and Chloe seemed to be doing okay. They'd come to terms with my absence and they were still a tight family unit—albeit smaller by a quarter now. I'd popped in last Christmas—their second since I died—and it had been a much merrier time. They did the tree and the decorations as usual. The solstice evening, and then the big turkey dinner and the presents afterwards. My parents were there this time, along with Charlie's mum and dad, and although they still missed me—still grieved for me—they were over the worst of it. They were at the stage where they—along with Charlie and the girls—could look back at their time with me, reminisce without the tears, and even laugh at funny things they remembered me doing.

I'd become that photograph in a frame on the mantlepiece. I was an old, much-loved memory movie that someone watched in their mind now that it was no longer painful to remember me.

I was okay with that, as long as it was true and they weren't still putting on a brave face. I don't think they were, but I wondered how Charlie was coping deep down. I had no way of knowing as I couldn't read him as well as I used to. There was a distance between the two of us now. In fact, I could feel a distance between myself and all of them. I couldn't quite explain it, yet it felt natural. Maybe, like them, I was also moving on.

~~~

They spent their Saturdays like anyone else. Off to Tesco for the weekly shop. All three of them setting off good and early before the roads got busy and the parking spaces were all taken up. Charlie would push the trolley and consult his list as he gathered the items on it, frowning as he searched for things and probably inwardly cursing when he discovered that the baked beans had been moved to a different aisle. I hated it when they did that.

Without me there to do the shopping, Charlie had become a modern-day hunter-gatherer. Hunting for sausages and bacon, and gathering boxes of cereal, cartons of milk and all the other staples required to feed his family.

When he wasn't looking, his two little helpers did some foraging of their own and sneaked packets of sweets, bars of chocolate and their favourite chocolate biscuits into the trolley. They'd be discovered at the check-out, but it would be too late to put them back and the big softie would go ahead and place them on the check-out conveyor belt.

Sometimes I joined them in the supermarket, frowning and tutting at some of the junk food he bought, but nodding in approval when he added a good amount of healthy fruit and veg to his trolley. Thankfully, the good food far outweighed the junk. Other times I stayed at home, enjoying the house once more and waiting for them to come back.

Today I decided to stay. I sat with Ross and watched him as he slept on his bed in the kitchen. I could sense he hadn't much time left and I knew my girls and their dad were going to be in for a whole lot of new grief and loss very soon. I whispered my own goodbye to my old fella and wondered if he would join me on my walks when he died. Two ghosts—one human, one a beloved pet— wandering the countryside together, just as we had done in life.

~~~

I heard a car engine outside. It stopped and I heard the sounds of car doors being slammed shut, followed by the back door opening and a flurry of tramping feet and chatter that told me they were home from Tesco. For a second, I forgot I was dead and jumped up to go and greet them, thinking I should have done the dishes instead of sitting watching my dog sleep in his bed. Then I remembered I wasn't really here and felt a bit stupid. I stood in the kitchen and watched them come in with their haul in large hessian shopping bags—the better-quality ones that the big supermarkets sell you. Charlie was carrying the heaviest ones and plonked them down on the floor near the fridge and cupboards. Ross climbed out of his bed, stretched his legs and walked over to Charlie. He wagged his tail, stuck his nose in one of the bags and had a good sniff around to see if there was anything in there for him. Charlie lifted the bag away from him and, set it on the counter, then knelt down and gave Ross a hug. He held his arms around him for a few moments, all the while telling the old dog that he was 'the best boy in the whole world.'

It seemed Charlie also knew that Ross hadn't long left in this world.

He was still eating well, though—Ross, not Charlie—and he wolfed down the handful of dog meal Charlie set down to him. He knew to feed Ross a light meal a few times a day now—probably on the vet's advice—rather than one big heavy meal that would be harder on his digestive system.

I watched Charlie as he put away the groceries. He looked good, as always, and I felt something I hadn't felt in ages—a pang of longing and desire for him. Or maybe it was the memory of that desire. Real or imagined, I wished I could kiss him and feel his strong arms embrace me. I could stand there in the kitchen all day if I was in Charlie's arms.

I sighed, but no one heard me.

Charlie yelled at the girls to come and help him put everything away. They'd disappeared to the TV room as soon as they were through the door, but they came back on his command and proceeded to help as I watched.

Chloe had sprouted like a weed this past year and had

almost caught up to Amy, two years her senior, who still had a couple of inches on her. Amy was looking very grown up and responsible, and I guess she'd learned that helping around the house made things easier for all of them. I hated that my girls had to grow up like this—learning to be responsible when they should be playing and having fun. My death had taken some—a lot—of their childhood joy away. It was something they'd never get back, but that's life—or death.

On the surface, Charlie was his old self—laughing and joking and being a responsible, yet kind-hearted parent. He was living a normal life with his work, his two young daughters, an elderly dog, and a cat that was having an on-again, off-again affair with some old tom from down the road. But Charlie was a single parent with all the added pressure that entails and I could see a weariness in his eyes that told a whole different tale to the one he told to the world. In his own private narrative, he still missed me and deep down he still grieved for me—and that grief wasn't going away any time soon.

Oh, he could still enjoy a pint or two with his mates down the pub when the girls were on a sleepover at Claire's. He could play with the girls and take them on outings and have fun with them. He could laugh and joke with people and have a good old time, but there was an undercurrent of sadness in his eyes—and in his soul—that was going to be there for a long, long time. Maybe forever.

It made me wonder if he'd ever consider someone else. Knowing Charlie as I do—did—I doubt he'd go looking for someone to replace me, but if they were to meet by chance and something clicked between them, I wonder if he'd take it any further. It would be hard to find a woman prepared to take on two small girls, and I hated the thought of someone new slipping into the role of their stepmother. My girls have a mother. She isn't around now but they spent some of their formative years in her care and they knew she loved them. This new woman couldn't possibly love them as much as I did—as I do.

Oh, I'm starting to well up again. Something I haven't done in ages. I'd accepted my lot and moved on, appreciating that I could still hang around my family and, even if I couldn't interact with them, I was still in their lives. But yeah, it still hurt a bit.

It's funny how reality comes back and slaps you on the bum just when you think you'd left it behind for good.

I refused to give in to it this time as I continued to watch my family going about their usual Saturday afternoon. Amy and Chloe were out in the back garden, playing in the makeshift tent Charlie had rigged up for them. Ross had joined them. It was a beautiful sunny day and they were taking it in turns to throw the ball for him. He refused to disappoint them and ran to catch it and bring it back. He didn't run so fast these days and I could see he was favouring his left rear leg, refusing to give in to the pain he must be feeling. The girls didn't know any better, and they called him 'Slowcoach' as they shouted at him to hurry up.

He fetched the ball back several times, then wisely called it quits and lay down on the soft grass. He was panting now and Amy got him a bowl of fresh water. He lapped appreciatively for a few minutes, then settled down for a snooze in the sunshine. Both girls seemed to know he was tired. They sat down beside him and chatted to one another while he slept, until Charlie called them in for their dinner.

I followed them inside and I was pleased to see that Charlie was still feeding them healthy food. It would have been so easy for him to slip into the habit of making something easy, or bunging a frozen pizza into the microwave. Instead, he'd prepared a salad with all fresh ingredients, cold cuts of meat and hard-boiled eggs. He had a mug of tea while the girls drank their fresh juice.

I noticed that Ross no longer joined them at the table, content to lie in his bed and watch them. I remember when he used to stand under the table, begging for treats that we never refused him. A piece of sausage, a crust of toast, and often a slice of carrot or banana. He loved bananas.

He was a crafty so-and-so. He would stand at my left side, get a treat from me, and then go over to Charlie for one. Instead of coming back round to me, he'd slip underneath the table and come around to my other side. We couldn't help laughing as it looked as though he was pretending to be a totally different dog in order to get an extra piece of sausage. As far as he was concerned it worked because he always got something extra.

He loved toast, and he loved the sound of the toaster popping. He would bounce from one paw to the other, barking madly. Even if he was in another part of the house, the popping toaster had him running like mad, sliding across the floor, and stopping in front of the worktop to sit down and wait patiently until he was given a corner of a slice, with only a scraping of butter because I didn't want to overdo the junk food.

One time I walked into the kitchen to find him sitting there, staring up at the toaster. I wondered what he was doing until I realised that I'd put a slice of bread in it, got a phone call and had completely forgotten about it. Ross hadn't, and he was still waiting for his share half an hour later.

~~~

When the girls had finished their lunch, and Charlie set his knife and fork down, he didn't even have to ask them to clear the table. I smiled as I watched them load the dishwasher for him. The three of them had this great routine going every day, and they had it perfected in much the same way Charlie and I had always moved in sync around the kitchen when we were making dinner, or tidying up afterwards. We called it the dinner dance, and now the three of them were dancing to a similar tune.

'You're doing okay, my love. I'm proud of you,' I whispered, but Charlie couldn't hear me as he went about his normal Saturday routine with what was left of his family.

Eventually, evening came and, after some TV, the girls went off to bed. The fresh air and all the running around they'd done had left them sleepy, and their eyes closed the moment their heads hit the pillow. Charlie kissed them both on the forehead, whispering 'Night, night. Sleep tight,' to them. He gently closed the bedroom door and went back downstairs to face the remainder of his Saturday with only the television for company.

This was when I saw the real Charlie. He didn't howl in pain or weep silent tears into a tissue, but he did pour a large whiskey, then made himself comfortable on the sofa and switched on the TV. He scrolled through the numerous channels but couldn't find one to spark his interest until he found a televised darts tournament. Charlie had only a passing interest in darts, but this seemed to be his viewing choice for the evening. He settled down, whiskey in hand, to watch a darts match he didn't have much interest in, while Ross slept peacefully at his feet.

This was when Charlie was lonely and blue. In company, he could smile and talk to people, pass the time with them and, for a little while, forget that I was no longer by his side. But in the evening, when he was alone, he allowed the mask to slip and I could tell he still missed me.

And I missed him.

I sat with him until he finished his drink and went to bed, leaving me on my own once more.

Chapter 25 – Goodbye, old pal.

About three weeks—it could have been longer, or indeed shorter—after I'd spent the day with my family, I was out on one of my usual early morning walks when a rustling noise behind me made me stop and turn around.

There he was. Racing hell for leather to catch up with me. His tail was wagging and his tongue was falling out of his mouth. We always joked that he would trip over it one day, the way it hung down in front of him when he was running at full speed, usually across the lawn to catch a ball or a frisbee.

~~~

They say the best gift you can give your pet is to be there for their final moments. They've loved you for all of their life. You've fed them, walked them and played with them. Taught them tricks and voice commands, and seen to all of their needs. They've loved you for every moment you gave to them, from the day you brought them home, either as a ten-week-old puppy, or as an adult dog you'd rehomed from a rescue centre. This last time will be the time they want, and need, you by their side the most.

It broke my heart that I hadn't been there, but I know Charlie wouldn't have failed in his duty. He might have taken the girls with him, but then again, he might think it would be too hard on them and, if they started crying, it would only cause Ross more distress. Taking Ross to the vets on his own was the sensible thing to do, and it was okay that it was just Charlie there so long as he held Ross in his arms until the end, said goodbye to him and told him what a great dog he was.

He's still a great dog, and I told him so as I knelt down and opened my arms to greet him as he rushed towards me. He put his paws on my shoulders and licked my face, whining and barking, and wriggling—completely overcome with excitement. I scratched behind his ears—which he loved—and kept my mouth firmly shut because when Ross kissed you, it was all about the tongue, and I really didn't want a mouthful of doggie tongue. I rubbed his ears and petted his back, and he was going nuts with excitement.

'Oh, you good boy. You are the best boy in the whole world and you have no idea how much I've missed you.' He'd settled down a bit and I was able to open my mouth to speak to him. That set him off in another whirlwind of frenzied barking and circling around. He was going crazy with the joy of seeing me again, and I'm guessing he had missed me as much as I'd missed him.

So, there we were. A woman and her dog who'd been best friends in life and were now two ghosts, reunited once more. We could do what we did in life—roam the hills and the dales together.

~~~

We did just that. We spent days with only each other for company and it was the best time ever. We walked for miles, neither of us tiring or feeling the need to stop, though we often did. It was nice to sit down for a while, usually on a large boulder in a spot that had a great view, or sometimes just on the grass at the foot of a big oak tree. I'd lean back against it and Ross would sit beside me with his body pressed against my shoulder. I'd put my arm around him and hug him tightly to me. He would turn his head to me and stare into my eyes and they were bright again, full of love and adoration. I wasn't a ghost to him. I was me again.

~~~

It was exactly like the old days when I'd set off early in the morning to spend the day taking photographs. Ross always came with me. In fact, when I thought about it, I couldn't remember a day when he wasn't walking by my side or racing on ahead when he caught an interesting scent, reluctantly turning back towards me when I whistled to him.

We carried on like this for the best part of two weeks, walking wherever our feet—all six of them—took us. We didn't feel hunger, or the cold, and we didn't get tired, but when evening came, we stuck to the routine we'd fallen into and stopped walking for the day. We found a nice, comfortable place to sit down, and together we watched the sun setting. Then, as night fell, we curled up together. I don't know if you'd call it sleeping in the true sense of the word, but we closed our eyes until it was morning again.

If it was raining, we went home and remained indoors. Ross whined a little when he saw Charlie and the girls. I was surprised because he seemed to understand that he was no longer there for them to see him and play with him, and he accepted this without complaint. But I could tell that he missed them.

~~~

On roughly the twelfth day of our ghostly journey

210

together, I turned to look at him and I noticed he was different. At first, I thought it was the way the morning sunlight shone on his coat, but on closer inspection, he seemed almost transparent as if he was fading from my sight. I blinked a couple of times and he was fully there again, wagging his tail and waiting for me to resume walking.

I shrugged my shoulders, tapped my thigh to bring him to heel and we set off along one of our favourite routes.

By that evening—when we came down from the high ground to the forest area—Ross was even more transparent, and I had to face the realisation that he would be leaving me soon. I sat down on the damp grass, under my favourite tree. It was an ancient, sprawling horse chestnut, and we used to collect conkers that had fallen from it in the autumn. Ross lay down alongside my legs with his chin resting on my thigh. I put my arms around him and the black and white of his coat seemed to merge together into a grey, swirling mist. I could barely see him now—he had faded so much.

Tears stung my eyes as I rested my head on top of his and held him close. I stroked and petted him. I talked to him and comforted him just as I would have done at the vet's surgery, if I had been alive and able to be with him on his final day. It seems we both had been given the chance to say goodbye.

'You are the best boy in the whole world,' I told him. 'Everything's going to be okay, and you just go for a nice, long sleep now, my old darling. I love you so much, Rossy-

Wossy. My big, beautiful boy. I've loved you all your life and I know you loved me back. And I'll love you forever. My Ross. My good, good boy.'

I buried my face in his soft fur—the soft fur I couldn't see or barely feel any more—and I sobbed quietly as the grey mist that was now my Ross curled around my hand, and I fancied he was licking my fingers the way he always did.

Then the mist that was once my dog dispersed into the air and he left me.

Chapter 26 – Back home again.

After the wonderful time I enjoyed with the ghost of my dog, I lost my taste for walking through the countryside, and I found myself patrolling the village all day and all night. I listened in on conversations at the bus-stop, in the post office, and even in the pub. I sat with my old team from work during the Thursday night pub quizzes, shouting out the correct answers even though they couldn't hear me. But after a few days—or maybe it was weeks, as I wasn't able to measure the passage of time the way I used to—I got bored with the gossip and not being able to participate in the quiz so I left them to win or lose without me. I still couldn't shift myself to do much of anything—not that I could actually do anything physically—but the walking had been wonderful and, although my time with Ross had been bittersweet, I was glad I'd had the opportunity to experience a few more days with him by my side.

I missed him more than I'd thought I would, and I couldn't settle for a long while after I said goodbye to him.

~~~

Back at home, Charlie and the girls were discussing whether or not they should get a puppy or check out the local animal charity centres for a rescue dog. It didn't surprise me one bit that they were begging for a puppy and I could see that Charlie was wavering between the sensible thing—getting a rescue—and what the girls wanted.

'Be strong, love,' I told him, hoping that even though he couldn't hear me, I might just plant the seed in his mind.

213

'A puppy is a lot of work, you know that. All that peeing everywhere and eating the furniture, your best shoes, the TV remote. And don't forget the training commands—Sit. Stay. Please. Oh, for fuck's sake, come back here, you little shit. Seriously Charlie, a nice, placid, child-friendly adult dog from the local rescue centre is the way to go. One that has already gone through its basic training.'

I don't know if my ghostly suggestion got through to him or not, but he told the girls that he'd have to think about it for a while and, in the meantime, they should get their coats on as they were already running late for school. I watched them stuff the last pieces of toast into their mouths, then grab their bags and coats as Charlie shooed them out the door and into the car. All talk of puppies put on hold for another time.

Deep down, I knew Charlie didn't want to get another dog. He would love to get one, but he knew he wouldn't have the time to look after it properly what with his work and running a home as well as looking after the girls. I also knew he felt it would be a betrayal of Ross to get one so soon. I hoped Amy and Chloe wouldn't pester him too much about it.

~~~

As strange as it may seem, I needed to get away from my family for a while. I knew I could pop back at any time, but I decided I needed a short break from them just now. For a moment, I considered going to Claire's house, then I remembered that I hadn't seen Mum and Dad for ages—so I took myself off to pay them a 'visit.'

~~~

Typically, they weren't at home when I got there. I wasn't surprised as Mum and Dad lived a fairly active lifestyle. They were always on the go, and had been since I left home—first for university, then to set up my own home with Charlie. I think they suffered a bit from empty-nest syndrome and found it difficult to sit still in a house that no longer had me running about—okay, I mean slouching about—and leaving dirty dishes in my bedroom, in the lounge and even outside on the small patio table. Not to mention clothes strewn over every conceivable space in my bedroom, apart from where they were supposed to go—in the drawers and the wardrobe. I was a teenager. Being lazy and untidy was a natural part of growing up.

When I left home for university, I think they expected me to move back after I'd graduated. They probably figured I wouldn't find a job immediately, and with my student debt—although it wasn't very high—I'd be skint enough to want to live at home for a while, to make full use of free lodgings, with the Bank of Mum and Dad ATM right there in the living room and available for cash withdrawals twenty-four hours a day.

Of course, I never did move home again. I met Charlie and we set up home together, so my parents had no choice but to become used to it being only the two of them. They were okay, though. They had their little dog, Cracker—my replacement—to keep them company and give them a reason to get up in the morning to take him out for a walk.

They didn't just walk the wee lad up the road to do his business and back again, though. They took out a lifetime membership of the National Trust and they already owned the camper van. Now that they were both retired, if the weather was fine—even if it wasn't—they would pack up the camper and, along with Cracker, set off to different places up and down the country. They'd visit stately homes and forest parks as the fancy took them. Sometimes, they'd go as far south as Devon and Cornwall, then the next time I heard from them they'd be up in Scotland, touring the Highlands and complaining about the midges, but otherwise having a good old time among the mountains, the lochs, and the heather, with faithful Cracker by their side.

At least today the campervan was parked in the driveway and Cracker was asleep on the sofa. Their car wasn't there, nor were the 'bags for life' that Mum kept in the utility room, so I assumed they were out shopping and would be home soon.

~~~

It was nice being back in the house I grew up in. Old and familiar like a well-worn, comfortable jacket. One you've had for years, but can't bear to part with simply because it is comfortable and familiar. Being back at Mum and Dad's house was that old coat. It was here that I'd been loved and nourished by these two people who'd adopted Little Orphan Lucy because they couldn't have a little girl of their own. They made me into the woman I became, and I knew I would always be loved by them, as I was loved by my husband and my daughters. Even though I'm dead, their memories of me with keep that flame of love burning forever.

As I thought about it, the realisation became clear to

me and I knew that this was what living forever meant. It was so obvious that I felt I'd always known it to be true—a sort of muscle memory, if you like. Maybe it was because I was dead and I now knew what death meant. It wasn't the end, but it wasn't quite what we had been led to believe— the whole born-again spiel about going to heaven, or hell, depending on how we had lived our lives. The bribery thing never sat right with me—be good to earn a reward? Why couldn't I just be a good person without needing a very dubious incentive?

But, to discover this to be a truth was a great way to lift the heart. To discover that we do live on was wonderful because—oh, it was so obvious—we live on through our people. Through our friends and our families, and anybody whose life we may have touched. We might only live for a generation in the memories—in the minds and the hearts— of those we shared this life with, but we live forever in the generations to come through our DNA. It was as simple as that. It gave me a warm fuzzy feeling to know that, in this respect, I would never die.

~~~

My musings were interrupted by the sound of the front door opening and a woman's giggle. A giggle? What the—? Then Cracker was up on his feet and racing for the door, his little feet scrabbling on the laminated wood flooring as he fought to gain traction on the slippery surface.

Mum walked into the kitchen, dabbing at her eyes with a paper tissue and setting her shopping bag on the counter, along with her handbag. Still wiping her eyes and laughing at whatever joke Dad had told her—he had quite the repertoire, some of which were quite dirty and some clean ones that he could tell to the vicar or the ladies during afternoon tea at the recently-built community centre—she knelt down to greet the frantic little dog who was trying to jump into her arms. He was that excited to see her.

'Oh, there's my darling boy. Did you miss me? Huh? Did you? Did you indeed?'

Cracker was yapping and spinning in circles on his feet and bouncing up and down on all four legs. At the same time, he was trying to lick Mum's face. He dropped her like a stone when my dad walked in, carrying several large bags of groceries. He rushed to Dad, then back to Mum again, as if he couldn't decide which of my parents he should greet and talk to about his day. You'd think they'd been gone for a week, not a couple of hours.

I watched them pack away the groceries, including several bottles of wine, a bottle of rum and a bottle of whiskey, plus bottles and cans of mixers. I wondered whether they were having guests for the evening, given they'd got that much booze. Mum and Dad had a fairly active social life when they weren't off in their campervan, visiting old castles and manor houses, and checking out how the other half used to live. They are members of various clubs—book clubs, movie clubs—and they regularly go to play bingo in the local church hall. Recently they joined the local Neighbourhood Watch scheme. Well, Dad signed up both of them to do it. He took to it like a duck to water, but Mum wasn't so keen. She considered her duty done by going door-to-door one Saturday afternoon and handing out leaflets that told people to be careful with their car keys and internet passwords, and to lock their doors and windows at night. As for my dad, well, it's not hard to imagine him skulking behind walls and hedges, torch and notebook in hand, as he searches for any signs of burglars, car thieves, or just teenagers messing about. I have no idea what conviction rate he has, if any, but I suspect it's around zero. Still, it gets him out of the house for an hour or two after dinner and out from under Mum's feet while she does the dishes and tidies the kitchen. He usually takes his trusty police sniffer dog—Cracker—along with him, for a sniff around and a pee on every lamppost.

Cracker hasn't managed to sniff out any bad guys yet, but I've no doubt they'll get a big collar soon, and there'll be a write-up in the local paper about their heroic exploits. Dad has it in his mind that one day he'll get an OBE and a subsequent visit to Buckingham Palace to receive his award for keeping the streets safe.

I used to look at my parents and wonder if Charlie and I would turn into them—two old fogies, settled in their ways, and content to visit old castles or take notes about what the neighbours were up to. Of course, I told myself that we would never let that happen. We'd raise the girls, send them out into the big, wide world and then we'd go wild—partying 'til dawn and getting kicked out of nightclubs in Ibiza because of our behaviour. I remember telling Charlie that I was going to get a tattoo, buy a Harley Davidson and a cool leather biker's jacket. Charlie said he'd do the same.

I wonder now, which of those two scenarios would

have been us—a version of my mum and dad scooting about in their campervan, or two crazy oldies living it up in Spain? It's a shame I'll never find out.

~~~

After she's done the tidying up, Mum left the kettle ready to boil and a mug and teaspoon on the counter for Dad, when he comes home from his patrol—along with a packet of digestive biscuits. She took one more look around the kitchen to check everything's in order, then she'd go upstairs to her 'office' and settle down in her favourite armchair with her Kindle and a pen and notepad resting on the table nearby. As she read, she would stop every now and then to jot down a few notes.

Mum's a voracious reader and always has been. She will read anything from horror and thriller books, true crime and cosy mysteries, to hot, spicy—often erotic— romances. She mostly reads books by indie authors—those that go down the self-publishing route—rather than those traditionally published because she feels they get overlooked by the wider reading public. She reviews everything—on Amazon and other platforms. As a result, she's become well known among the online indie author community. She has a Facebook group that has thousands of followers where she posts her reviews and recommendations every week. Her followers are both authors and readers, and she encourages the authors to post their book links so she and the other readers can download them. She's been considering setting up Instagram and TikTok accounts as well, but hasn't made up her mind yet.

So, while Dad's out sleuthing, Mum is curled up with

her trusty Kindle in her lap, and I'm happy to see them again, and know they're okay. They still visit my grave every Sunday morning—except when they're off on their jaunts—and they're regular visitors at my house to see their granddaughters and have a catch-up natter with Charlie—which can get a bit emotional now and then—but I can tell they're doing okay without me.

They still have all their wits about them and they have a good circle of friends for companionship and activities. That, plus their travels, and their wee dog, keep them from stagnating on the couch in front of the television.

They're young at heart and reasonably fit and healthy—at least for the time being. I just hope Amy and Chloe will be there for them when they need help in their old age. I think they will because my girls adore their 'Granny' and 'Gramps.'

~~~

I spent a few days with my parents until one morning when Dad checked the weather for the week and decided it was high time they were off on their travels once more. He had a hankering to go back to Wales on this occasion but Mum wanted to visit Scotland again. There were still a few old castles she hadn't visited yet, it seemed.

The van they'd bought was compact but comfy, and it was small enough that Dad could manoeuvre it without too much difficulty. They had all they needed under one roof and on four wheels. It even had a roll-up canopy that they could pull down to use as an outdoor area when the weather was fine. They loved it. It was their home-from-home and they could put what they needed in it, start the engine and go off to see the world—or at least see a good part of the UK—and still have their groceries in the small larder, their milk in the little fridge, and a kettle plugged in should they decide to stop along the roadside for a brew and a biccy to dunk in it.

I watched them pack up. Cracker must have known what they were planning as he was so excited, I thought he was going to pee himself.

And then they were off. I waved from the window until I couldn't see them, then I stretched out on the sofa for the rest of the day.

~~~

I was pleased that my parents were getting on with life. They were doing okay, but I knew they still missed me. Every now and then my mum's face would go blank as if she had been switched off and I knew she was thinking of me and missing me. My Dad would rub her shoulder or put his arms around her and tell her he loved her.

'Chin up, lass,' he'd say, and she'd sigh and smile wistfully as she glanced at my graduation photo. It sat beside a couple of others—one of Charlie and I on our wedding day, and a formal portrait of the four of us. Charlie had on a suit and tie and I'd put on a dress and wore my hair up. Amy and Chloe were also in their good clothes—their 'Sunday Best,' as Mum called it, although in our house, 'Sunday Best' usually meant tracksuit bottoms and tops, and old cardigans or sweaters. Chloe was smiling sweetly for the camera but Amy's lips were turned downwards and she looked as though she was about to burst into tears. I can't remember why she seemed upset.

Maybe she was feeling poorly or maybe I'd scolded her for something. I don't know.

~~~

I went upstairs to my old bedroom which became Mum's office after I left home. She'd cleared it out when I moved in with Charlie, and I'd helped her because I took a lot of my stuff with me. She'd kept the bed though, in case things didn't work out between us and I needed to come home to lick my wounds. After I got married, she took the few remaining items—the single bed and the small cabinet—to the charity shop. She painted the walls a nice neutral colour, then bought new curtains and a new carpet. Next, she installed a sofa bed—just in case I ever did come home—and an office table for her laptop and notebooks, along with a comfortable office chair. She added a bookcase and one of those mother-and-child floor lamps that had an uplighter, and a flexible reading light behind the sofa bed and added some cushions and a footstool. This became her office—her reading room. She kept it spartan, with only one or two canvas prints on the walls and, after I died, she placed a photo of me on her desk. It was here that she'd read and write her book reviews when my dad was watching sport or one of his favourite documentaries on the History Channel.

It was similar in idea to what I'd created in the back room at home where I'd binge-watch shows on Sky, Netflix or Amazon while Charlie watched the football in the lounge. My room was less spartan than my mum's though—less office-like—and much more a cosy living-room with a wood stove and more comfortable furniture.

223

Not to forget that my room had, as well as a bookcase and a coffee table, a large-screen Smart TV with a Sky box hooked up to it.

I think that after Amy and Chloe were born, the penny dropped that I had no intention of dumping my man, and my parents finally accepted the fact that I wasn't moving back in with them any time soon.

Mum did love Charlie. She thought he was the bee's knees. So did my dad, but I guess that deep down she—both of them—always wanted their little girl back in the house she grew up in, with the parents who loved her.

~~~

I wandered around the house for a few hours, but it was lonely with them gone and I decided I wanted to be somewhere else. Plus, I felt the urge to go for one of my long walks again. I closed my eyes and screwed up my face in concentration—or clicked my heels, or whatever it was that I did to get from place to place, I still don't know quite how I do it—and there I was, back on my beloved hills, relishing the thought of a nice, long walk.

Chapter 27 – *Grand Designs* and a massive memory reset.

Of course, it had to start raining the moment I arrived. Nowadays, rain doesn't affect me in the slightest because I won't catch a cold if I get a soaking, and my make-up is hardly going to run. My clothes will get wet and my hair will be plastered to my scalp, but once the rain stops, my clothes will be the same as before and my hair will revert back to the way it was—long and mostly straight, and tied back in a ponytail. I don't know why that happens, but it does, and I'm not complaining.

But I still don't like being out in the rain. It could be a residual emotion from back when I was alive—I disliked getting wet then—and I often sought shelter at the first drops.

The heat or the cold didn't affect me either. Nothing did, really. I had a limited sensation of touch, which I didn't have at the beginning, but it was very limited. I could feel rough bark on a tree, or hard concrete on a wall, but more subtle textures escaped me. Pain didn't exist—except in my heart—so I didn't feel anything if I banged my knee or my elbow on something, nor did I get sunburned in the summer or frozen in the winter. I even stopped wearing shoes or boots for a while. That was cool—feeling the grass and the soft earth under my feet, as though I was still grounded to this world. I was tempted to go completely naked a few times, but I didn't. I don't know why I didn't. It just seemed weird.

My eyesight and my hearing were, if anything, better

than when I'd been alive. My sense of smell was about the same and, as for taste, well I haven't put anything in my mouth to test it. I've no desire to, either.

Some might think I lived—not sure if that's the correct word—a lonely existence, but I didn't. Although I couldn't interact with them, I still had my family and friends. I could observe them, smile with them, and be sad with them. No, while I did miss them, I definitely wasn't lonely. It wasn't something I dwelled on much. I couldn't change anything, so there was no point.

But ghost or no ghost, I still didn't like getting caught out in the rain.

~~~

One of my favourite places—haunts—was an old, derelict farmhouse. It was damp and musty, and almost ready to fall down, but it was a place I'd grown to love over the last two—almost three—years, and I hung out there a lot.

It was a standard sized traditional-style farmhouse with a big kitchen that held an old, rusty range, the remains of a sofa and a broken chair. Upstairs was empty and awash with damp patches and bird droppings where a part of the roof had collapsed, leaving it open to the elements. Beside the house there was a massive barn and I'd often go in there to shelter rather than use the old house.

I hadn't a clue who, if anyone, owned it. I never paid much attention to it when I was alive, other than exploring it to take a series of photos of it, and the surrounding area, at different times of the year, and in different weather conditions—sunshine, snow, fog. I even took a few in the rain. But since I died, it had become one of my favourite places to, well—haunt.

I'd sit there and wile away the time by imagining how I'd renovate it, if I had the money to do so. And if I was still alive, of course.

First of all, I'd gut the place—rip everything out. Then I'd fix the roof and the walls. Do a complete rewire. Sort out the plumbing as it was ancient. Put in new windows and doors and replaster the walls. Then I'd run a connecting passage—with glass walls and a tiled floor— from the house to the nearby barn, and I'd use the barn as our main living area. The house itself—with its two bedrooms, small bathroom and an en suite added to one bedroom, a living room and a kitchen diner—would be a self-contained area for guests. Or maybe I'd use it as a holiday let as that would help pay for the renovation work. I know, I know. I've watched a lot of property shows on TV.

The massive barn would be completely converted, after I'd fixed the roof and installed the electricity, plumbing, and a decent wood floor. I'd make it open-plan downstairs, with the living area at one end, but taking up most of the available space downstairs. It would have a floor-to-ceiling window—the view was magnificent—and I'd put a state-of-the-art kitchen at the other end with a utility room and downstairs loo off the kitchen. I'd put in a second floor for the bedrooms and bathrooms—which I'd set behind a mezzanine balcony with a wood and steel staircase leading up to it and have it overlook the extensive downstairs living-space. I'd put beams across the ceiling

227

and have low hanging lights—big industrial ones—maybe hanging from thick rope. The balcony would be wide enough for two comfy armchairs and a coffee table, as well as a bookcase because I figure it would make a lovely reading nook.

Yep. I had it all planned, built and decorated in my mind. It looked great.

I'm pretty sure this project would be made into an episode of *Grand Designs*. I had a thing for Kevin McCloud, and I watched every episode religiously. Getting on that show would have been a dream come true. It would also have royally pissed off 'Just call Me Cyn' who claimed she'd almost been on the show with her big, bland house, her expensive boots and her snooty airs and graces.

~~~

I leaned back against the old stonework, waiting for the rain to stop, and I let my imagination soar.

I mucked in with the work, scratched my head as I tried to interpret the architect's plans, sourced the best materials, and successfully project-managed the whole thing to fruition without going a single penny over budget.

Cyn probably didn't watch the episode, but if she had, she'd be spitting nails.

Kevin McCloud was well impressed.

~~~

It must have been the countless walks through the countryside that did it.

I was out early one morning and it was shaping up to be a fine day so, as usual, I was up there tramping through the trees and stepping over the small streams as I made my

228

way along. I was higher up, where the ground was rockier and heather grew everywhere, and following a narrow trail—made by years of sheep and people—that twisted and turned, this way and that, around the rocks.

I wasn't really thinking about much in particular—just letting my mind wander from one thought to another—when I stopped to look around me. The countryside stretched out in all directions and I did a full three-sixty turn to take it all in. In one direction the sun was rising, in the other I could see, in the distance, the visitor carpark where I used to park my old Land Rover.

And then I remembered.

I remembered all of it.

~~~

Stepping in that stupid hole in the ground, twisting my ankle and then hitting my head on a rock as I fell. Cursing my clumsiness as I checked that my camera wasn't damaged. Worrying about my ankle being broken and how to walk back to the car if it was. No phone signal meant I could be stuck on these hills until my family wondered why I wasn't home yet. I should have been home—it wasn't like me to be late—and when they gave me another hour and I still hadn't shown up, they'd call out a search party— although it could take them hours before they found me.

There was nothing for it but to try and walk back down to the carpark.

I remembered the pain in my ankle as I tested it with care, found it painful but bearable, and slowly made my way to the carpark, Ross walking by my side. Then driving home at a crawl and telling Charlie what had happened and him sitting me down and putting a bag of frozen peas on my foot. Then I sipped a glass of wine and he cooked the steaks. My ankle was sore but the ice was helping and the bump on my head only hurt when I touched it.

~~~

Now, I sat down on a rock and allowed the memories to come back to me. Maybe it was the same one I sat on that day when I stopped for lunch.

The memories were as clear as crystal as they came back. I remembered us eating outside that evening, drinking wine and watching the setting sun—followed by some sweet love making afterwards and then falling into a deep sleep in Charlie's arms.

~~~

As the details of what had happened to me returned bit by bit, I began to piece it all together. The ankle I twisted when I fell hadn't been my only injury. I didn't know it that evening, but the bump to my head when I went down had caused a brain bleed. A subdural haematoma is the medical term for it. I had heard of it before, but I didn't know very much about it.

Basically, striking my head on a rock had caused bleeding between the skull and the brain, as well as swelling. My symptoms were slow to emerge and, as a result, I felt fine. Charlie and I had spent a lovely evening together—wine and good food, followed by love-making and then a good night's sleep. I had a bit of a headache just before I fell asleep but I blamed it on the wine because I did have rather a lot—which is par for the course for me on an evening when I don't have anything to do but relax and enjoy myself.

I felt fine the next morning. I didn't have a hangover, but I did have a mild headache, and I didn't know anything was wrong until I got a severe pain in my head. I collapsed and suddenly everything became as wrong as it could possibly become.

I hadn't known about it because I was unconscious, but I was taken to hospital, where all the usual scans were carried out, confirming what was wrong with me, and they rushed me into surgery.

Again, I have no actual recollection of any of it, yet I seem to know what happened—or maybe I'm just assuming that this was the procedure. I mean, it's common sense that it would be what they'd do. We've all watched years of medical dramas on television so we're all pretty clued up on what happens. I know I was.

The memory of the pain in my head when I collapsed was so clear that I could almost feel it now, as I touched the ragged scar on my head where they'd cut me open to try and fix me. They'd failed, but they didn't know that then. They told Charlie—and I knew this from the telly—that I'd be placed in a medically induced coma to allow my brain to heal. This would last for a while, until they decided to bring me out of it slowly to see if I'd recovered. I don't know if they tried this and it killed me, or if I just didn't heal and died naturally. I just know I was in that coma—drugged and unconscious—and, while I was in this condition, a very strange thing happened to me.

I met this woman named Jennifer.

~~~

231

Just to clarify, I didn't actually meet her—that came later, sort of—but I learned who she was in the dreams I had about her. I got everything. From the moment she met Ilan to the night their car overturned and she suffered a head injury not unlike the one I'd suffered.

I saw her life in Cyprus with my own eyes—but through hers—and I learned how much she loved her job as an interior designer and how much she enjoyed living there on that beautiful sun-kissed island where the locals treated you like a beloved family member, and the pace of life was still slow and easy-going.

My pulse quickened at Jennifer's first sight of Ilan as he leaned against the bar, drank his whiskey and, like most of the other patrons that evening, watched the match on the wall-mounted TV above the bar. I could tell she was already falling for this handsome stranger by the time he bought her a drink and they sat down together. They chatted forages and they got on well, but she was suspicious when he sidestepped her questions about him.

In each of my dreams I learned more about them, and I could feel their passion as well as Jennifer's hesitation. Then he finally told her what he worked at—he was a Mossad officer, how cool is that? I laughed myself when Jennifer told him she'd thought he was a criminal. No way. No one that sexy could be a criminal. Well, he probably stole a few hearts in his time, and any 'Most Wanted' list he's on would be one compiled by love-hungry women.

The sex. Ah, now that was well—weird. It was good, though, but it was mind-blowing for two reasons. For one thing, Ilan was really good at it. He had Jennifer—and me—climbing the walls. Did they teach that at Mossad School? Where do I sign up? Secondly, it was disturbing in some ways as I dreamed my way through their almost-insatiable passion for one another—because I was there. I was feeling everything Jennifer was feeling. Every single touch and kiss and nibble. His teeth, tongue, fingers, his gentle hands and every sensation they sent through her—I got it all, in full technicolour, high definition, with surround sound for every gasp and moan and whimper, and the added bonus of an, as-yet-not-invented, in-the-flesh-reality experience that was genuine, not virtual. By heck, it was disturbing, but I couldn't deny that it was good. Great, even.

Jennifer wanted Ilan with a passion that bordered on full-blooded insanity, but she kept her cool and loved him when he was with her, then hated him when he disappeared—sometimes for weeks on end. Well, she didn't really hate him. She hated him going away, but she knew what he worked at, she knew how dangerous it was, and although she got on with her own life, she was the proverbial spouse—sitting at home, waiting and worrying about her man. That's the part she hated.

I was there when she had to deal with their house purchase while he was off saving the world, and I was an uninvited, invisible guest at their wedding, such as it was. I dreamed about all of their life together—and then I discovered that she was dreaming about me too.

That came as a shock. She knew all about the house and the work we'd done when we bought it to make it our own. She dreamed about the births of my two daughters, and she was there when I decided to give up teaching to pursue my photography career.

She didn't seem to like me very much. She thought I drank more than I should—oh, she was one to talk—and I got the impression she thought she was better than me.

Near the end, we dreamed that we'd decided to meet up and discuss our situation. We met in one of my favourite places—a picnic spot at our nearby forest park. I loved it. The wooden tables and bench seats were near a fast-moving stream that raced down over the rocks and pooled into a wider area before coursing on down to join a larger river a mile or so in the distance. The trees at the water's edge gave sun-dappled shade as they danced in the soft breeze, and the sound of the water was peaceful. We often came there for days out and picnics—Charlie and I and the girls—and sometimes I'd go there for a break when I was out in the area with my trusty camera. I'd sit there alone with my flask of coffee and my sandwiches, with Ross by my side—content and at peace with the world. It was one of the most beautiful places I'd ever found.

~~~

It was interesting to discover that Jennifer perceived the place we both had chosen for our meeting was a city centre café, with all the hustle and bustle of people and traffic. But I suppose that was just our different personalities.

Either way, we were sitting down together, each in our perceived place and, while it was pleasant for both of us, it was anything but normal.

There was waiter service for a start. I've no idea how,

but he appeared before us—a rather stuffy, bad-tempered waiter who seemed to read our minds. He gave us each a menu and asked us if we'd like anything to drink. We both ordered wine, and when he came back with it, we ordered salads. The salad was the most delicious I've ever tasted, and the wine went down a treat, too.

Our conversation was stilted and there was no bonhomie between us. We didn't greet each other with hugs and, 'Oh, it's so good to finally meet you,' smiles. It wasn't quite hostile but it wasn't friendly either. Jennifer mentioned the beeping noise and I told her I had heard it too, but it seemed to have stopped. I didn't know it then, but I stopped hearing the beeps—the sounds of the hospital equipment we were both hooked up to—because I was slipping away.

I did try to fight it. That's why Jennifer and I discussed who would live and who would die because both of us believed we had a choice. But the truth is that we didn't have a choice, and the supposed conversation with the woman whose life I shared in dreams was, in fact, my brain telling me that it was shutting down—and with it my body. There was nothing I could do about it. I was going to die. I tried not to believe it, but I think I knew deep down that I was going to pass away very soon. I also knew that Jennifer was going to survive, wake up and live out the remainder of her life.

There was no battle on another plane over this. Although we were sharing the same experience there was no sisterhood-type bond between us, in which we vowed to be strong for one another and help each other. I think I realised that as we finished our lunches, got up and went our separate ways.

It was a simple case of my injury was so severe that I couldn't survive it, whereas Jennifer's wasn't, and she would live.

Shit, as they say, happens.

Chapter 28 – Going places.

The best part about remembering Jennifer was that she was living in Israel, and now I had somewhere else to go. In addition to the area that surrounded my home, and my parent's home, then spreading out to the surrounding villages and towns, I now had another place—another country—to visit and explore. I've already covered most of Yorkshire, especially the moors, and honestly, it never occurred to me that I could go anywhere I wanted. My ghostly persona had evolved to the point where my days of being bound to the village and my home were long gone, and I was a bit bored, if I'm honest. That's the downside to being a ghost—okay, one of the many downsides—there's so little to do, and it does become a tad dull when I'm wandering around on my lonesome all the time.

It was either spread my wings a bit more—no, I don't have actual wings because I'm not an actual angel—to go and explore a foreign country, or join my parents up in Scotland.

I decided to go to Israel and see what the J woman was up to.

~~~

Not much, as it turned out.

She spent a lot of her time moping around the house and, to be honest, I got bored very quickly. I left her to it and played tourist in Israel for a while—visiting Jerusalem and the surrounding areas. I had a long walk around Tel Aviv, and I went to Haifa. I stood on the shore of the Dead Sea, dipping my toes into the salty and mineral-enriched water, and I explored many other top tourist attractions. I even hopped on a couple of tour buses and listened to the guides as they explained the history of the various places. It was all very interesting and I enjoyed all the sightseeing. I also got a kick out of doing it all for free—one of the very few perks of being a ghost—but for some reason my thoughts always brought me back to Jennifer and I couldn't help it, my curiosity got the better of me, and I slipped back into Jennifer's life. Just to see how she was doing. Nothing else. Don't get me wrong, I was still a tad angry and jealous that she'd lived and I'd died, but I didn't hate her. I didn't like her very much but I didn't hate her. After all, my injuries were more serious than hers and, if I had lived, I would have been severely impaired for the rest of my life. I overheard Charlie telling someone that the doctors had said my injuries were catastrophic and it was surprising that I'd lasted as long as I did.

Basically, Jennifer was luckier than me.

Nevertheless, I wanted to see her again. To find out what she was up to, and if she was still with that sexy Israeli. So, I popped into one of her dreams and hung around at her place for a while.

Honestly, I wonder why I bothered. It was so boring. If you think being dead is as dull as dishwater, go and visit Jennifer. The expressions – 'watching paint dry' and 'watching the grass grow' spring to mind. I've read the back of a cereal box that was more interesting.

Admittedly, in those first few weeks and months, she was still healing, both physically and psychologically. When she wasn't at her physiotherapy sessions or getting counselling, she sat around the house in the grip of depression, and usually with a glass in her hand. Poor Ilan did his best, but she wasn't having any of it. She ignored him and sank lower into whatever it was that was pulling her down.

She was drinking a fair bit, and I don't condemn her for that, because she was suffering from terrible nightmares and it was obvious that her survivor's guilt was the root of her problems.

She had this recurring dream about me in which I grabbed her by the throat and choked the life out of her. I hissed at her, called her all sorts of terrible names, and told her I was going to kill her, and that I should have lived and she should have died. All fair points if you ask me, but I never did any of those things to her. Hand on my heart— the cold, dead one, as I've mentioned before—I never once got into her dreams and shouted at her, or tried to choke her. It was nothing more than her own mind manifesting her guilt in her dreams.

It took her a while but eventually Jennifer got herself together, in both mind and body, and she began to pick up the pieces of her life. Ilan had weathered the storm, and you could tell a weight had been lifted from his shoulders. He looked younger and more relaxed, and that gorgeous smile appeared once more. From the moment I first met him in the dreams Jennifer and I shared, I always fancied him a little. Nothing serious, though. I mean, I wasn't going to dump Charlie and run off to Cyprus to steal him away from her, but I did enjoy seeing him in my dreams of Jennifer's life.

Speaking of Cyprus, Jennifer was heartbroken when Ilan explained that they could never go back, and that an offer had been made on their house there. An excellent offer—well above the asking price. He took her hand in his and told her that they had to accept it.

'We'll find another house here. One that we can make into a home,' he told her.

She didn't argue, didn't reason with him and plead for him not to sell their house. She merely sighed and nodded in agreement. I really felt for her. It was a lovely house.

They did find a nice place, in a quiet, secluded and well-to-do neighbourhood in Tel Aviv. It was spacious, private and had a big garden. It didn't take them long to settle in.

~~~

Jennifer seemed to have turned a corner shortly after this and she began to go out more, mostly hiking and swimming with Ilan, to improve her fitness. It was helping her mental health as well. She smiled more; she engaged more in conversations. She even got a job—in a rescue centre, working with dogs. Ilan's daughter gave her two kittens and I often watched her playing with them and laughing at their antics.

At the rescue centre, she really bonded with this old dog—or he with her, depending on how you look at it. He was deaf and he hated cats, and Jennifer wished she could adopt him but she couldn't, because of her cats. Besides, he was what you'd call institutionalised. The centre was the only home he'd even known and, while he probably would have been happy with Jennifer and Ilan, he seemed content to remain there, and looked forward to her feeding him and taking him for a walk every day.

Ilan was desk-bound now, at Jennifer's insistence. I thought it was a shame because that man was James Bond personified and I couldn't imagine him hunched over the paper he was pushing, like some bored civil servant who could only dream of seeing action in the field. I didn't want to. I preferred to swoon over his delicious hotness, as he chased the baddies through narrow streets in a sleek supercar. Or maybe stripped down to his boxers to dive into the water to rescue me. Oops, I mean the girl that the bad guys wanted to kill. Any scenario was better than him sitting behind a desk in a stuffy office.

Unless I was his secretary.

Yeah, that would work.

~~~

But Jennifer's life was a bit humdrum, and I found my interest in her quickly waning. I did pop in every once in a while, but those instances became fewer and fewer and, in the end, I parted company with her and I sort of forgot about her completely.

Imagine my surprise when, over three years since I died, she appeared in my house. I was sitting at the kitchen table, reminiscing about the morning I was waiting, and panicking, over opening the envelope containing my A-level results. I was a nervous wreck because I was convinced that I'd failed them, and my chances of getting into university were well and truly screwed. If the results were bad, it would be no one's fault but my own for not revising enough.

Boyfriend or geography? Geography or boyfriend? I was seventeen, almost eighteen, and I'd been dating Craig since Christmas. Because of him, I wasn't as interested in geography, maths and English as I should have been. It was all about the teenage hormones—maybe I should have studied biology, ha-ha—and I couldn't get him out of my mind. It was all hearts and flowers and soppy love songs because he was such a honey. Tall and dark, with the most gorgeous brown eyes and a smile that melted me. And boy, he could kiss.

Craig wasn't my first boyfriend, but he was my first— er—you know what I'm talking about and, despite my love for Charlie, he still holds a special place in my heart, even though I haven't laid eyes on him since I left school. I have no idea if he's alive or dead, married or divorced, rich and famous, or poor and working for the council on a bin lorry, but I occasionally still have a soppy, out-of-focus memory of him.

I was never the most studious pupil in school, probably because I was a fast learner and absorbed everything quickly—meaning that I didn't need to over-study. Plus, I hated homework with a passion. As far as I was concerned, the minute the bell rang at the end of the day, school no longer existed. I did what I had to do—the very minimum—and, in the end it was enough for me to scrap through my A-levels—only just passing, but it still counted—and secure a place in university studying to become a primary school teacher. I'd already decided I wanted to do this even though I didn't particularly like the idea of becoming a teacher, but hey—long holidays.

I was remembering all this when I heard a creak behind me and I jumped in fright.

I heard soft footsteps in the hallway and I went to see who it was. It was her. Jennifer. My old comatose-dream pal.

She was dripping wet. Apparently, it was raining outside—or wherever she was in her dream—and she looked cold, wet, and frightened to death as she stood there staring at me. Although I was grinning from ear to ear, I didn't quite know how I felt seeing her there in the flesh. A bit of anger with a pinch of jealousy thrown in summed it up pretty well. But in general, I didn't feel any real animosity towards her. She lived, I died. It wasn't her fault any more than it was the man in the moon's fault. It sucked. It would have been nice if both of us had survived, woken up and carried on with our lives. I wondered if we would have remained aware of each other, and would we have made contact? Emailed or phoned once a week? I doubt we'd have become friends. We'd probably have been nothing more than two people who shared an out-of-body experience—a bit like the people you meet on holiday and you get on great with them while you're there, but you don't want any more contact once you get home. That, in itself, is a bit of an out-of-body experience, in my opinion.

Jennifer and I had—in our respective dreams— wondered what it would be like to meet up. Maybe even go on holiday together somewhere. Charlie and me, plus the girls, and Jennifer and Ilan. It would have been okay, nice even. But it would probably fizzle out naturally, apart from the odd email every now and then.

I did wonder now though, if she'd died and was trapped like me, or was I in her dream? Time to find out.

But, first of all, I sent her upstairs to see my family and how they were coping without me. It was spiteful I know, but I had to let her know the consequences of my death, and the effect it had on my family.

When she came back downstairs, she looked miserable as hell. Good.

I nudged the chair out from the table with my foot and invited her to sit down.

Surprisingly, she didn't bolt, although she didn't look too happy, but she sat down opposite me.

I pretended to be angry for a while—okay, I *was* angry, but not as much as I let on—and I was a bit bitchy. Eventually she told me what was happening. Ilan was missing in action, and she was trying to find him in her dream so they—Mossad—could go and rescue him. This was her first attempt, she told me, and it seemed to be going all wrong.

Okay, now I felt sorry for her, and I was worried about Ilan. He was my dream lover after all. I told her that I didn't hate her and that I hoped she figured out how to do what she needed to do and she managed to find him, safe and well.

~~~

We ended up on good terms. We even hugged. Why shouldn't we? It wasn't her fault that I was the one who ended up dying.

She lived, I died. There was nothing more remarkable than that. Shit happens, as they say. Still, it would have

244

been nice if it had happened the other way around and I'd been in my kitchen making a brew when her ghost appeared.

Anyway, there was nothing else to do about it so, we hugged. I wished her all the best, and she walked out through the door, leaving me alone with my musings about Craig and my A-level results.

Chapter 29 – She spies with her sleeping eyes.

Personally, I thought Jennifer was a right bitch for treating Ilan so badly. He'd come home in a bad way and, after being away for so long, I might have expected her to be a bit more caring and considerate. And a bit more pleased to see him. But no, she was angry and could barely speak to him. When she looked at him, her face told him she was looking at something she didn't like very much.

I knew the reason why, as did she, but poor Ilan was clueless.

Jennifer was going through some hard stuff herself. She wasn't able to forgive him, or even talk about what she went through while he was missing in Syria, and because of that—as well as what transpired when she met him in her dream in Syria—they were on the verge of breaking up. She wanted him back but she couldn't—or wouldn't—allow herself to relent. As a result, she had turned into a really nasty cow towards him. I know because I was there in their house, watching it all unfold. Plus, she was drinking far too much, way more than she ever did before, and this was making her worse. Poor Ilan hadn't a clue what was wrong. He only knew part of it and he did feel guilty, because he was the reason Jennifer now worked on the Dream Catcher Program and spent her nights spying on the dregs of society through their dreams. The things she'd seen weren't doing much to improve her mental state and, if anything, they were making her worse. But it was what she wasn't telling Ilan that was the real cause of her problems, and until she did, things wouldn't get any better for the two of them. She needed to sit down and explain about what had happened when she'd met him in a dream in Syria, and how she felt about it. I know she'd talked it over with her shrink friend, Miriam, but she really needed to talk to Ilan.

I suspect she was afraid that he'd think she was being silly—it was only a dream after all—and that's why she was unable, or unwilling, to tell him. Even if it was only a dream, it was real to her and she couldn't move on until she got it off her chest.

~~~

It got slightly better after a while, and she was making an effort, but I could tell Ilan wasn't happy. He wanted his wife back, not this woman—this stranger—who was living in his house and sharing his bed. Just about sharing his bed, mind you. She spent more nights at Mossad HQ than she did at home.

Of course, that was her job.

Then the Coronavirus spread across the world and everybody had to stay in their homes, Jennifer and Ilan included. I left them to it because I needed to check on my own family. They were fine. The girls—surprisingly— escaped it, but Charlie caught it. Thankfully, he wasn't too ill and was up and about after a couple of days. Mum and Dad were careful in the extreme, and it missed their house, and that of my in-laws, but both my parents and Charlie's parents were heartbroken at the loss of several of their close friends. Gavin, Claire and their three children also took lockdown to the extreme and didn't catch it. Claire's mum—who thought it was all fear-mongering—caught it, and although she was very ill, she eventually made a full recovery.

A lot of people died. Far too many lost their lives because of the government's ineptitude. Actually, that's too mild a word. It was more a case of bloody crooks feathering their own nests and not giving a flying fuck that people were dying in their tens of thousands.

My family survived, and for that I was thankful, but they could easily have become another number in the total death toll.

Once I knew they were all okay I went back to Jennifer and Ilan. I fully expected to find two corpses in the house after they'd fought to the bitter end and died from their wounds. But no, there they were, sitting out on the patio and, like everyone else in the world during lockdown, boozing from lunchtime onwards.

They must have realised that lockdown was the make-or-break moment in their marriage, and both of them knew they wanted their marriage to recover so, without any words spoken, an uneasy truce had been agreed between them.

Of course, Jennifer still had to work. Criminals, terrorists and traitors didn't let a little thing like a pandemic stop them from going about their nefarious schemes, and she still had to go into their dreams in order to find out what they were up to. Under the strict social distancing regulations, of course.

Jennifer did see some terribly disturbing things in her dreams. I saw them, too, through her. There are some sick, evil bastards out there. Some of them—the ones passing their countries' secrets to the enemy—might claim they were justified, their defence being that they were in it for the money to pay for the kids' schooling, or for love, or any other reason they could come up with. The why didn't matter because Jennifer was able—through her ability to get into their dreams—find out what they were up to, pass on the details via her boss to the necessary authorities, and they'd be arrested and hauled away.

I bet they spent many hours in their prison cells wondering how they were caught. I bet they wouldn't believe it if someone told them that an Englishwoman had dreamed about them.

~~~

There was one horrific event in which Jennifer caught a serial rapist and killer. I won't go into the details because it is just so disturbing, but let's just say that it frightened Jennifer very much. It was one of the worst cases she had dealt with and I was concerned about how it would affect her, emotionally and psychologically.

I heard all the details as she told Ilan about it over several glasses of gin and tonic—each one becoming more gin than tonic. He didn't ask her questions, but merely sat beside her, taking small sips of his whiskey, and allowing her to relate her experience to him in her own time. It was only when she'd finished telling him that she looked at him, smiled and said that she felt better because he didn't push her to talk, then she took his hand in hers and told him she understood him so much more now. She told him that she now realised how he coped with trauma, how he dealt with it mentally and compartmentalised it in such a way that it didn't impact on his everyday life.

I got a bit misty-eyed when he said that this was why he wanted her to quit the Dream Catcher Program, but it was also the reason why he didn't want her to quit.

I knew then that they'd be okay.

It didn't stop me thinking about her dream experiences—this one in particular—and, for the first time ever, I was glad I'd died and that she had lived, or else I could have ended up in her shoes—or pyjamas, to be exact—dreaming for MI5 or 6. Or even the local bobbies down the nick.

~~~

It was at times like these that Jennifer and Ilan found their way back to one another and, once lockdown ended, they spent many of their days outside. They'd visit markets because Jennifer loved shopping and Ilan loved taking her shopping. They'd visit the usual tourist attractions and places of interest, and they would go hiking off the beaten track, or spend a day horse-riding, or on the sea—swimming, sailing and scuba diving. The companionship they shared on these trips brought them together and, in no time at all, they were back in love like never before.

It was on one of their days out that she told him what had happened in her dream when he was in Syria, and how much it had frightened her when she though he was going to kill her. Ilan was horrified, but it broke the ice between them and they began to open up and let the love back in.

They were lovers again. Their days were spent enjoying the actives they both loved, but their nights were full of passion and romance. They couldn't get enough of one another.

As for me, I turned into a real pervy ghost as I watched them getting it on night after night. I told myself I was justified because this was the closest I would ever get to getting laid again.

~~~

Jennifer and I did meet in a dream again. It wasn't a nice experience. Something had happened during her last Dream-Catcher job, and I had to step in as there was a chance that she could end up in serious trouble because of it.

She was a bit shocked to see me after all this time, but she heeded my warnings and I think she learned her lesson. I just didn't think she'd go to such extreme measures to get herself out of trouble.

Once I knew she'd sorted everything out, I left her and Ilan to themselves and decided to go home again. To be honest, I was becoming a bit bored with all the sex. Bored, and more than a little jealous.

What I really needed was a sexy man-ghost to cuddle up with. I haven't found one yet, but I haven't given up looking.

Chapter 30 – R.S.V.P.

Well, of course I went to the wedding even though I wasn't invited. I wasn't going to miss this for all the tea in China, or cheese on the moon, or cows in the field. I needed to be there, and I decided I was going to gate crash it. Then, when they got to the part about anyone knowing why these two shouldn't be joined in matrimony, I planned on jumping up and shouting that he was mine and she couldn't have him. That would have worked a treat if I'd been corporeal, but I wasn't. I could jump up and down and shout all I wanted but no one could see or hear me. All I could do was sit there fuming as the ceremony went on without me.

My Charlie—my husband, Charlie—was marrying my best friend, Claire.

~~~

I knew he was looking for someone. I'd seen him more than a few times searching through dating sites on the internet, swiping left or right—or whatever people did on those apps—as he looked for another me.

Then he found someone, and they began dating. It was casual for a while. She wanted to take it to the next level but Charlie was hesitant. A part of him was still reluctant to move on—to let go of me.

She wasn't going to give up so easily and, eventually, they began dating more seriously—though I suspect it was more to do with her pushing him than any desire on Charlie's part for them to be a couple.

Then along came the mid-term holidays and the girls

were spending their time out of school with my mum and dad who had decided on a few days touring Cornwall in the campervan. The girls were still too young to consider travelling around the countryside with two old fogies boring, and they were loving their time with their grandparents.

As for Charlie—oh, I don't even want to think about it—he was spending a few days on a city break with this new girlfriend. They were getting on well and he'd agreed finally to go somewhere with her, although I don't think Charlie was serious about a long-term relationship. He enjoyed her company and they were having fun in the bedroom, but that was all. So far.

I didn't know how I would feel if their relationship became serious. On the one hand, I wanted him to be happy but, on the other, I still didn't want to share him with anyone.

I decided to wait and see.

~~~

Claire and Gavin have always had what you'd call a volatile relationship and, although they loved one another deeply, they often fought like cats and dogs. It was never physical but they did a hell of a lot of yelling at each other, and sometimes Gavin would take off in a sulk for a few days. At other times, Claire would disappear—sometimes to stay with us, or to her mum's, and once she took herself off to Gran Canaria for a week. She got a last-minute holiday cancellation for pennies, lay on the beach all day and drank sangria all evening. She came home a bit hungover from her week of binge-drinking, but in a much better mood. She also came home with a lovely tan that made everyone envious because it was November and all of us were pale and miserable as we shivered in the cold and the rain.

But mostly, when they had a row, they yelled for an hour or so, sulked for a while, then got back to normal.

~~~

I couldn't believe it, and I kicked myself for not seeing it coming. I'd been spending so much time in Israel with Jennifer and I guess I'd taken my eyes off the ball where Charlie, and especially Claire, were concerned.

Jennifer and Ilan's relationship issues were as good as any soap on the telly for me, and I was totally engrossed in their little domestic saga, so much so that I was unaware of what was going on not a few miles from my own home.

~~~

Claire and Gavin were chalk and cheese. Gavin was the quiet one. His idea of fun was a long walk through the woods or a gruelling hike up over the moors. He enjoyed hiking, kayaking, fishing, and bog-snorkelling of all things. Basically, he loved any kind of outdoor activity. Claire, on the other hand, hated getting mucky or wet or cold. Her perfect outdoor experience was lying on the sun-lounger, sipping something cool and alcoholic and reading a good book.

They'd been fighting a lot more recently. Other than the times she took off for a few days, one of the reasons Claire managed to keep it together in the past was me. When she was pissed off with him, she always talked her issues out with me, either over the phone or in person. She got everything that was annoying her out of her system and went home, usually to a contrite and apologetic Gavin. They kissed and made up and everything was fine—until the next row, and the next phone call to me.

But there was no me to talk to any more, and Claire was stuck with her feelings—her resentment and her anger—with no release. So, instead of blowing off steam by telling me what a piece of shit he was, and describing all the many ways she wanted to kill him, she allowed it to simmer until it blew up in the worst way possible.

During one of their fights, Claire began listing all his faults and Gavin—maybe in the heat of the moment and probably not intentionally—let it slip that he finally knew what love really is. And he wasn't referring to the song.

Both of them stopped shouting and stared at one another and—I think—Gavin just decided he'd had enough. He took a deep breath and told Claire that he'd met someone, he was in love with her, and he wanted to spend the rest of his life with her.

With that he stormed out of the kitchen, slamming the door behind him.

Claire was gobsmacked.

So was I.

Both of us stood there in her kitchen wondering what to do. Well, she wondered what to do. I wondered what would happen next. I got my answer pretty quickly for Gavin came back with not one, but two suitcases.

He grabbed his car keys off the kitchen counter and stormed outside, without saying a single word. He got into his car and drove off, throwing up a good amount of gravel with his spinning wheels as he floored it out of the driveway, and out of his marriage.

Claire went as white as a sheet and stood there, paralysed. I wished with all my heart that I could go to her, put my arms around her and tell her everything would be okay.

'He'll be back when he cools off,' I'd say. 'You know what he's like. He's probably gone to Gran Canaria, just like you did.'

Or maybe he'd gone to be with his new and true love.

Claire blinked a few times and looked around the kitchen as if she was in a strange, new place. In many ways she was.

Her eyes landed on the mug Gavin had been drinking his tea out of not twenty minutes earlier. She reached out as though to pick it up but swiped it off the counter. His Inverness Caledonian team mug crashed to the floor and shattered into pieces. Just like her heart.

Claire's heart would shatter many more time over the coming months.

~~~

I stood at the back of the registry office as I watched them repeating their vows. They looked happy. I couldn't be angry or hurt because of what both of them had been through—Charlie losing me and Claire losing everything.

~~~

The floozy, slut, tart—there's another word I'd like to call her but it's the only swear word I don't ever use, so I won't—that Charlie had been seeing turned out to be a gold-digger of the highest order. She wanted him to marry her as soon as possible. They even got engaged, and I stood there and watched her complain that the ring he wanted to buy wasn't expensive enough. She pointed to one that had a diamond twice as large and a price tag that was equally as massive. Charlie told her he'd think about it.

She gave him twenty-four hours, then dragged him back to the jewellers in town and told him she loved him with all her heart, and she wanted this ring. I could tell his heart wasn't in it, but he bought her the ring and she put it on. He didn't ask her to marry him, I noted. He just bought her the ring, but as far as she was concerned, they were engaged.

She dragged him to the nearest, half-decent, restaurant for a slap-up lunch to celebrate.

A week or two later, she offered to do his books for him. Charlie said that his accountant did everything and she replied they could save money if she did it. Charlie replied that his accountant didn't charge too much, and he was always confident that everything was in order at the end of each tax year.

Then I caught her eyeing up some of my photos on the walls and checking me out online to see what they might be worth.

The girls hated her and avoided her as much as they could.

Thankfully, Charlie came to his senses and dumped her. It was coming up to the anniversary of my death, when he always took the girls to the cemetery and they'd place a big bunch of flowers on my grave.

Her Ladyship—see, I didn't use the bad word—told

him that this was a waste of money and he'd be better off spending their hard-earned cash on a meal for two in some expensive restaurant. *Their* hard-earned cash. She actually used that word.

I never wanted to be a poltergeist as much as I did then. I wanted to wreck the house with her in it. I'm sure she felt my waves of anger washing over her because she did frown and glance around the room a couple of times.

Charlie took a long, hard look at her and I think he compared her standing there to me standing there, and he couldn't picture himself living with this woman in the house—the home—that he and I had made together. He couldn't imagine living with her anywhere.

And just like that it was over between them.

Oh, she made a big fuss. Shouting and screaming and calling him all sorts of names. Then she cried and pleaded and told him she loved him. I fully expected her to tell him she was pregnant even though I knew she wasn't. But Charlie stood firm and she realised she was on a hiding to nothing. She began to tug the ring off her finger.

'Keep it,' Charlie told her. 'Just get the fuck out.'

We never saw her again, but it knocked Charlie back a bit, and he went back to evenings spent staring into the fire and drinking whiskey. I wasn't too worried. He'd come out of it before and he would come out of it again. Maybe next time, he'd find someone decent to love.

But did it fucking have to be Claire? My best mate?

Chapter 31 – A shoulder to cry on.

I could see them getting closer, but I didn't think anything of it. Claire was a mess and Charlie, being the kind-hearted soul he was, stepped in to help her in any way he could. It's what we both would have done, if I'd been alive.

Claire was down a deep, dark well and she was struggling to climb out of it. Gavin had meant what he said about being in love with someone else. She didn't hear from him for over a week. His phone went to voice mail and he ignored her texts and WhatsApp messages. He even blocked her on Facebook—the only social media account he had.

She put on a brave face in front of the children but they knew something was up. No amount of telling them that 'Daddy was working away from home for a while,' could convince them that things were okay.

He must have been keeping an eye on her and her movements because he came home when she was out shopping. He took everything that belonged to him—all his clothes, books, fishing gear, toolbox, and everything else in between. He didn't leave a note, but he left his house keys on the table. That, in itself, was as good as any note.

Funnily enough, Claire took it well. Not great, but she didn't weep and wail. She accepted that her marriage was over and she had no choice but to pick up the pieces and move on.

The first thing she did the following Monday morning was contact a solicitor who specialised in separations and divorces. She booked an appointment, then made the kids their dinner, sat them down and told them the truth. She didn't gloss over it. I suspect she decided they were old enough to know the truth, so she told them straight that their dad had met someone else and wasn't coming home any more.

Lots of tears ensued, but she eventually got them settled and off to bed. Then she poured a glass of wine and phoned Charlie.

'Do you want me to come over?' he asked when she told him that Gavin had moved out permanently and that she'd already contacted a solicitor. 'I mean, I'll need to bring the girls with me, but—'

'No. I'm fine. I just wanted to let you know, and ask you if he'd been in touch.'

'He hasn't, Claire. Honestly. I'd tell you if he—'

'I know you would, Charlie. I appreciate it.'

'Are you sure you don't want me and the girls to come over? I'll bring pizza for all of us and we can talk while they hang out in the playroom.'

'It sounds good, Charlie. Great, in fact. But maybe another time? I have the kids settled down for the evening, and tomorrow I'm going to have to sit down and have a serious talk with them. I've told them the bare bones—that he isn't coming back—but it hasn't sunk in yet and I need to take time with them and explain it all properly. Lily will be devastated as she's such a Daddy's girl. The boys will be as bad. They love him to bits.'

Claire's voice caught in her throat and a sob escaped her lips. Charlie offered again to come over but she told him no.

'I need to be alone tonight, Charlie. Maybe another evening.'

Charlie reluctantly gave in but he told her to call him anytime—night or day—if she needed anything, or just wanted to talk. He signed off with a promise to relay any conversations with Gavin back to her. If there were any, that is. I suspected there wouldn't be. I had the feeling that Gavin was gone for good and had cut all ties with his life in Yorkshire, including the people he knew there.

~~~

I was only partially correct, for three days later Gavin returned when Claire was at work. Although he'd left his house keys, he must have had a spare, and it hadn't occurred to Claire to change the locks. He returned in his own car—followed by a bloke in a large van—and took what he considered to be his share of the household items. He took the fridge and the microwave and other assorted items from the kitchen. The suite, coffee table and the television from the living room, plus other odds and ends such as towels and bed linen from cupboards. This was bad enough, but he also took all the furniture, toys and clothes that belonged to the children.

Everything was loaded securely into the van and, after a brief discussion about routes, the two men got into their respective vehicles and drove off, the van following for a few miles before Gavin turned towards the village. The van driver had been instructed on where he was going, and that he'd be driving for several hours before he reached his destination. He also knew that Gavin had one more errand to run before following the van on the same route.

Claire was in shock when she arrived home to find an empty space where her sofa and chairs used to be, and the contents of the fridge sitting on the kitchen counter beside the space where the fridge had stood. They'd bought a chest freezer during the covid lockdown and she checked the garage to find it still there with the contents inside, so at least there'd be something she could cook from frozen for their dinner. She was as mad as hell and cursing herself for not changing the locks as she checked to see what else was missing.

She was about to open Lily's bedroom door when her phone rang.

She frowned as she recognised the number. She answered it and her world fell apart.

~~~

I sensed her anger and her anguish as if it were my own. She shouted down the phone at the unfortunate staff member who told her that Gavin had collected the children, citing some family emergency that he hadn't time to explain. He'd merely said that he needed them to come home with him immediately. When the children were brought to the office, they rushed to him, glad to see their father once more. They thought he was back home again for good, even telling him that Mummy would be able to stop crying now that he'd come back to them.

But something in his manner, his sense of urgency, and a furtive look that the school secretary saw in his eyes prompted her to pick up the phone and call Claire—but only after he'd left and she'd thought about it for half an hour.

'Why the hell did you let him take them if you thought something was wrong?' Claire yelled through her tears.

'Because he's their father and he's on the list of people authorised to collect them,' the woman told her. 'Along with your parents and Charlie Wilson, poor Lucy's husband.'

She knew who I was from back when I worked there, and of course, my girls go to the same school. Like I said, it's a small village.

Claire realised she'd screwed up by not removing Gavin from the list. The bastard had not only had an affair, dumped her and run out on her, but he'd sneaked back and taken half of her furniture. And now he'd stolen her children. God knows where he'd taken them.

She sank to her knees, the phone falling on the floor beside her, and she howled in agony.

~~~

When Charlie got home from work that evening—it was the Friday of a Bank Holiday weekend, and his parents were taking Amy and Chole to the seaside until Sunday— he found Claire's car parked in the driveway and she was sitting on the doorstep with a bunched-up tissue in her hands. Her eyes were red from crying and she had a look of utter desolation on her face.

He was out of the car in a heartbeat, the beer and pizza he was planning for his dinner-for-one forgotten.

Once they were inside, at his insistence, Claire told him everything. She poured out her grief and her anger, and her fear. Charlie stood silently, allowing her to get it out of her system.

When she finished speaking, she seemed to deflate as though the life had gone out of her with each word.

'He's taken my kids, Charlie,' she said and her tears began all over again.

Charlie pulled her to him and she wrapped her arms around his waist and laid her head on his chest. He stroked her hair as she sobbed. Neither of them realised it, and I certainly didn't—I guess my intuition must have died along with me—but this was the moment their relationship began.

Chapter 32 – My best friend's wedding.

I wasn't a happy bunny when she moved in with Charlie, though I wasn't completely surprised. I could see it coming from a mile off.

When she discovered that he had taken the children back to Scotland, Claire fought Gavin as hard as she could. But Scottish law differed from English law, and she didn't have the same clout in a Sheriff's court as she would have had in an English court. They—the other side—argued that her children were half-Scottish, being Scottish nationals on their father's side. Furthermore, they were residing in Scotland—having been taken there legally by their father as no order was in place that gave sole custody to the mother—and, since they were currently residing there, the courts decided residence—the term used in Scotland, rather than custody—in favour of Gavin. His barrister cemented the argument by saying that they would receive a superior education and have better life opportunities if they remained in Scotland with their dad, who loved them very much and wanted only the best for them. The Sheriff—the Scottish equivalent of an English judge—was of the same opinion and sided with Gavin regarding education, having been to school briefly in Manchester. He'd been failed miserably, due to economic cutbacks and the lack of teachers with even a smidgen of interest in teaching their pupils, before his parents relocated back to Edinburgh, where he began to excel at school, passed all his exams, and then went on to study law at Dundee University.

As a concession to the tear-filled eyes of Claire, he

granted residence to her every other Christmas and for half of each school holiday period. Gavin very reluctantly agreed to this. It wasn't what Claire wanted. She'd asked for full custody on the grounds that their father had abandoned her and kidnapped them, and she wanted to appeal. Her lawyer, who was more honest than most lawyers, told her that, technically, it wasn't kidnapping and this was the best they were going to get. An appeal in a Scottish court, he told her, could result in Gavin getting full custody.

~~~

Once the dispute over the children was sorted out, the divorce was relatively easy—or as easy as divorces can ever be. Claire was still angry, but also heartbroken and bitter over the loss of her husband, her children and her home. It had come completely out of the blue—she had no idea that Gavin was having an affair, never mind leaving her and then taking the kids with him—and it left her shell-shocked and bewildered.

As a result, she turned to Charlie more and more for advice and support. When the house was sold and the mortgage repaid there was very little left over. Claire had to quickly weigh up the cost of finding somewhere to rent—somewhere with enough space for her three children when they were allowed to visit—or moving back in with her parents. The latter was not something she wanted to do, but the costs of a decent rental property were too expensive.

'Why not move in with me,' Charlie said to her one Saturday afternoon when she'd called in for a coffee to cheer herself up.

She looked at him in shock.

I looked at him in shock.

'No. I don't mean move in with *me* in that sense, if that's what you're thinking. I mean move in here. I've plenty of space. You'll have your own bedroom and en-suite, and you can use the back room—the snug—for your own living room. All we'd share would be the kitchen, and let's face it, you eat here most of the time these days anyway.'

'I don't know what to say, Charlie.'

I was a bit speechless myself. I mean, it made good sense. Claire was homeless, or would be in three weeks when she moved out of the house and the new owners moved in. But, although I knew Charlie was just being kind to a friend in need, and I would have done the same myself, I wasn't entirely comfortable with Claire living under the same roof as my husband.

I didn't like it but there was nothing I could do about it.

~~~

It went to plan for a while. Claire kept to herself, licking her wounds and missing her kids. She would join Charlie and the girls for breakfast and again for dinner, then she'd do the washing up and excuse herself before disappearing to her bedroom or to the back room where she could read, watch TV, or cry for the remainder of the evening.

Gradually though, a shift occurred and she began to spend more time with my family in the evenings. She helped the girls with their homework, played or talked to them. They were older now and they appreciated a woman in the house to talk about the things they couldn't discuss with their father. Besides, they'd known their 'Auntie' Claire since they were babies and had loved her for as long.

Periods. Make-up. Boys. All the things they were supposed to learn from their mother they now learned from Claire. She made sure they knew what was what. She bought pads and tampons, lipstick, mascara and hair products. Grown-up clothes, or at least more teen-oriented clothes, and bras.

I hated her. But I loved her, too. She was looking out for them. She could have been substituting them for her own children, especially Lily, who'd be going through the same thing with her new stepmother—Gavin married his bit on the side as soon as the ink was dry on the decree absolute. I knew it wasn't just that, though. Claire had always loved my girls, just as I'd loved hers. She was my best friend—my kids were hers and hers were mine. I just didn't believe for a single moment that one day this 'hers is mine and mine is hers,' thing we had going for all of our lives would apply to Charlie.

It seems I was wrong.

~~~

I took off in a sulk when Charlie asked Claire to marry him and she threw her arms round him and grinned from ear to ear as she squealed.

'Yes. Oh, yes, yes, yes. I love you so much, my darling.'

I knew they were sleeping together. She'd moved into his bed about four months after she'd moved into the house. I was surprised it took that long. I think both of them were hesitant because there was still so much of my presence in the house. I don't mean I appeared every time they got close, or threw ornaments at them—I'm not that kind of ghost—but both of them were never able to forget that I had lived in this house at one time.

I was also jealous that they were now a couple. She was the one sharing his bed at night—making love to him, curling up beside him, listening to him snore.

Despite being jealous, I knew I could live with it—what choice did I have? Charlie needed someone. So did Claire, and they—I hate to admit it—they fit together nicely.

Then he proposed to her and I was heartbroken. I was angry too, which was stupid because I wanted Charlie to find someone. He needed someone. He needed to not be alone for the rest of his life. He needed to be happy again. But, by heck, did it have to be Claire—my best friend since primary school? Oh, I was fit to be tied.

I got out of there as quickly as I could, and left the happy couple opening a bottle of Prosecco that Charlie had bought and hidden in the fridge earlier. They popped it open, laughing as it sprayed over them, and filled two flute glasses to the brim. Those were my flute glasses. There used to be six in the set but, over the years, we'd managed to break two of them.

I stormed out of the house and headed to where I knew I'd find some peace and quiet—my old, abandoned farmhouse.

~~~

It was stupid to be this upset. I went over their timeline again—sorting it out in my head. They'd been a couple since a few months after Claire's divorce. They sort of slipped into it gradually over the summer and autumn, and by winter—with Christmas almost on them—I could see them falling in love, and I knew it was only a matter of time before the relationship became serious and they became a couple. I just assumed they'd live together—the way they had been doing—so Charlie's proposal was a big surprise.

~~~

Gavin had come to his senses regarding allowing the kids to spend their allocated time with Claire. At first, he'd been awkward, always leaving things such as travel arrangements until the last minute, then telling her they needed to be home a few days early because he'd arranged some activity for them as a treat before they went back to school. He was just being nasty and petty, and for a while Claire played him at his own game—and between the two of them they were making matters worse. It was the children themselves who put a stop to their parents' antics.

Basically, Lily, Cameron and Alastair told their parents to grow the fuck up.

Out of the mouths of babes, you could say.

It worked. There is nothing like a child playing the adult to make the supposedly real adults come to their senses.

With all this behind her, Claire settled down into her role as a part-time single parent. Although she missed her kids when they weren't with her, she had a great time when

270

they were—spoiling them rotten and making sure they were happy, well-fed and safe in the knowledge that their mum loved them very much. They loved living with her and their 'Uncle' Charlie and, of course, they'd known their 'cousins'—Amy and Chloe—since babyhood.

Claire was over Gavin—or that piece of shit, as she called him—and she began to enjoy herself once more. She even went out on a couple of dates, but none of them stuck and she often came home alone to find Charlie waiting up for her. It was at moments like these that they found themselves growing closer together.

It was a late-night glass of wine after a summer's evening when they'd eaten their fill, played with my girls until both of them began to yawn and rub their eyes. Charlie packed them off to bed with a promise that they'd do the same thing tomorrow night, and the next night, and every night when Claire's kids joined them at the end of the week. This was met with sleepy cheers and complaints about having to double up with Lily so the boys could have a room to themselves.

It was Amy who planted the seed.

'Daddy? If Auntie Claire slept in your room, then Lily can have hers and we won't have to share because there isn't enough space in our room. You have a big bed, so there's lots of room for Auntie Claire.'

Embarrassed, Charlie had laughed and told her to go to sleep.

~~~

Maybe it was the wine and the romantic summer sunset, or maybe it was the seed that Amy had planted in his mind, but something in Charlie heart awakened and he began to see something in Claire that he wanted. I wouldn't call it love—not yet—but it was more of a need, a desire for a friend and a warm body to hold.

He relegated me to the roll of a memory of times past and he knew it was time to forge a new future with someone else. He stood up, pulled Claire to her feet and put his arms around her. His lips were gentle as they met hers, and she didn't pull away.

~~~

I lay on the sofa bed in my old bedroom, now converted to Mum's office, thinking how ironic it was that she'd always kept somewhere for me to stay if I ever did need to leave my husband and children and come home again.

I didn't cry. I didn't swear. I was numb. And I wasn't totally surprised. But I still didn't want to see or even think about him taking her in his arms, kissing her and leading her to his bed—our bed. I knew this day would come. He was hers now, and I needed to stay away from them for a while.

~~~

Six months later he told her he loved her and proposed. I took off again, to my house up on the hill.

~~~

I did go back for the wedding. And yes, I was angry. Not at them, but at the fact that I was dead and they—my husband and my best friend—were now a couple. I wanted to scream and shout that it was wrong and they shouldn't do it because he's still mine. But that whole ghost thing—

invisible and can't be heard—got in the way.

~~~

It was a quiet affair. They held it at the house—beautifully and tastefully decorated—with a marriage celebrant performing the ceremony, and only friends and family in attendance—about twenty-five in all—to see the happy couple tie the knot. Mum and Dad were there, too. For the most part, they were delighted for both Charlie and Claire, but every now and then I could see a wistful expression on Mum's face—on Dad's too, though he was better than Mum at keeping it hidden. I knew they were thinking of me. I suspect everyone was to a degree, probably even Charlie and Claire had a moment when I crossed their minds.

I was angry in the lead-up to their 'big day' and even during the ceremony, I was still a bit pissed off. But afterwards, I settled down and watched the party unfold. Everyone, even Mum and Dad, congratulated them and wished them well. There was enough food to feed a small army and the amount of booze could have filled a swimming pool. There would be some serious hangovers in the morning.

The girls along with Claire's three children, spent the day and the evening filling their faces with food and running around with the other children who were in attendance. They were staying tonight but going to stay with my parents tomorrow and for the next two weeks while Charlie and Claire flew off to Greece for their honeymoon. Claire's kids would be looked after by her mum until it was time to go back to their father in Scotland.

I stuck around for most of the evening, then I didn't know what to do. My girls loved their new 'mum' and I knew she loved them back. They'd be well looked after. Charlie had found my replacement and, yeah okay, I was a bit miffed that he'd chosen my best friend, but overall, I was happy to see him happy.

It occurred to me that evening that it was time to let them get on with their lives, and that's what I did. I finally left home.

I stayed away for many years, but I knew I'd come back one day to see my girls again.

Chapter 33 – Something old, something blue.

'No.' I screamed as Chloe put her foot on the bottom rung of the ladder that led up to the attic.

I knew she didn't hear me—she couldn't possibly hear me—but something made her stop and think about what a stupid thing she was about to do. I breathed a sigh of relief because my youngest daughter was eight and a half months pregnant and climbing a ladder was a recipe for disaster. Served with potatoes, a creamy blood-and-broken bones sauce, and a side order of premature labour topped with a potentially dead baby.

And usually, it's Chloe who's the sensible one.

'Ames? Are you still up there? What are you doing?'

'Yeah. Hang on a mo,' Amy called back.

I could hear the sounds of boxes and crates being moved about and I could tell Amy was searching for something.

'What are you looking for?' Chloe asked. She was looking up, and she still had one foot on the bottom rung of the ladder.

'Found it,' Amy said as she began her descent with an old cardboard box tucked under her arm.

She was covered in dust and cobwebs, and Chloe wrinkled her nose in disgust and fanned the air in front of her face to make her point.

'So, what's in the box?'

'Oh, yeah, we'll get to that. Look at what I found.' Amy held up the small lapis lazuli bracelet.

I remembered it. Charlie had bought it for me when I

275

was going through a 'Blue is my all-time favourite colour' period. I wore blue jeans with blue tops. I had blue trainers and a blue ribbon to tie my hair back—even my nails were blue. I'd decided that I wanted to repaint our bedroom walls blue. Charlie refused point blank, which set me into a sulk for a day or two, and he bought the lapis lazuli bracelet as both a distraction from my re-decorating ideas and an inroad into my good books again. He got it on eBay for a fiver and I wore it every day. Right up to the moment I decided that green was my favourite colour. I have no idea how it got up there, and I'd even forgotten I had it, but I had a fair idea why Amy wanted it.

'Ahh, something old and something blue.' Chloe reached to take the old box from her sister.

'Exactly. And I'm stretching it a bit, but it might be something borrowed as well.'

'Nope. All Mum's stuff belongs to us so it doesn't qualify as borrowed.'

'We could pretend it's yours and you can let me borrow it.'

'Okay. That'll work. So, what's in the box?'

'The coolest thing ever.' Amy grinned. 'Come on. Let's go downstairs and I'll show you.'

Intrigued myself, because I couldn't remember what was in the box, I followed my daughters down the stairs and into the kitchen. The house was mostly the same as it had been when I was alive but some things had changed over the years I'd been away. Claire had made her mark on it, by changing the colour scheme in the living room—a change I actually approved of—to more vibrant shades, and she'd replaced the furniture, which had grown old and tatty over the years. Her kids, when they came to visit, had commandeered the spare bedrooms—the boys in one and Lily in another, which meant Amy and Chloe had to remain in their own room together. Fortunately, they got along and were happy with the arrangement, and besides, it was only for a few weeks every year. But during those few weeks, my two along with Claire's three made one big, happy family that I could visit now and then and see them growing into beautiful adults.

~~~

The kitchen had been upgraded and modernised. The fridge was the biggest I'd ever seen, and they had all kinds of gadgets for making coffee and cooking food that were totally alien to me. The dog bed in the corner was long gone as they'd never gotten around to getting another dog, although there were two cats now.

Charlie and Claire were happy together, and I was pleased because I didn't want either one of them alone and unhappy. They kept my photo on the mantlepiece and, every now and then, they still remember me.

~~~

After Charlie and Claire got married, I stayed away for a few years, but as my daughters grew towards womanhood, the urge to see them again, and find out how they were doing, never left me. So, every six months or so I came back to do just that.

~~~

I leaned against the kitchen worktop as I watched my girls make themselves tea in preparation for the opening of the old box. I remembered what was in it and I couldn't help smiling at the memories it brought back.

'Do you miss her?' Amy asked.

Chloe took a sip of her tea as she thought about the question. She set her mug down on the table.

'Honestly? Not really. I think we've been so used to her not being here that it's normal. I mean she's been dead for well over half of our lives, and my memories of her are sketchy now. But I do miss not having had the chance to grow up with her in my life. It would have been nice to have been a teenager with her around. Crazy nice, but sweet nice too. Someone to talk to when I came out. I would love to have introduced her to Cathy and told her this was the girl I was going to marry, and then when I was pregnant with Sebastian, I would have loved to sit down and ask her questions about how she felt when she was carrying me.'

'Probably horrified,' Amy said with a grin.

'Nah, she adored me. You were the weird one that she was frightened of. The way you used to sneak around the house never saying anything. You were dead creepy and you made her jump all the time. She thought you were some sort of undead, little monster kid and she was terrified of you.'

'She was not.'

'She bloody was.'

'Wasn't.'

I had to laugh as I listened to their back and forward banter. This was them all over again, except when they were kids the whole was/wasn't thing usually ended in

278

hair-pulling and lots of tears. Now, it was just for fun.

'Seriously though,' Chloe said after a moment of remembering their childhood. 'Don't get me wrong, Auntie Claire is great, and I love her to bits—always have, and I always will—but she isn't Mum. And that's what I miss.'

'Yeah, me too.'

'So, what's in the box? Or don't you know and you're afraid to open it without your big sister to hold your hand in case something jumps out.'

'I had a peek when I found it in the attic,' Amy told her. 'You are so going to love it.'

Amy opened the box carefully, so she wouldn't cause too much dust to scatter in the air, and lifted out a pile of old papers and notebooks.

'You found them.' Chloe's eyes were wide with delight. 'I thought they'd been chucked away years ago.'

'So did I. They were behind a box of old clothes, and a stack of left-over wooden flooring. We seriously need to spend a day up there, clearing it out.'

'Hel-lo. Heavily pregnant woman here. I doubt I could squeeze through the trapdoor, never mind get up the ladder.'

'Well, we'll do it after the baby comes, then. You never know what we might find. Now, let's see what we have here.' Amy handed one of the small notebooks to her sister, opened another one and began to read. I wondered if she would struggle to make out my handwriting. It was never the tidiest and I used to get pulled up at school, and at work, because nobody could read it.

Amy didn't have her reading glasses handy—she had

a habit of putting them down somewhere and forgetting where she'd put them—and she was squinting. I could tell she was struggling to read the faded print on the paper.

Chloe, on the other hand, had no trouble reading my writing. She'd put her feet up on one of the chairs to ease her swollen ankles, and she was giggling with laughter as she read.

'Bloody hell. This is going to send me into early labour if I'm not careful,' she said as she put the notebook down and wiped away the tears of laughter. 'Do you remember these?'

'Some of them, yes. Which one are you reading?'

'It's called "Ee-wees or Yoos" and it's all about you. I remember that you called the ewes ee-wees, because you pronounced it phonetically. Even though everyone we know calls them yoos, you insisted everyone else was wrong and you were right.'

'Well, at least I learned from my mistakes, and the correct pronunciation is yu, so we all got it wrong. These books are great. This one has nearly all the little poems and songs Mum used to sing to us. I remember them.'

Chloe nodded, and I knew she was thinking wistfully of her childhood—her own and that of her sister—back when they were young and they had me there to tuck them in every night, and make up a song or a story for them as they drifted off to sleep.

'We should type these up on your laptop and maybe publish them. What do you think?'

Oh, fuck no. Chloe, please don't. They're not that good. Amy, tell her it's a daft idea.

280

But Amy couldn't hear me, and I could see the cogs grinding in her mind as she smiled and nodded her head in agreement.

'That is such a good idea, sis. Mum would love it.'

Oh, no I wouldn't. Right now, I wished I could snatch up the notebooks and chuck them on the fire, where they belonged. I stood there cringing as they spent the remainder of the afternoon, and carried on well into the evening, talking and reading through the rest of the notebooks. Every now and then, as they read, they let out peals of laughter that were interspersed with solemn moments and more than a few tears. I think I'd a total of about thirty poems, silly verses and stories, and some of them might not be at all suitable for kids.

Even though I cringed as they read my stuff aloud, I couldn't help but admire the two beautiful young women sitting at the kitchen table. Two young women that Charlie and I had created out of our love for one another and although I wasn't with them as they grew from children to teenagers and then into womanhood, I'd set the groundwork for the wonderful people they'd become. They were beautiful, and both had a sense of humour that matched my own. They had the work ethic of Charlie and they lived their lives the way they wanted. Chloe, with her career in accounting, with Cathy, the wife she adored by her side and between them, their young son, Sebastian. Now another baby was on the way and they couldn't wait to welcome him or her into the world. Neither could I.

Amy was about to fly the coop to be with Stevie who she met and fell in love with while they were both at school. They parted for a while when he joined the Army and was deployed abroad, but they picked up where they'd left off on his return to the UK. They haven't been apart since.

Stevie is a local and 'farm-reared' as they say, and he is absolutely gorgeous. Tall, fair-haired and handsome, with a smile that melts you where you stand. He's a shy big lad—doesn't have a lot to say, but when he does speak, people sit up and listen. He knows all the ins and outs of animal husbandry and growing veggies. He plays the guitar and has a singing voice that would put him at the top of the charts every week should he ever decide to pursue a career in the music business.

Sounds perfect, doesn't he? Well, he is. If I were still alive, I'd be the mother-in-law I hope he'd want to—ah, never mind. I'm too old for him, besides he only has eyes for my eldest daughter.

It's his dream one day to own his own small-holding. It's long been Amy's dream, too.

~~~

Dreams do have a way of coming true though, as Amy and Stevie discovered about eight months ago when they'd just announced their engagement.

There's an old farm just up the road from us and part of the farm land borders the bottom of our garden. When they were younger, both girls would spend their holidays working on the farm. They fed the chickens, helped with the sheep, and Amy even learned to milk one of the three dairy cows. She took to it more than Chloe and could often be seen in welly boots and the youngster's version of my old wax jacket. At her insistence, Charlie had kept mine and, once she was big enough to fit into it, it became hers. She would be found walking over the fields and sometimes just gazing at the sheep as they chomped and nibbled the grass. When lambing time came along, both of them spent their days and nights in the shed, assisting the births when necessary and bottle-feeding any lambs that needed help. Chloe did it because the animals were cute and the pocket money was great, but Amy saw it as an opportunity to learn about self-sufficiency farming—and I knew before she even voiced her ambitions that this was what she wanted to do with her life.

The elderly farmer and his wife had no kids of their own so my girls became their stand-in daughters. Arthur's wife, Hillary, took both Amy and Chloe into her kitchen and taught them how to make butter—actual, real butter—and how to bake the most delicious bread, scones and cakes. In the summer, they gathered buckets full of blackberries and she taught them how to make jam. In the autumn, they learned to made apple tarts. She also showed them how to make the most wonderful stews that could be frozen and kept for the cold, dark winter days.

Both girls loved these lessons but Chloe quit when she walked into the farmhouse one morning to find three dead rabbits lying on the kitchen table, waiting to be skinned and prepared for a hearty rabbit stew.

She'd always been a bit queasy when it came to plucking and preparing chicken and even pheasants, but she managed it because she loved the taste. The rabbits, on the other hand, were too cute to eat and she took off for home.

Amy, on the other hand, got stuck right in.

Sadly, Hillary passed away a year and a half ago and Arthur, lost without his wife, followed her three months later. They left most of the farm to a nephew a few miles away, but the twenty acres near us that included an old barn—not unlike the one I imagined I'd converted on *Grand Designs*—was left to Amy and Chloe.

Chloe already had a home, a wife and a son, and she was more than happy to sell her half to Amy and Stevie for a nominal fee. They applied for planning permission—which was granted—to convert the old barn into a residence and build a new barn, where they would keep a few sheep, a couple of cows and some hens. The renovations were almost complete. The vegetable garden was already planted, and it was only their impending nuptials that was preventing them from ticking off their list, the few small things—mostly decorating—they still needed to finish.

So, in a way, my fantasy barn conversion finally became real.

~~~

Although never an avid reader as a child as Chloe had been, Amy's passion for reading had awakened in her teenage years. This, in turn, led to a degree in English Lit. and several qualifications in editing. She now worked as a freelance editor. She kept her rates competitively low and this gained her the attention of many independent, self-published authors such as Laura Lyndhurst. On the advice of Laura—who became a multi award-winning best-selling author with her *Amanda Roberts* series, and again with her

Criminal Conversation series—she branched out into online marketing services—such as book trailers, promotional posters and videos, and anything she could think of that would help the indie authors on their literary journeys—again keeping her prices as low as possible and therefore, affordable.

Laura never failed to recommend her to any newbie authors and, as a result, Amy was a popular addition to the indie author community, not only utilising her skills to help them but also teaching them to make their own marketing materials.

The two of them became great friends and any time Laura was 'up our way' she and Amy would meet for lunch and a glass or two of wine. Amy returned the lunch and wine meet-up on the occasions she was down south, and they could easily wile away the afternoon discussing the latest new authors as well as their favourite books.

But the farming life had a strong pull. Amy knew it was something she could do well, and something she could do alongside her editorial and marketing work, and the more she discussed it with Stevie, the more they knew this was what they wanted to do.

It's funny because, as a small child, Amy was a little horror and we joked that she'd grow up to be a psychopath or worse still, a politician. Maybe it was her younger sister's influence—Chloe was the quiet, bookish one as a child—and maybe Amy learned from her and she settled down considerably. I also think that some of Amy's personality rubbed off on Chloe because, as she grew up, she lost her shy ways and became more outgoing and gregarious.

~~~

Chloe found her niche in numbers, and accounting was the career she chose. It was where she met Cathy, an estate agent. They fell in love and, so far, they're living the dream—happily ever after. They have good careers and an affluent lifestyle—which is reflected in their beautiful contemporary modern home that everyone loves, me included. They take several holidays to far-flung places each year, although this urge to travel was first tempered somewhat by the arrival of little Sebastian—Seb for short—and now put on hold for the foreseeable future by another little one on the way.

When she married Chloe, Cathy became my third daughter. Beautiful and smart, she's a born prankster and has a wealth of smutty jokes that match my father's—they even compete against one another to see who can win the most giggles and guffaws, and the air can get very blue sometimes.

Chole and Cathy's son Seb, is a little darling and Charlie adores him. He loves his grandpa and I think he's inherited Charlie's building skills because he's obsessed with his toy bricks. He's always making things out of muck and sand with his spade and toy digger, and dressed in his little workman's boots with his little yellow safety helmet on his head. He's even suggested that Charlie should take him to work with him some day. Knowing Charlie, that day isn't too far off.

Despite being two years younger than Amy, I always knew Chloe would be the one to settle down first, so I wasn't surprised when she married Cathy and Amy was her bridesmaid.

~~~

As she grew up, Amy changed and put away her cheeky, often disobedient, behaviour. She became the happy, country girl she is today, working alongside Stevie with the animals, getting mucky and walking the moors with their two rough collies, Riley and Lass. She even likes country music, for fuck's sake.

Chloe is the image of her father and has the sense of humour to match, whereas Amy favours me in her looks. She was never really a psychopath—Charlie and I just joked about that aspect of her personality. It was a standing joke when I was alive, and for a few years afterwards.

Charlie and I made two beautiful, strong women and I'm so proud of them. I know Charlie is too. I see it in his eyes every time he looks at them.

~~~

'I need a drink,' Amy said as she closed the last of the small books. She got up and took a bottle of wine out of the fridge and poured a hefty measure into a glass. 'After the wedding, I'm going to put these into some semblance of order and type them onto my laptop, and then I'll look into publishing them.'

'It's a terrific idea, and I'll help where I can,' Chloe told her. 'Speaking of weddings and husbands-to-be, aren't you supposed to be meeting Stevie later this evening?'

'Yeah, but he's coming here, so I can have a few drinks.'

'I wish I could have one along with you, but I'll have

to wait until this one pops out.' Chole patted her large baby bump.

'Chloe?' Amy's face grew serious. She took a large mouthful of wine and gulped it down. 'Did you ever see or hear Mum when we were growing up?'

'How do you mean?' Chloe frowned at the question.

'Okay, I know this sounds weird but, over the years, I thought I saw Mum out of the corner of my eye a couple of times. But when I turned around there was no one there. Obviously. And sometimes I thought I heard her voice saying goodnight to me. It happened a few times. Did anything like that ever happen to you?'

All of a sudden, Chloe became very interested in the buttons on her cardigan. She cleared her throat a few times before looking at her sister.

'Aye, right. Ask me a question like that when I'm pregnant and can't have a glass of wine for courage.'

'Well, did you see her?'

'Did you?' Chloe shot back. 'Or are you just winding me up?'

'No, but I think I almost did a few times. I swear I could feel her beside me when I'd get up early in the summer and go for a walk. Or when I was checking the ewes that were ready to lamb up at Ivan's place. God, that was a distance to walk up to, especially in the winter. I wish Dad had hung on to Mum's old Landi. I could have used it back then. And sometimes I thought I heard her whisper my name, or I'd think I could see her out of the corner of my eye but when I glanced round, there was nothing. I dunno, maybe it was wishful thinking, maybe not. I just know I sensed her near me. What about you?'

'Um. Sort of. I didn't see her or hear her, or anything like that, but I sort of felt her presence a couple of times. It's like she was there when I needed her. Remember the time I fell of that stupid horse and broke my stupid leg in two places?'

Amy nodded.

'I thought I was going to die because I hit my head when I fell. Just like Mum did.'

'You were wearing a helmet, Chloe.'

'I know that, but these things go through your mind when you're lying in a hospital bed, and that's when I got the feeling that she was there with me.'

'Like a creepy feeling? Or like you were going to die and she was there to help you—move on, or whatever?'

'Bloody hell, no. It was nothing like that at all. But it was so comforting and, even though I was in agony and Dad didn't know what to do or say—he kept pacing instead—I felt Mum was there holding my hand. And I knew I'd be okay and my leg would heal. Then when I was in labour with Seb, I got the same feeling. I've experienced her near me a few times over the years, not just those times, but when I was happy or just going about my normal day, I felt she was there beside me.'

Oh, I was. I was always here for both of you. I've spent so much time with you as you both grew up, and I've been happy and occasionally sad in your presence. When you were in labour with Seb, you swore as much as I did when I was delivering Amy and then you. I laughed so much at that, even though you were in so much pain and

289

demanding drugs just like I did when I was having you.

~~~

The thought that my daughters knew I was still around pleased me no end. They took comfort from me and they knew I loved them so much that I could never totally leave them.

~~~

Both of them had tears in their eyes. I was welling up a bit, too.

'She was a great Mum, even though we only had her for a while,' Chloe said with a hitch in her voice.

Unable to speak, Amy nodded.

'And if Bump here is a girl,' Chloe stroked her swollen belly. 'I'm going to call her Lucy, after the granny she'll never get to know.'

Okay, now I was bawling my eyes out. Where was Depression with her box of tissues when I needed her?

Actually, I didn't need her. I was crying with happiness because I knew then that, even though I've been dead for many years, this is what they mean when they talk about living forever. This is why I will live forever.

Chapter 34 – Mum's stories.

The following few pages contain a selection of the short stories, poems and nursery rhymes that our mother, Lucy Wilson, used to tell us—and sometimes sing to us—at bedtime to lull us off to sleep, or on a rainy afternoon when we were bored. The stories were great, the singing not so much—she had a voice like an animal in agony.

We didn't know she'd written them all down and kept them, until I found them in a box in the attic. My sister Chloe and I had some great laughs, and we shed a few tears too, as we read them again.

I remembered most of them, but there are a few that I've never heard. Obviously, Mum thought the ones she didn't tell us were too scary, or too complicated for our age group, or just too weird for our tender years. Or maybe Dad intervened before we ended up having nightmares because some of them are definitely frightening.

They were handwritten in old notebooks and it's great that we have this literal treasure trove of something tangible that was part of her. Mum wrote about thirty in total and we are only releasing these few for now as a tribute to her. The remainder we want to keep for ourselves, for our own kids and grandkids. We might publish them. I don't know—Chloe and I haven't made up our minds yet. Though if we do, we'll probably have to add a caveat that they are absolutely *not* for kids.

Chloe's little boy, Sebastian, and her daughter, Lucy, who she named after Mum, have already been lulled to sleep by one of Mum's more terrifying songs. Thankfully, they are too young to understand the words. LOL!

Mum wrote a few personal comments on the pages in between her stories, and we decided we wanted to preserve everything that she'd written in her notebooks. We've included one or two of them but the rest we will keep private.

Most of you know what Mum was like so, when you read them, you'll know what to expect. You have been warned!

Amy Kennedy

1. The Fowl and the Sleeping Cat.

It was a lovely, sunny day in the Wilsons' back garden. Phil the pheasant was happily scratching the grass in his search for tasty bugs and insects to eat, along with the seeds that had fallen from the small bird feeder among the grass and weeds that grew along the hedge. There was always plenty of food to be found in the garden and he came every day for lunch and dinner, before setting off to find a nice spot to roost in amongst the trees and hedges.

He was pecking away when he spotted something that made him stand completely still. Lying in front of him was a sleeping cat.

Phil was terrified, but he knew to stay still and not let out a loud squawk.

The cat was asleep in the warm sunshine, but she must have heard Phil for she opened one eye and stared at him.

'Is she going to eat him?' Chloe asked.

'She might. If she's hungry.' Chloe's Mum replied.

Phil was thinking the same, and he didn't know what to do. Stay still and hope the cat went back to sleep, or take off and fly over the hedge and away to safety.

The cat stretched out her front leg and dug her claws into the ground.

Is she looking for bugs, too? Phil wondered.

But no, she wasn't looking for bugs. She was just stretching as cats do. She'd had a good breakfast and she wasn't hungry. She was content to snooze in the sunshine, so she yawned, closed her eyes and curled up to sleep again.

Phil breathed a sigh of relief as he carefully turned and walked away to the safety of the taller hedge. He didn't feel so hungry after almost becoming dinner himself.

2. Our Day at the Beach.

We found seaweed and shells of all kinds of shapes as we played on the beach. And we built a big castle with our buckets and spades. Then, with sand in our toes, we walked along the shore. Then we splashed and jumped into the water. It tasted salty.

We swam at the edge where the water was shallow and warm. Then we swam out a bit more and we heard Daddy yelling, 'No.' So, we came back to land and we sat at the edge. And the waves were all around us.

We climbed on the rocks and found fish in the pool, and shells stuck to the rocks, and the starfish stayed still. We watched the fish as they swam to and fro, and we sat there for ages, until we got bored.

Then Mum called us back and we hurried to her. She had cake and juice in the big freezer bag. She rubbed suncream on our arms and our legs, our shoulders and faces and the tip of our noses, as we sat down to eat.

It didn't taste salty.

When it got late, we packed up our stuff, got into the car and Daddy drove home.

And that was the end of our day at the beach.

As told by Chloe and Amy,
with a little help from their mum.

3. The Snowman Who Hated Being Cold.

Snowy was miserable. He was freezing outside in the snow and the cold, biting wind. All he had to wear was a bowler hat and an old football scarf. His poor hands were numb and felt like the small branches from a nearby tree. He thought they looked the same, too.

His nose was raw and red and, when he crossed his coal-black eyes to get a look at it, it resembled a carrot. He sniffled, and wished he had a hanky because his nose was running and icicles had formed on his top lip.

And his left foot was yellow because the dog had peed on it.

He really wasn't having a good day at all.

~~~

His day didn't get any better because a big, black crow landed on him and tried to peck at his nose, thinking it was a tasty carrot. Yes, a crow was picking his nose! How disgusting. He wanted to flap his arms and stamp his feet, and shout at the crow to go away, but he was frozen to the spot. He couldn't even speak.

He wished he wasn't a snowman, and he wished he was anywhere but the garden in the middle of winter.

Just then a fairy flew down from the treetop. At least he thought it was a fairy. It was hard to tell because she was bundled up in a long, woolly coat, and she was wearing a woolly scarf, hat and mittens.

She waved her magic wand and snowflakes scattered around him.

'I am here to make your wishes come true,' she said.

'I will grant you three wishes.'

Snowy thought about it for a moment. What did he want? What was his deepest wish?

He had to pick only three so he knew he'd better pick three good ones.

'I wish I was a sandman,' he announced.

The fairy waved her magic wand and more snowflakes danced around him, and poof! He was made of sand. He was a sandman. How cool is that? No more freezing in the cold winter and shivering all day and night.

But, wait. He might not be a snowman now but he was still standing out in the snow, and he was still freezing. He needed to use his second wish pretty quickly.

'I wish I could live on the beach, someplace where it's always warm and sunny.'

The fairy shrugged her shoulders—most people wished for fast cars, mansions and a whopping big bank balance—but if this guy just wanted to be a beach bum, it was his choice.

She held up the wand and waved it again.

Poof!

Snowy, now named Sandy, was sitting on the beach. It was warm in the bright sunshine and he put on his sunglasses and smiled as he gazed out over the beautiful blue ocean.

The fairy took off her woolly coat, hat, scarf and mittens and stood beside him, waiting patiently for him to tell her the third wish. After five minutes she coughed to get his attention.

Snowy, now Sandy, looked up in surprise. He had

forgotten all about the fairy that had gotten him out of the cold.

'Oh, sorry. I have a third wish. Right?'

'Yes. You have one more.'

'Okay. I wish for a—no, hold on. Let me think. Okay, got it. I wish I had a choc ice.'

The fairy rolled her eyes. Most people want a fridge stocked with the best champagne. This guy wanted a choc ice. What a weirdo.

The fairy swivelled her magic wand one last time and Sandy got his choc ice. Then she disappeared. Her work was done.

Sandy smiled. He'd always wished he could be out of the cold. Now, here he was sitting on the beach and enjoying a choc ice as he watched the tide going in and out.

He was a very happy ex-snowman.

4. Shooting Star.

There's a shooting star and it travels so far,
Across the darkest night.
And as I look up, I see it's light,
A streak in the night-time sky.
Where is it going? And where will it end?
As I lie in bed it speeds overhead.
Will I see it tonight when I turn out the light?
But no, it has gone,
Left me all alone.
Goodbye, my lovely shooting star.

5. Pete, The Helpful Poltergeist.

Every night when the family have gone to bed, the little poltergeist sneaks out from its hiding place and into the house. He's a different kind of poltergeist. He's not at all like the other types, who throw things about and open cupboards and drawers, and pull out the tea towels, the spoons and even the can opener, and leave them lying on the worktops in the kitchen. They also scatter toys and shoes and magazines everywhere and leave dishes unwashed in the sink—and they even hide the TV remote.

This little poltergeist is called Pete, and he likes to tidy up.

He folds up the tea towels and puts them back in the drawer. Gathers up the spoons and the can opener and puts them in their proper places. He washes and dries the dishes and takes tomorrow night's dinner out of the freezer, puts it on a plate and leaves it in the fridge to defrost. He checks the fridge and makes a list of anything that has run out. Then he wipes down all the worktops, mops the floor and puts the kitchen chairs back where they should be.

After all that, he goes into the living room and lifts all the toys, finds the remote and puts it beside the TV. Then he gathers up the magazines and books and puts them in a neat pile on the coffee table, before plumping up the cushions and using a brush and pan to sweep up any crumbs that have fallen.

He checks all the doors and windows are locked, that the car keys are where they should be, and gives the dog a fresh bowl of water.

At the weekend he does the laundry and dusts and vacuums the whole house—but this is a weeknight, so he just does a general tidy up and, when he's finished, he takes one last look around to make sure everything is done. He disappears before morning.

Our mum tells us that she does it but we know it's really Pete, the helpful Poltergeist.

6. Rossy Wossy.

'Rossy Wossy, you're so bossy.
You bark all day and you bark all night.
You bark behind me and give me a fright.
You bark at trees and you bark at cars.
You bark at people and even the stars.
You beg for a treat, and sit there so sweet.
And then you lie down, asleep at our feet.
Rossy-Wossy, we love you.
Even when you roll in poo!'

7 – The Little Lost Boy.

It was Christmas Eve. It was snowing outside and it was the perfect winter wonderland. The family—two girls aged six and eight, and their mum and dad—were gathered in the living room. The tree, adorned with lights and tinsel and decorations, took pride of place near the front window. The kids were watching *The Snowman* on TV, while Mum and Dad listened to Johnny Mathis crooning *The Little Drummer Boy* on the stereo. Mum was wearing her new reindeer sweater—almost fainting with the heat of it combined with the warmth pumping out from the central heating—as she sipped from a glass of eggnog. She hated eggnog, but it was a Christmas tradition.

Dad was enjoying a whiskey, and looking forward to another later when he drank the one left out for Santa at midnight. He'd dump the shortbread biscuits in the recycle bin after he'd placed all the presents under the tree, and the kids would think there really was a Santa Claus.

Santa Claus may or may not exist. But other things do.

~~~

Johnny Mathis had switched to *Silent Night* when a knock on the door disturbed the silence. Mum looked at Dad, who shrugged his shoulders and took another mouthful of his drink.

Mum sighed and got up to open the door. It was probably a neighbour with a last-minute gift, or maybe a friend with a bottle of wine.

She opened the front door and looked out. There was

no one there. At least no one of her height she could see.

A giggle made her look down, and there on the doorstep was a little boy.

He was wearing pyjamas but his feet were bare. The funny thing was, he didn't melt the snow around his toes. His face was pale with the cold and he had the most unbelievable angelic smile.

'Hello,' said the mother. 'What are you doing out here all alone at this time of night?'

'It's Christmas Eve, and I have nowhere to stay,' the little boy replied. A big tear trickled down his cheek.

'Oh, you poor little thing. Come on in and get warmed up and we'll see if we can find your mummy and daddy.'

The little boy stepped over the threshold and followed the mother into the living room. Everybody looked up to stare at him.

His angelic smile turned into a hungry grin.

None of the family survived.

And the moral of that story, my darling daughters, Mum wrote in her notebook at the end of this story. *Vampires are not sparkly classmates, and you can't teach a werewolf not to pee on the carpet. The former will rip open your throat because he's thirsty and he 'vants to drink your blud' and the latter will rip open your throat because he's a hungry doggie and he wants to eat you!*

7 - There's a mousie in the wall.

I can hear it scratching and I wonder how it got there. Did somebody leave the back door open?

That's how they get in, you know.

And they live in the wall and they watch you until you fall asleep. And when you do, they come out of the walls and they explore the house. They find the kitchen and they open the cupboards.

Snacks are what they're after.

They love chocolate digestive biscuits and lemon drizzle cake. Cheese is a firm favourite, too. They love sugar but they don't like coffee or tea.

And they'll eat and eat all night long, until there's no food left for little girls who leave the back door open.

You have been warned.

8 – Some of the comments Mum wrote about us in her notebooks.

"I'm trying to relax and watch *Line of Duty* in peace and if those two brats I spawned don't stop chattering and settle down to sleep immediately, I swear I'm going to phone Social Services and get them to take the pair of them into care."

~~~

"Toys left on the floor at night time will be chucked in the bin."

Signed,
The Management.

~~~

"Ask your dad. Oh, he said no, did he? Oh, well. I guess it's a no from me too, then."

~~~

"I love my daughters so much, it hurts."

~~~

"I want to grow old and play with my grandchildren. Then, when they crap in their nappies, I can hand them back."

~~~

Chapter 35 – Proud Mum.

I watched my two beautiful, beautiful daughters as they laughed and cried over the words that I had written for them so long ago. Amy was particularly weepy when she read my poem about Ross. Chloe was also tearful but I think his memory got to Amy the most, even though she has her own dogs now.

They have grown into the most remarkable young women. Chloe, at twenty-five is already a mother of two. Amy, who will be twenty-seven in a few weeks' time doesn't seem to have the motherhood gene and is quite content being an auntie to Chloe and Cathy's children, and a mother to her animals on the farm she works with her husband, Stevie.

I am so bloody proud of them. Charlie and I got them started on their journey through this life, and Claire took over from me and steered them around, over, and under the troubles and hazards of their teenage years. Between the three of us, my girls got there—safely into adulthood as thoughtful, kind, sensible young women. Oh sure, there were bumps on the roads they travelled—there probably would be a few more ahead of them—but they had their dad, their 'Auntie' Claire who is now their loving step-mum, and their own respective partners—Cathy and Stevie—by their sides.

What more could I ask for?

~~~

Well, I could have asked to be with them, but I couldn't find that option anywhere. Instead, I had to watch them from afar. But that was okay, and now I can relax in the knowledge that they'll be fine as they travel through their lives.

They were smiling through their tears. Chloe blew her nose with a tissue while Amy discreetly wiped her face with her sleeve. Wouldn't they be gobsmacked if they knew I was sitting right here with them?

I held out my arms as though to hug my girls, and I could see I was slowly becoming transparent—like Ross had when he finally left me. My hands were like the early morning mist on the moors, and as I reached to caress the cheeks of both of my darling daughters, I fancied they could feel my fingertips touching them as I whispered my last goodbye to them.

The end.
Amanda Sheridan
July 2023.

About the author.

Amanda Sheridan, a retired civil servant, lives with her husband and their two rough collies, Riley and Lassie on the beautiful Ards peninsula in Co. Down.
She is a dedicated motorsport fan as well as being an avid reader.
She began writing in 2017 and published *Rapid Eye Movement* in March 2020. *The Dreaming* followed a year later and the third part of the story – *Dream Catcher* was published in June 2022.
Bad Dreams is a spin-off from *Rapid Eye Movement*.

If you enjoyed this book, please leave a review. Reviews are the lifeblood of indie authors.
Thank you. xx

Acknowledgements.

A big thank you first of all, to my husband, Hugh—always supportive and encouraging, despite not being a reader himself. Likewise, my brother, Reuben Sheridan.

A massive thank you to my Australian cousin, Alannah Sheridan, for the beautiful silver Dream Catcher necklace she made and presented to me when she was visiting in June of this year. You can see a photo of the necklace on my Facebook page – Amanda Sheridan Author.

My beta reader and good friend, Laura Lyndhurst—always supportive and a terrific author herself. Go check her out, and read her books.

All the other indie authors out there. Always supportive, always welcoming, and a great bunch of people.

I can't finish without a word about the local traders I've come to know at the markets and crafts fairs I've attended over the past couple of years. Another lovely bunch of good people.

Original Cover Image by SuperHerftigGeneral on Pixabay.

Printed in Great Britain
by Amazon

28148416R00179